Paris Time

Lost in Time – Time Travel Series
Book 2

Belle Ami

ARE YOU SIGNED UP FOR DRAGONBLADE'S BLOG?

You'll get the latest news and information on exclusive giveaways, exclusive excerpts, coming releases, sales, free books, cover reveals and more.

Check out our complete list of authors, too!

No spam, no junk. That's a promise!

Sign Up Here

www.dragonbladepublishing.com

Dearest Reader;

Thank you for your support of a small press. At Dragonblade Publishing, we strive to bring you the highest quality Historical Romance from some of the best authors in the business. Without your support, there is no 'us', so we sincerely hope you adore these stories and find some new favorite authors along the way.

Happy Reading!

CEO, Dragonblade Publishing

Additional Dragonblade Books by Author Belle Ami

The Lost in Time Series
London Time (Book 1)
Paris Time (Book 2)

CHAPTER ONE

Present
New York, New York

J ENEE LAZAAR WAS determined not to cry. It was something she hadn't done since she was a child and lost her parents. Crying represented defeat and weakness to her. It wasn't that she was heartless. She held no prejudice against someone else's tears, but in her own life, she had never found anything positive from salty water running down her cheeks or indulging in self-pity.

That was how she survived med school, and that was how she survived the barbs and hate that were spewed against her. Born in Algeria, Jenee grew up in Paris after her parents, both university professors, immigrated there. Jenee got a full scholarship to the University of Southern California Keck School of Medicine and fell in love with L.A. After her parents were killed in a bomb attack at a friend's restaurant opening in Paris, Jenee was devastated. But she was a fighter. Rather than move back home to Paris after she graduated, she decided to make America her permanent home. Ten years later, Jenee was a successful dermatologist with a thriving practice.

She dug her nails into her palms as she gazed at the painting. Why? Why did Allegretto's painting make her feel such sorrow? Yes, she thought it was a hauntingly beautiful series of paintings. She loved the bestselling novel inspired by the paintings, *The Time*

Traveler's Lover, just as much as her besties, Emily and Gabriella. But Jenee wasn't a die-hard romantic like Gaby and Em. Emily had developed a tough skin when it came to men since she had caught her (now ex) fiancé cheating on her. And Gaby hadn't had much in the way of relationship experience. A chef's life wasn't conducive to love. But both women did believe in true love.

At some point, she would do the artificial insemination thing because she did yearn to be a mother, but she didn't need a man for that, just his sperm. For now, it was full speed ahead in her career. Jenee had worked hard to reach the pinnacle in her field. Hell, she was known as the Pimple-popper to the Stars. Her Beverly Hills-based clinic catered to A-list celebrities, top social media influencers, and the richest of the rich. Regularly featured in fashion magazines such as *Vogue*, *InStyle*, and *Cosmopolitan*, Jenee had become a celebrity herself. The media referred to her as the hottest doctor in Los Angeles. Her "supermodel" looks, thanks to her Algerian heritage and sexy French accent, also gave star power to her persona.

Jenee had everything she wanted in life, except someone to share it with. As she gazed at the five-hundred-year-old painting by Allegretto, her heart clenched. She'd never truly fallen in love. Oh, she had a very active social life, but she'd never truly experienced the beauty of true love. Soul mate love. The realization flooded her eyes with tears.

"Are you all right?" asked Emily, sweeping a strand of blonde hair off her cheek.

The girls' weekend was Emily's idea when she snagged the coveted tickets to the highly anticipated opening of Renaissance master Marco Allegretto's *The Three Stages of Love* series at the Metropolitan Museum of Art. The paintings featured Allegretto with a beautiful, mysterious woman with red hair. No mention of the artist's muse had ever been discovered; the only proof of her existence was the paintings themselves.

Emily Christie, a British transplant, was the editor of the hugely successful online magazine *MFL*, which stood for *My Fair*

Lady. She'd invited her besties, Gaby and Jenee, to stay in her swank Manhattan apartment with her for the weekend. The night before, the girls had sipped champagne, gorged on lasagna, and giggled the night away. Their friendship was forged in a mutual love of good food, fabulous shoes, silly humor, and books. That they lived in different cities—Los Angeles, Chicago, and New York—made no difference. Regardless of their physical distance or busy lives, they honored their gift of friendship.

The trio had met in an online book club and become fast friends. Reading *The Time Traveler's Lover* had cemented Emily, Jenee, and Gabriella's friendship. The novel, a tragic, romantic time-travel tour de force of love and loss, was based on the paintings. It was a love story that took the world by storm. The fictionalized fantasy based on Marco's paintings had spawned multiple theories about who the authoress was.

Gaby wrapped her arm around Jenee and handed her a tissue. "It's okay, honey. I'm crying buckets here, too."

Jenee chuckled through her tears. Gaby was all heart. She was one hundred percent Italian, from her long, dark hair to her Sophia Loren-like curves. And in typical Italian fashion, Gaby mothered everyone she cared about. Also in typical Italian fashion, Gaby was a fantastic cook. In fact, she ran a successful restaurant specializing in traditional Italian cuisine and eclectic cultural mashups.

"I hate being emotional, especially since I have everything to be grateful for," Jenee said.

"You're talking to the hand, *ragazza. Un amico a portata di mano è meglio di un parente a distanza.*"

"What does that mean?" asked Jenee.

"It means, 'A friend at hand is better than a relative at a distance.'"

Gaby's late *nonna* had been a font of wisdom, and she was always relating her grandmother's stories and flavoring her sentences with Italian proverbs and solutions for whatever life presented. Her old-world charm and old-soul spirit often made

Jenee wonder if Gaby was channeling a past life.

Jenee looked at the painting. "Do you think they ever found their happily ever after?"

"I don't know if we'll ever know," said Emily, "but I'd like to think so. I guess it gives me hope."

Jenee felt another swell of emotion in her chest. *I need to get up and walk around before I break down and start sobbing.* "Hey, gals, I'll meet you back here in an hour. I need to be alone for a few minutes." She needed to breathe, think, and assess this life she'd created. It was her way of dealing with uncertainty and adversity. It was the scientific, analytical part of her brain that she trusted. Emotions got her in trouble. Logical, methodical insight and analysis never failed her in making a diagnosis or treating a patient, and that was where she turned when her personal life presented a dilemma.

"Are you going to be okay?" Gaby asked.

"I'll be fine." Jenee winked so that her friends wouldn't worry. She wandered through the galleries aimlessly, barely glancing at the masterpieces on the walls. The people around her might as well have been invisible. Like a dropped bag of marbles, her thoughts zigzagged in every direction. Distracted, she bumped into a stranger and walked on without apology.

"An *excuse me* might be nice," the stranger's voice broke in. "You should consider adding those two words to your vocabulary."

She might have ignored him, but his reprimand was not meanspirited, and a hint of laughter echoed in his deep vibrato. She turned and found herself face to face with the bluest eyes she'd ever seen, and a clear complexion the color of a toasted biscuit. Being a dermatologist, when she looked at someone, the first thing she noticed about them was their skin. While most people remembered names, eye color, and hair, she remembered complexions. The handsome man whose brows were lifted in question had the same skin tone as hers, with the natural glow of a desert sun.

"I beg your pardon?" she asked.

"Ah, she isn't sleepwalking. I said, you might want to add *excuse me* to your vocabulary."

Her breath caught in her throat. *Gleaming smile, high cheekbones, chiseled Don Draper jaw, and eyes the color of the Mediterranean Sea.* "I'm so sorry. Forgive me. My mind was elsewhere." She hesitated, wondering if he would ask her what she was thinking, make a comment about the artwork, or offer up another quip…

He seemed to pause as well. For a moment, he just stared into her eyes.

And she stared back. *Who are you? And why do I feel like I know you?*

He smiled again, but this time it was more subdued; perhaps he was realizing they had never met before. "No problem," he said. He gave her a slight nod, turned, and strode away.

And that's that. Case closed. Jenee stood momentarily and watched the tall, broad-shouldered stranger, deciding whether to follow him, but before she decided, he was joined by a redhead who possessively took his arm. The redhead must have seen their exchange because she turned and gave Jenee a withering look as if to say, *Stay away, he's mine.*

You almost made a fool of yourself. But, oh my, those eyes. Those incredible eyes. She exhaled a deep sigh. *They're probably married. All the good ones are taken, and what did you think Mr. Blue Eyes was going to do? Drop to his knees like Marco Allegretto, kiss your hand, and ask if you believe in love at first sight?*

A snort of laughter escaped her, and she covered her mouth. A quick glance around told her no one had heard her guffaw. Correction—except the gallery attendant whose censorious gaze pinned her like a butterfly to a spreading board.

Sheesh, it's not like we're in a library. Jenee made her way down the aisle and stopped in front of a painting on loan from a private collection. The museum label read, *Pablo Picasso, Painted in 1900. Nineteen-year-old Picasso, recently arrived in Paris as a journalist to cover the Exposition Universelle, fell in love with the city, its people, and its art.*

Jenee studied the painting and found it nearly as upsetting as Allegretto's series, but for an entirely different reason. She looked again at the label and read the title and the translation of the painting, *L'etreinte Forcee, The Brutal Embrace.* The portrait of a man and woman dancing in a dance hall made the hair on her nape stand on end. What might have been a sensual and beautiful depiction of a couple dancing in a nightclub was portrayed in a raw, aggressive manner. The man's hands mauled the woman, grasping at her private parts, yet, given her lurid smile, she seemed to be enjoying it.

What was Picasso trying to say in the painting? His talent was undeniable, as was his uncanny ability to capitalize on his talent. But also undeniable was his misogyny. *Genius certainly comes in many forms.* The French had a moniker for men like Picasso: *L'Enfant Terrible*, the terrible child, which in its very name was a forgiveness for whatever ill deeds a person did.

Jenee shook her head, dispelling the grotesque image from her mind, and forced herself to walk away. She took a deep breath and regained her composure. How different Picasso was in his disdain for women in contrast to Allegretto and his pure reverence and adoration of them.

Why did she always meet the Picassos of the world and not the Allegrettos? Whispering under her breath, *"Que sera, sera,"* she headed back to the gallery where she'd agreed to meet Em and Gaby. Throwing a glance back over her shoulder, she nearly laughed. Trailing her was the museum attendant.

I didn't make an impression on Mr. Blue Eyes, but I certainly made one on the security guard.

Her impish side thought about leading him on a wild goose chase, but her friends would scold her. She reached the bench and plopped down in front of *The Three Stages of Love.* Em and Gaby were probably still wandering around. She looked at the three paintings again, wanting to erase the lurid Picasso from her mind.

The Three Stages of Love: La Sedia, Il Divano, Il Letto—The Chair,

The Settee, and *The Bed*—were shrouded in mystery and controversy, having disappeared several times since Allegretto first painted them in 1503. Much speculation had circulated over the years about the mysterious paintings. One story had it that *La Sedia* had been sold at auction in London in the late 1800s to the Duke of Shrewsbury, then disappeared along with the duke. The second painting, *Il Divano,* appeared at the 1900 Universal Exposition in Paris and vanished, too. No one knew anything about where they were or who possessed them until all three paintings were discovered in a villa in Tuscany after World War II.

But the biggest mystery was contained within the paintings themselves. Why was the unattributed female in the portraits fading into a ghostlike image, and why did she continue to fade? Mystified art conservators and restorers could not pinpoint the cause and stop the deterioration. Jenee read in the brochure that many had suggested touching up the paintings and restoring them to their former glory. But the caretakers since World War II, the Uffizi Gallery, had so far refused to tamper with them. Even with the defects, the paintings were still considered unequaled masterpieces, mesmerizing in their emotional truth and captivating brilliance of execution.

Jenee gazed at the three paintings, wondering about the love affair depicted on the canvases before her. Was this the artist's fantasy of his ideal woman, or had she been a living person? She studied the first painting, *La Sedia.* Allegretto knelt before the seated woman and kissed her hand, his unwavering gaze one of complete love and adoration. In the foreground, to the right of Allegretto, was his easel and the painting on which he'd begun mirroring the moment. Beside the woman was a delicate table on which a wine glass and vase filled with irises rested. The redheaded woman dressed in an off-the-shoulder gown of lilac silk reflected his adoring gaze in what could only be described as one of the most romantic declarations of love ever painted.

In the second painting, *Il Divano,* the same woman, the object of the artist's fascination, reclined on a divan with Allegretto's arms encircling her. He was poised to kiss her, and they gazed at each other with such passion that it felt like the painting might incinerate itself. It was enough for Jenee to fan herself with the brochure.

In the third painting, *Il Letto*, the beautiful redhead was lying nude on her side on a bed with a sheer swath of red silk draped over her hips, barely covering her private parts. It was impossible to ignore the come-hither look in her eyes. Allegretto, shirtless and wearing only tights, was turned with his muscled back to the viewer. A burning candle provided a shimmering glow, casting chiaroscuro contrasts over the two figures. The artist matched his emotional storytelling with the technical skill of creating three-dimensionality with light and darkness.

Jenee's hand rose to her heart, and her other hand gripped the bench. A strange premonition grew inside of her, and she trembled. *How odd.* At first, she thought the painting made her tremble, but as the tremor continued, she realized the bench was shaking beneath her. California had its share of earthquakes, and Jenee was used to tremors, but she had never heard of earthquakes in New York. She looked around, wondering if anyone else had noticed, but the few people in the gallery showed no sign of anything amiss.

Maybe they don't feel it because they're moving. I wish Emily and Gaby were here.

Jenee looked at her watch and froze. Her heartbeat spiked as if she was in the path of a speeding car. The hands on the dial of her watch were spinning counterclockwise.

Mon Dieu, *what is going on?*

Goosebumps rose on her arms as a low hum echoed around her. She stood and looked about. Where had everyone gone? The entire gallery was empty. Not even the snooty security guard was around.

The buzzing grew louder, sounding like a gigantic hive of bees barreling toward her. She caught a movement from the corner of her eye and turned to see Allegretto and his muse kiss.

It can't be real. I'm hallucinating. Jenee fixated on the sensual kiss between the lovers and saw that the ghostly woman grew more vivid with every passing second, as if Allegretto's mouth infused her with life and color. Her faded tresses turned flaming red, and her eyes, which remained open as he kissed her, became as emerald-hued as the shamrocks of Ireland. Spellbound, Jenee could not draw her eyes away.

What is happening to me? The woman Allegretto was kissing transformed into her. Jenee blinked rapidly to dispel the hallucination. She couldn't process what was happening. *This is madness.* From her long black hair to her crème caramel skin, the woman in the painting had become her, and Jenee couldn't tear her eyes away from the handsome artist who gazed at her with such unrestrained passion.

The logical medical practitioner realized she had to be in the grip of a mental breakdown to project herself into the painting. She covered her mouth as nausea seized her, and the ringing in her ears rose to an unbearable decibel level. Marco Allegretto broke the kiss and stared into her eyes. His strong arms clung to her, pulling her closer, and his eyes, the color of a storm-tossed sea, darkened with his demand. *"Aiutaci! Aiutaci! Tu ci devi aiutare!"*

Jenee, who spoke several languages, including Italian, understood precisely what Allegretto was saying: *"Help us!"*

Help them? I must help them, but how?

An icy chill filled her veins. She rubbed her arms, and then her hands flew to cover her ears as the vibration and Marco's plea became a roar. The world around her began to melt like a Salvador Dali painting; an explosion resonated around her, with flying debris and shards of glass. Was this what her parents had experienced before they perished in the bomb attack all those years ago?

My God, it must be a terrorist attack. I have to find Em and Gaby.

Jenee looked around, but the explosion had caused a swirl of smoke and fog as thick as pea soup. She held her hands out, trying to find her way out of the gallery, but a sudden wind whipped her around and sucked her into a spinning vortex. She screamed as she was hurtled through what felt like a long black tunnel. The darkness gave way to flashing lights as Allegretto's words echoed in her mind: *Aiutaci! Aiutaci! Aiutaci!* She spun and spun and spun until she was so dizzy that she felt herself losing consciousness…

Jenee woke up coughing and trying to catch her breath. She rolled onto her side and sat up on her knees when a massive concrete slab crashed mere inches away from where she'd fainted. *Shit! What the hell?* Had a terrorist's bomb caused the collapse of the building?

Shaking from her narrow escape, she stood and looked around her. The ringing in her ears dimmed, and an eerie silence descended. Broken and jagged slabs of concrete and metal lay scattered around her. Distant cries and moans reached her ears. *Gaby! Em!* She turned, trying to find a way through the devastation, a way to the voices that called out for help. She pulled up her blouse to cover her mouth as she slowly moved through the heavy black smoke.

As blackness dissipated, Jenee's vision began to clear. Hearing a moan of pain to her left, she turned and gasped in shock. Falling to her knees, she looked up and could not believe her eyes.

How is this possible?

Just a few yards away stood the Eiffel Tower.

CHAPTER TWO

April 29, 1900
Paris, France

I'M IN PARIS!

How was that possible? How could she have been in New York minutes ago and now be looking at the Eiffel Tower? *Yellow?* It was not the Eiffel Tower she knew so well. This Eiffel Tower was painted bright yellow.

Even so, this was Paris, the city she grew up in. Jenee stared at the wrought-iron tower with its lattice girders and metal trusses rising above the Champ de Mars in a towering monument. She rubbed her eyes, managing only to cloud them with dirt again. *Merde.* But there was no time to contemplate the occurrence that had transported her to Paris or that the Eiffel Tower was yellow. What she needed to do was understand the nightmare she found herself in.

Cries of human suffering pierced the silence. She took the Hippocratic Oath upon becoming a doctor, and now that oath demanded that she do something. Taking careful steps, she clambered through the wreckage and searched for the source of the piteous voices that cried for help.

Jenee covered her mouth as she saw a pair of feet wearing an odd pair of button boots protruding from beneath a concrete slab. A clip from the movie *The Wizard of Oz* played in her head. Unlike in the movie scene, this Wicked Witch of the East's feet didn't roll up and disappear beneath the house. Jenee hadn't been swept up in a tornado, dropped from the sky, landing on a witch. These feet remained motionless, silently bemoaning that their owner was dead, and no munchkins bursting out in song would change that irrefutable truth. Jenee could be of no help to this poor soul. She swallowed the bile burning in her throat and moved on.

After discovering several more bodies, she found a woman covered in dust whose lips flapped open and closed as if she were a fish out of water trying to breathe. Jenee knelt to the semiconscious woman and laid her ear to her chest. She was relieved to find a faint pulse, but the woman barely breathed. There was no time to think. She opened the woman's mouth, cleared it, and tilted her head back. Pressing her mouth to the woman's, she filled her lungs with breath. The woman's chest rose, and Jenee pressed the heel of her hand to the center of her chest and pumped in and out in an even rhythm. She counted off thirty times. Again, she tilted the woman's head back and administered breath resuscitation, alternating back and forth from breath resuscitation to cardiopulmonary resuscitation until the woman began to breathe on her own. The woman's eyes fluttered open, looking at Jenee as if she were a ghost or perhaps an angel.

"What happened?" She coughed thickly.

"I don't know, but thank God you're alive. I need you to take even breaths while I check to see if you have any broken bones." Jenee had no inkling as to what had caused the catastrophe. She was so caught up with helping the woman that there was no time to address the strange way the woman was dressed, as she was completely coated in a layer of dust. Caught in the exhilaration of saving a life, she had nearly forgotten that she had been in New York and not Paris minutes before.

A man took her arm and lifted her to her feet. "Mademoiselle, thank you for what you're doing." He motioned to two men wearing white uniforms. "My medical response team will take over now. We are moving the wounded to the Saint-Jean ward at the hospital. Are you hurt in any way?"

"No, monsieur, I seem to be fine."

"Thank goodness." The mustachioed and bearded man held out his hand. "I am Dr. Gilles de la Tourette, the chief surgeon here at the fair. What is your name? Are you a nurse?"

"My name is Jenee Lazaar. I'm a doctor."

His brow arched skeptically, and she instantly regretted her honesty. She was on the other side of the looking glass, and it wasn't wise to reveal anything about herself until she figured out where she was and how she got here. She wanted to ask him what fair he was talking about, but she didn't dare, fearing he'd think her crazy. Fortunately, the doctor was too busy to question her as he directed the rescue effort.

Two medical attendants lifted the older woman onto a stretcher.

The woman grabbed her hand. "What is your name?" She was American, and Jenee detected an upper-crust Boston accent.

"Jenee Lazaar."

"Jenee, my name is Constance Shipley, and I'm renting a house at 12, Rue Odinout in Faubourg Saint-Germain." She squeezed Jenee's hand, just managing to eke out her words before being overcome by a coughing fit. "You must come to see me tomorrow. Promise me?"

"I-I… Yes, of course. I'll come tomorrow. Be well."

Jenee watched the men carrying the stretcher with Constance carefully climb over the rubble. She needed to get her bearings and figure out what she would do. She was totally perplexed by everything happening to her and around her. She was not hallucinating—the Eiffel Tower was still to her left, and still yellow, but when she circled to see what else she might find, she felt her legs give out again.

To her right was a blue and gold painted globe that had to be more than one hundred and fifty feet in diameter. The giant planet was mounted on a concrete structure supported by four columns. She vaguely remembered seeing it before, but she didn't know where. It was painted with constellations and zodiac signs. She saw dozens of people leaning over the balustrade surrounding the globe, staring down at her, their faces reflecting all the stages of witnessing a disaster and realizing it could have been them. This was not the Paris she knew. Maybe she had traveled over the rainbow.

Jenee looked beyond the broken concrete to the Quai d'Orsay, the walkway that bordered the Seine River. She saw women in old-fashioned long dresses carrying parasols and men sporting top hats, straw matelots, and French straw boater hats, strolling leisurely upon the Quai de Billy. Hundreds of feet high, a giant Ferris wheel, loaded with people, slowly spun, silhouetted against a Robin's-egg-blue sky.

Her breath caught in her throat. Nothing made any sense. Buildings she had never seen before lined the banks of the Seine. She shook her head, trying to clear it, but her eyes did not deceive her. Along the river were elegantly dressed men, women, and children who didn't seem to be walking yet were moving. It took a moment for her to realize they were riding on a moving sidewalk, much like the moving flat escalators that shuttled people to their gates at airports.

It's impossible.

"*Excusez moi,* mademoiselle. *S'il vous plait,* may I help you get away from this quagmire?"

"*Oui bien sûr.*" She turned and saw his face, and her knees buckled. Completely confused, she stumbled into his arms, her face inches from his.

"Mademoiselle, are you all right?" His strong arms held her, and he searched her face.

Those blue eyes! She wanted to kiss him. He looked like the man she'd encountered at the Metropolitan Museum. The man she'd run into in the gallery.

Her excitement at seeing a familiar face was so great that it didn't bother her that he didn't remember her. She grabbed the lapels on his suit and tried to speak, but nothing came out. Her voice was trapped inside her, and all that came out was a squeak, which was so embarrassing that she could feel the heat climb up her neck and paint her cheeks.

Perhaps there was an explanation for what was happening to her.

She barely noticed that he was dressed differently, formally, wearing a high-collared white shirt and tie with a three-piece suit of gray worsted wool. A flat cap kept his dark curls in place on his head. She didn't recall him having a mustache, but what of it? His pale blue eyes were unforgettable; she would have recognized those eyes and his biscuit-hued skin anywhere. *It's him. It has to be him.*

Even as she latched on to his lapels, she realized that nothing was as it should be. How could he have grown a mustache and changed his clothes in minutes? And where was the redhead?

She glanced down at herself. She was still wearing a navy suit, but it was tattered and covered in debris. She pushed away her doubts and clung to the hope that all would return to what had been. Mr. Blue Eyes would take her hand and lead her to safety, back to her friends, and back to New York. And she and he... Well, she shouldn't think that far ahead.

"My name is Xavier Doumaz." He looked around, taking in the scene. "A terrible disaster. I ran over here when I saw the pedestrian bridge collapse." He removed his hat as he introduced himself. "I'm an off-duty officer with the Prefecture of Police of Paris. I heard concrete cracking and saw the walkway to the Globe Céleste come down. What a terrifying experience for you."

She just barely got the words out. "*Oui*, terrible." Her relief faded as quickly as it had come.

"*S'il vous plait*, let me escort you to a café and offer you an espresso so you might recover yourself. Can you walk?"

Jenee nodded. She felt faint and confused and scared. But his kind offer would give her time to think. She'd gone into medical mode, and that had taken precedence over any thoughts about what had happened. Maybe Blue Eyes could provide the answers to the questions now bombarding her. But she would have to be careful—he was a policeman, and it would be risky if she revealed too much or asked too many odd-sounding questions. She was literally on shaky ground. Nothing about Paris looked the way she remembered. The world was upside down, and she had no idea how to turn it right side up.

He held her arm, and she leaned on him as they walked away from the turmoil and destruction that the police were busy cordoning off to keep the curious out. The area was inundated with police, medical personnel, and other officialdom. She found it odd that nobody questioned them, letting them leave the scene without so much as a word of inquiry. She chalked it up to his being recognized as law enforcement, but still, she wondered at the lax protocols.

As if to distract her, Xavier kept up a steady stream of conversation. It occurred to her he was purposely calming her and keeping her mind preoccupied with inane observations. Was it to relax her guard? She glanced up and caught him studying her with his observant eyes, trying to see into her mind.

They walked for a few minutes to Avenue de la Bourdonnais and arrived at a typical French café with a hanging green awning that read *Café des Terres*. In front were chairs with green and white backs and seats woven in cane like a lattice pie crust. The chairs were occupied by people who sipped coffee at white marble wrought-iron tables.

Everyone was dressed like they were actors in an old-time movie, reminding her of the film *Meet Me in St. Louis*. The waiter who took their order wore his hair parted in the middle and slicked back. The ends of his waxed mustache looked sharp enough to core an apple.

Have I landed on the set of a movie? Is that why everyone is dressed in old-fashioned garb with old-fashioned hairdos and mustaches?

When their coffees and croissants were delivered, Xavier lifted his cup and set it in his saucer after taking a sip. "As the cloud of dust cleared, I saw you standing amidst the destruction;

it was almost as if you appeared magically, out of nowhere. How you were not harmed is a miracle."

"Yes, I-I don't know how I survived. One minute everything was normal, and the next, it was complete chaos."

"Forgive me, but I don't believe I caught your name."

"Jenee Lazaar. I'm sorry, I should have introduced myself."

"An easy mistake, given the circumstances. Do you live in Paris?"

"I—uh, I was born in Paris, but I live in California." *Oh, God, would it have been easier just to say, yes, I am from Paris?* Her blunt honesty was going to get her in trouble. The only thing to do was go on the offensive. "So much has changed in Paris since I was last here. It's almost as if I arrived at the city of my birth at a different time in history." Jenee picked up her cup and sipped her coffee as nonchalantly as possible, but her shaking hand gave her away.

Xavier seemed not to notice. To all outward appearances, they might be any couple enjoying a Sunday afternoon of leisure.

If she had to be honest with herself, living in L.A. was wonderful, but she often missed the unharried lifestyle of living in Paris. The pleasure of sitting in a café and watching the world walk by. Life in L.A. was all about making deals and making contacts, all for the purpose of either breaking into an industry, whether it was movies or real estate or, as in her case, the business of beauty.

"Everything has changed, indeed?" he said, eyes boring into hers. "Imagine how much it's changed since the Third Republic, when the communes fell. Buildings were bombed and looted, and much of Paris was destroyed until order was restored and the city was rebuilt. And now, Paris has taken her rightful place as the most beautiful city in the world. I believe we have truly entered the golden age of prosperity. Have you visited the Gallery of Machines on the Left Bank, with all its marvels of industrial technology? It truly heralds the forthcoming twentieth century and the future beyond."

Jenee choked, spewing coffee all over herself.

Xavier jumped up, patting her on the back. "*Ma chère fille*, are you all right? Breathe."

But Jenee couldn't breathe, and her head was spinning. *How could I not see the signs?* The strange attire of everyone around her and the differences in the architecture and the vehicles. The lack of modernity. It was impossible to wrap her head around what was so obvious.

My God, what am I going to do? Not only had she been transported from New York to Paris, but she'd been transported to the Paris of 1900 and the *Exposition Universelle*, the grandest and most successful of the three expositions that Paris had hosted before the turn of the century—the twentieth century.

Jenee shivered, contemplating the impossibility of having traveled over one hundred and twenty years backward in time. This wasn't a dream she would wake from. Xavier wasn't the man in the Metropolitan Museum, even if he looked like him. It was no wonder he didn't recognize her. She saw him now with fresh eyes. Maybe the man in the museum was a reincarnated version of him. Was he trustworthy? Would he help her? Even though she was alone and had no one else to turn to, a voice in her head cautioned her to be careful. Who would believe such a story? Even someone who was seemingly forward-thinking, as Xavier was. He was still a police officer. He could very well arrest her, and she could end up in prison for the rest of her life, or in a mental institution.

Thinking back to what had occurred in those seconds before she disappeared into that frightening vortex, she realized that her hurtling back in time had something to do with Marco Allegretto. She recalled the artist's words to her: "*Aiutaci! Aiutaci! Tu ci devi aiutare!*"

Am I supposed to help Allegretto and his muse? How could she possibly do that when she had no idea what he wanted her to do? Fear churned in her stomach, and she fought not to double over. She sensed the only chance to return to her life in the twenty-first century was somehow tied to Allegretto's paintings. In the meantime, she needed to survive, to find a place to live and a job.

At least I'm in Paris. Yes, it was Paris from a different time, but it was the city she grew up in. The city her parents had called home before they were brutally killed in a bombing. Oh, how she wished her parents were here!

She needed a haven and a place to think and plan. A light bulb flashed in her mind. Constance Shipley! The woman whose life she saved. Constance said she was staying in Faubourg Saint-Germain. It was one of the wealthiest neighborhoods in Paris. Maybe Constance would help her. Tomorrow she would call on her and appeal to her as a woman and a fellow American.

In the meantime, Jenee turned on her famous "L.A. charm" for Monsieur Xavier Doumaz. She would need his help too. It could not have been a mere coincidence that she'd met his future doppelganger at the Met only minutes before Allegretto flung her back in time. She had no idea what the connection was and why, but she was damn well going to find out.

CHAPTER THREE

April 29, 1900
Paris, France

EVERYTHING ABOUT JENEE heated his blood and raised his suspicion. Xavier Doumaz sipped his coffee and ignored his desire to shut Jenee up with a kiss. He listened to her feed him what he knew was a pack of lies. He was no fool and believed very little of what the beautiful young woman told him. None of what she said made any sense. His work as an undercover agent for the Prefecture of Police of Paris, and more directly for Direction Centrale des Renseignements Généraux, the intelligence service of the French police known as the RG, had refined his skills as a detective and sharpened his instincts and powers of observation.

Xavier was proud of French law enforcement and proud to be a member of what was considered the most advanced police force in the world. His career as an inspector defined him, and it was the brightest star in an otherwise lonely life. His undercover identity was known only to the director of the RG, who was the only person he answered to. To his fellow officers, he was a chief inspector.

His current assignment placed him at the very helm of Paris security. Although he was intrigued by Jenee's beauty and felt an inclination to protect her, he was wary of the professed French-born woman. With every word she uttered, he grew more suspicious of her. He suspected she might be tied to terrorists.

The investigation he was involved in had brought him to the exposition, and now the worst had happened. Even as he sat here chatting with the enchanting young woman, his men were plowing through the rubble, searching for proof that the fall of the walkway leading to the Globe Céleste was not a random accident but the result of a bombing. Of course, if it was an act of terror, the public would not be apprised, since it would only lead to panic and affect attendance at the exposition.

Too much was invested in the success of this event. The city of Paris would suffer an unbearable loss if word got out that an act of terrorism had occurred. He knew his superiors would insist they report the collapse as a failure of materials and, in the meanwhile, continue to investigate and stop any further attacks. The risk was significant, and heads would roll if there was another incident. His position might become precarious. It was always the lower ranks that shouldered the blame.

HQ had received a tip that a bomb had been planted at the exposition by a cabal of Algerian zealots who sought independence from French rule. Xavier and his men had rushed over from the Préfecture de Police and their headquarters on the Île de la Cité, arriving just moments before the collapse of the pedestrian ramp. Unfortunately, not in time to stop the terrorist act, but in time for Xavier to see the concrete fall and for Jenee to emerge unscathed from the dust.

"I saw what you did for the American woman. I've not seen that technique of resuscitation used before, although I have read about it. Where did you learn to do that?" As cool as a cucumber, he kept all suspicion out of his voice.

Jenee sat up as if expecting to invite his censure. "I am a doctor, monsieur. I learned my skills in the United States, and it is a relatively new procedure that is very effective."

"I see." Xavier could hear the defensiveness in her voice, and he could guess why. He found it reprehensible that the French, unlike the U.S. and Britain, did not welcome females into the profession of medicine. His adopted country lagged when it came to the advancement of women. Xavier was a man who understood well the burden of inequality and ostracism. During the pacification campaign in Algeria, his father, a French soldier, fell in love with a Jewish Algerian woman and returned to Paris with his infant son and new wife in tow.

His father had joined the civilian police, called the *Sûreté*. At a very young age, Xavier learned about the prejudice against Maghreb immigrants and the anti-Semitism experienced by Jews. It was a battle he'd fought since he was a boy in the schoolyard.

The ongoing Dreyfus affair made the precarious standing of Jews even more prevalent, elucidating Xavier's own struggles. The trial had torn France apart. From the miscarriage of justice at the trial of the Alsatian military officer of Jewish descent, Captain Alfred Dreyfus, and the verdict of treason for passing French military secrets to the German Embassy in Paris, the trial had divided the entire country, and anti-Semitic riots had broken out in more than twenty French cities. To Xavier's disappointment, several people had also been killed in Algiers during riots there.

For Xavier, "*L'affaire*," as it was called, was a stain of dishonor on his country. Last year new evidence had come to light clearing Dreyfus, and he'd been brought back from Devil's Island, where he'd been sentenced to four years. The second trial was as corrupt as the first, and Dreyfus was again found guilty and sentenced to ten years of hard labor. Fortunately, he was pardoned but not exonerated.

One day perhaps this wrong will be righted.

Xavier's childhood was fraught with anti-Semitism. He'd fought against it not only with his words but with his fists, often coming home from school battered with a bloody nose or a black eye, or worse. He'd channeled his anger by following in his father's footsteps and entering law enforcement. Xavier had fought his way up the ranks and achieved many accolades, despite jealousy and hatred from some of his fellow officers.

He vowed to make a difference in his country with determination and hard work. When his parents had arranged a marriage to the daughter of a well-to-do Algerian merchant, Xavier had gone along with it, despite his misgivings. He respected his wife and grew to respect her, but his marriage lacked any sort of meaningful union.

After his daughter was born, Xavier vowed to change and try harder. He adored his little girl and would have done anything for her. He was devastated when his wife and daughter perished in a fire that also killed his parents. He'd failed to protect them and failed to save them. He'd sworn never to marry again.

To make up for his failings, he'd dedicated his life to the safety of his adopted homeland and changing the mindset of the xenophobes.

Xavier studied Jenee. Her clothing was torn and covered with dust, but he'd never seen women's clothing like what she was wearing. It was a suit of some sort, with a jacket tailored to her slender frame and a jaw-droppingly short skirt. Had the explosion torn away the rest of her dress? He couldn't help but notice her stunning long legs and delicate ankles...

Nom de dieu de merde, get a grip on yourself, man! She's not the first beauty you've ever encountered.

Xavier forced himself to focus on essential matters, including her medical expertise. He was a fervid student of the emerging science of forensics. The man he admired most was Louis Lépin, the head of the Préfet de Police, who had taken him under his wing and not only encouraged Xavier's meteoric rise in law enforcement but urged him to devote himself to the study of criminology. Lépin and Xavier believed law enforcement was on the brink of a revolution in solving crime.

Xavier could not get out of his mind the way Jenee had saved the woman's life. But what intrigued him was how she could possibly be aware of, let alone use, this life-saving procedure. He had only read about it and never seen it performed. He was determined to find out everything there was to know about Jenee

Lazaar.

Xavier's relentless search for the truth had defined him and resulted in his meteoric rise to chief inspector. However, he was not without his detractors. Some were jealous of his success and resented his rapid ascent. Again, anti-Semitism raised its ugly head. The lesson reinforced by the Dreyfus affair was that, as a Jew and an immigrant, he must always be on guard.

"Did you have to leave Paris to pursue your dreams?" He was curious and knew women faced different prejudices that barred them from most professions. He was conservative in his values, but having experienced firsthand the harshness of oppression, he was more understanding than most. He believed pursuing one's calling shouldn't be deterred by gender, race, or ethnicity.

"In Paris, I wouldn't have been able to get my degree." Her tight-lipped response told him all he needed to know. *She bears scars much like I do.*

"It is our loss, I'm sure, mademoiselle."

It was the first smile she gave him, affecting him more than he would have liked. His attraction to her was more than physical; he admired her intelligence and the way she carried herself with dignity and grace. It was impressive to what ends she'd gone to follow her dream. Leaving her homeland to pursue her calling and succeeding in a man's profession was a testament to her self-determination. He knew very few women like Jenee, which raised his estimation of her.

She shrugged. *"C'est la vie."*

A smile tugged at his lips from her casual acceptance. "Are you visiting family?"

"Non." She bit her lip and averted her gaze, not meeting his eyes. Was she worried about what he might ask next? She was hiding something, he was sure. But was it something personal, or was she in league with the terrorists? He needed to get at the truth, or he might be unable to stop the terror group and prevent further attacks. But he had to proceed with caution, or this little bird might fly away.

Sweetness would bring him more than harshness. *I must break down her defenses and gain her trust. Woo her if need be.*

Even though his interest was for the sake of his investigation, he could not help the pang of guilt. It had been a long while since a woman had captivated his senses as Jenee was doing. Passion, let alone happiness, was a weakness he rarely allowed. He didn't love. He should have perished in that fire along with his family. And he never allowed himself to forget it. His work was the only thing left to keep him from madness.

He was cursed. Better to live alone with the ghosts that haunted him than to put another life in jeopardy. He was resolved to his fate. He did not deserve anything more, especially not this beautiful and intriguing woman across from him. A woman who could be hiding deadly treachery.

"Where are you staying, mademoiselle? I will see you to your hotel. You cannot walk about the city dressed like this." He would see her home safely and find out where she was staying. That way, he could assign one of his men to watch her comings and goings closely.

He needed to return to headquarters. Even now, the terrorist group might be plotting another bombing. With thousands of people visiting Paris, they needed to apprehend the bombers.

He wanted to believe Jenee was just a visitor to Paris who'd been in the wrong place at the wrong time, but he could not rule out that she was somehow involved. She was of the right ethnicity, and one never knew what motivated someone to violence or rebellion. It was as easy to choose the wrong path as the right one.

Jenee didn't answer his question. Instead, her face suddenly flushed red, and her hands searched her jacket and then around her on the ground. "My purse, it's gone!"

"Are you sure?" He searched the ground, but he didn't recall her carrying anything.

"Of course I'm sure." Panic was in her eyes.

"You must have lost it during the chaos of the sidewalk collapse."

"You don't understand. All my money, my identification, everything is gone. What am I going to do?" She covered her face with her hands, and her shoulders shook. Xavier wasn't sure whether it was a performance worthy of the finest stage actress or a genuinely scared young woman. His heart squeezed, and his first reaction was to enfold her in his arms and offer comfort, but he refrained. He would play along and see where she led him.

"Please, allow me to be of assistance." Xavier reached across the table and patted her arm. After a few more shudders, her hands fell into her lap, and she looked at him with tearful eyes. "If you need a place to stay, I can arrange something. I will not abandon you to the streets, mademoiselle."

"Your offer is most generous, monsieur, and I would be a fool not to accept. Tomorrow I will find a way to free you from my imposition on your kindness. I am sorry, but I have no way to repay you." She managed a small smile, and he realized how that token of her affection swelled the yearning inside of him for more.

"Ah, but you do."

Her brows rose quizzically, and a delightful blush filled her cheeks. "And how is that?" Her voice sharpened, and he wondered if all American women had her backbone.

"You can teach me this method of medical procedure of breath resuscitation you used. I am certain it will come in handy in the future and will help me save many lives."

The color in her cheeks darkened as she lifted a regal brow. It was easy to surmise she understood his meaning completely. He held his laughter in check as she regarded him with narrowed eyes and gave a little humph.

"I suppose, if your intention is noble, I can give you a lesson," she said stiffly. "But it will have to be tomorrow, for as you can see, I have been through enough today."

Oui, tomorrow it is. I admit I'm looking forward to that lesson, Mademoiselle Lazaar.

CHAPTER FOUR

April 29, 1900
Paris, France

THEY TOOK A fiacre, a one-horse carriage, to Montmartre. Xavier stopped briefly at HQ to find out what had been learned from the investigation into the collapsed walkway. He told her the investigation was proceeding and that evidence was still being collected.

Jenee did not expect him to confide in her or share anything about what he was working on. She was simply grateful that he had offered to help her, although she sensed he did not trust her.

Narrow streets and alleys shot off the Rue Novins, the main road that climbed from Paris proper to Montmartre. Jenee looked out the carriage window and could see the white travertine stone façade of the Basilica of Sacré Coeur. The church sat on the highest hill in Paris and, when finished, would offer a commanding view. She'd been to the basilica and Montmartre many times, but seeing the landmark church with its dome not built yet seemed eerie.

"It is a shame they couldn't finish the construction of the funicular in time for the exposition," Xavier observed.

She turned, and his face was impossibly close to hers as he peered out the window on her side of the carriage. He was so handsome it made her knees quiver. The cab was narrow, and their shoulders rocked against one another as they traveled over rutted dirt roads.

"I don't imagine there will be many visitors to our fair city who will trudge up the endless steps and steep roads to visit a bohemian commune, even such a charming one." He smiled, clearly having a fond spot for the working-class hamlet. "It is a shame, as Montmartre is a lively place with much to recommend."

Between the buildings, they passed rickety-fenced vineyards and gardens of vegetables and flowers where the sweet smell of blooms and fruit battled with the more pungent scents of manure and sewage. Montmartre was a patchwork quilt of poor working-class walk-ups, artists' studios, bars, and cabarets. Nothing like the upscale, gentrified neighborhood it would become one day.

"I love Montmartre. It feels real to me. Common folk struggling to make their way and keep their families fed. Like so many of those that come from humble origins, they dream of a better life but are in a daily struggle to maintain the one they have. Having come from humble origins, I have a great affinity for them." She turned her face back to the window, not wanting to miss a single moment of this ride through a historically significant neighborhood and afraid of the heat that poured through her body from Xavier's nearness.

He interrupted her introspection. "A charming observation. Few see beyond their own troubles in life."

Her eyes met his, and Jenee felt pulled into their pale blue depths.

The carriage jostled her against him again, and she grasped the window frame beside her, worried he'd think she was trying to come onto him. She looked out the window and watched the city go by. Two women stood on a corner holding shopping sacks and chatting while a young boy chased a little girl around a tree. A small dog barked at their feet. The girl's squeals rose above the barking, kindling visions of Jenee's childhood. The loss of her parents in that restaurant bombing was eerily parallel to her near miss when she landed smack dab in a bombing at the exposition. Losing her parents had been the most painful time in her life.

Although Jenee had settled in L.A., she felt an acute desire to keep her parents' memory alive. She truly believed that they were with her wherever she lived, firmly entrenched in her heart. Her love for them was integral to who she was. But if the last few hours had taught her anything, it was how fleeting life was.

Her determination to become a strong, financially independent woman was no longer necessary. It was more an excuse she wore like a suit of armor, a shield she used to protect herself from risking her heart. What a foolhardy notion. Where had it gotten her? She was unworthy of the gift her parents had given her by example, of knowing what a loving relationship could be.

Xavier thumped the roof of the fiacre, signaling they had arrived. He jumped out of the cab, handed her down, and then paid the driver.

The street was lined with eighteenth-century townhouses with colorfully painted shutters and doors, and from where they stood, Jenee could see the red-tiled roofs and wings of two windmills turning.

Xavier took her arm and led her down a narrow offshoot alley, and they climbed stone steps to the butte. "The rent is cheaper the higher you go, but it is not for the faint of heart. Are you okay with the climb, Jenee?"

"I am certainly young enough to not tire from a little exertion." She laughed. "It's quite invigorating."

"I only meant that after today's experience, you might be fatigued."

"Your friend is an actress?" She ignored his concern and tried to control the quiver that ran up her arm from his touch.

He nodded. "Of sorts. Lulu Lelouch has mostly achieved small roles at the Théâtre du Châtelet. She is an aspiring *dames entretenues* searching for a patron."

"A *demimonde*? How very interesting."

"You are not ashamed to meet her?"

"Not at all. I've always been curious to meet a *demimonde*. In truth, if a woman in these circumstances is lucky enough to gain a patron who is kind and generous, it would give her more freedom than most other women experience. Wouldn't you agree?"

His brows drew together in a frown. "I would hope this is not something you would aspire to."

"Me?" She laughed at the foolish notion but even more at detecting his disapproval. "She is your friend, monsieur. I would expect you to be more understanding, or do you preach reform to your *amie* while at times sampling her pleasures?"

His brows rose as if he were insulted, but the truth often evoked denial. Perhaps her rescuer was not as altruistic as he portrayed himself to be.

His face flushed, and his eyes sparked with anger.

Jenee felt a tightening in her chest and a wave of guilt for accusing him. *Maybe he's truly in love with her. It's none of my business, in any case.* "I'm sorry, I was impertinent to intimate such a thoughtless accusation. I hope I have not offended you."

"Understandable, mademoiselle, that you would jump to such conclusions," he said in a clipped tone. "I am a friend to her, someone she can trust. Lulu would have thrown herself into the Seine had I not come upon her at that fateful moment. It happens more often than you can imagine, especially to young women with no family and no support, struggling to make their way in a cruel and indifferent world. My intervention was a fortuitous event that changed the course of her life."

Jenee felt another wave of remorse at questioning Xavier's moral integrity, but he seemed too good to be true, and no one had more trust issues than she. "I should not have questioned your intentions. And certainly not accused you of any improprie-ty."

He nodded and directed her through an iron gate, up a walk-way, and into a four-story building. "After you, mademoiselle." She looked up the stairs and began the ascent. "Lulu lives on the top floor," he called behind her.

The stairwell was dingy, the wallpaper of rose bouquets faded and peeling. Jenee was out of breath by the time they reached the top. Usually, four flights of stairs would not have winded her, but Xavier was right, she was exhausted between the time travel, the explosion, and the emotional upheaval.

Xavier knocked on the door, and a lilting feminine voice called, *"Arrive."* A minute later, the same voice, now closer, asked, *"Qui est-ce?"*

"It's Xavier."

The door flung open to a charming squeal of delight. *"Mon ami,* Xavier. I haven't seen you in so long." Slender arms wrapped around Xavier's neck and pulled his face down for the requisite kiss on both cheeks. *"Entrez, entrez."*

Stepping into the apartment, Jenee came face to face with Lulu, and they eyed each other curiously.

"Lulu, this is Mademoiselle Jenee Lazaar. She had an unfortunate experience today, and I need your help."

Lulu's sapphire-blue eyes regarded Jenee from her head to her shoes, and she tsked, shaking her head. Jenee could only imagine what she thought. Lulu looked like a siren from an old movie, wrapped in a red silk kimono, tied snugly at the waist, making no secret of her voluptuous figure. Her thick red hair was held in place with combs, and her flawless skin and cheeks made Jenee think of whipped crème fraîche and strawberries. The *pièce de résistance* was her charming dimples, so deep they looked as if someone had stuck their fingers in the young woman's cheeks and left a permanent impression. Jenee had had a few clients in L.A. who'd paid thousands to get dimples like that. But Lulu was all natural and utterly beautiful and feminine. She was also clearly besotted with her savior. Xavier could have Lulu if he chose. Why he wouldn't or didn't was beyond belief. Was it due to a lack of funds to support a mistress?

Jenee gave herself a mental shake. *You only met the guy a few hours ago. What he does or doesn't do with Lulu is none of your beeswax.*

She turned on her L.A. smile and offered her hand to Lulu. "I'm pleased to make your acquaintance, Mademoiselle Lelouch. Xavier has spoken of you as a trusted friend."

"*Merci*, please call me Lulu. Everyone does." Lulu reached up and caressed Xavier's cheek. "You are lucky to make a friend of *Inspecteur en Chef* Doumaz. He is the kind of man any woman wants on her side." She giggled and, standing on tiptoe, kissed his cheek, leaving a perfect red imprint of her lush lips.

Xavier reddened, and he wiped away the smear of lip rouge. "You are an unrepentant flirt, Lulu."

She dismissively waved her hand. "One day, Xavier, you will release yourself from your prudish bonds and find pleasure where it is offered."

"Lulu, you are not on stage in a performance."

"If only I were, but the director is stingy, casting the plum roles with his latest paramour."

Jenee found Lulu's machinations amusing. Her flirtations were clearly for Jenee's benefit. The actress was marking territory. It was the aspiring *demimonde*'s way of subtly laying claim to Xavier. Jenee sensed a gauntlet being thrown down, and competition for Xavier's affection had begun. She reminded herself it wasn't any of her business whether Xavier enjoyed sex or anything else with Lulu.

So why did her pulse race in the carriage whenever his arm bumped hers?

Stop with the pining, Jen. This dude is clearly off-limits. Besides, even if she was back home in Paris, it was a completely different world, and one that she had no intention of staying in. She had to figure out how to get back to her own time. Emily and Gabriella must be worried sick about her. She could imagine the headlines: *Pimple-popper to the Stars Vanishes Without a Trace.*

"Come and sit down." Lulu waved them to the sofa. "A glass of wine, *chérie*?"

"Yes, thank you."

Lulu turned to Jenee. "Mademoiselle?"

"Oui, merci."

While Lulu fetched glasses and wine, Jenee looked around the apartment. The furniture was a bit frayed and worn, but Lulu had thrown beautiful silk scarfs over everything, which provided a colorful gaiety that lifted the gloom in the run-down place. Candles glowed, and the walls looked newly papered in a yellow and white stripe that brightened the room. This upper loft must surely be light and airy in the daytime. From where they sat on the sofa, she could see a small kitchen with two chairs and a café table, where an Art Nouveau metal vase filled with pink roses perfumed the air.

Lulu returned and handed them each a glass of burgundy-colored wine. Then, after retrieving her own glass, she draped herself over the divan across from the sofa, reminding Jenee of Theda Bara, the silent film vamp. Jenee had to hand it to Lulu: she was a skilled seductress. She must always be playing a part, always alluring, and weaving a web around those within her orbit. Jenee knew the drill well, having witnessed it a thousand times in the behavior of her patients.

"Lulu, *mon amie*, Jenee needs attire to see her through the next couple of days," Xavier said. "I told her no one has a better sense of fashion or more articles of clothing than my dear friend Lulu."

"But what has happened to you that you are in such a *prédicament?*" Lulu asked.

"I-I—"

Xavier interrupted. "You might have heard about the walking bridge that collapsed at the exposition today. Jenee was in the thick of it and was lucky not to be killed, but tragically, nine others were not so lucky. Jenee has just arrived from America, and her handbag lies beneath the fallen concrete. I've offered her a place to stay until we find her a more suitable situation."

Lulu's eyes flashed. "How kind of you, *mon amour*, forever rescuing damsels in distress. Well, we must see to this immediately. Come, mademoiselle, and we will dress you so you can go anywhere in Paris."

"*Merci*, Lulu. I will find a way to repay you," Jenee said.

"*C'est rien.*" Lulu waved her hand dismissively. "Although I commiserate with your plight, I do this for the inspector." She turned her winning smile on him and blew him a kiss.

Xavier cleared his throat and changed the direction of the conversation. "I am starving, *chérie*, and I could use a bit of distraction after the week I've had. In honor of your kindness, why don't we celebrate, and I will treat you lovely ladies to a meal and some dancing? I'm sure Jenee will enjoy seeing a bit of the liveliness of Montmartre."

Lulu clapped her hands. "What a delightful idea. Come, Jenee, we must fix you up. One never knows who one will meet among the bohemians."

Jenee imagined Lulu would be pleased if she met anyone other than Xavier.

CHAPTER FIVE

April 29, 1900
Montmartre, Paris

JENEE'S CHEST FLUTTERED with excitement as they walked down the hill to the center of town and approached the corner of Rue Saint-Vincent and Rue des Saules, where the restaurant and nightclub Au Lapin Agile stood.

Jenee's mother, Aida, had been an art history professor, and her father, Sami, had taught literature and creative writing at la Sorbonne. Jenee's childhood had been full of wonder, with almost weekly trips to the Louvre, the Musée d'Orsay, and the Musée de l'Orangerie. Her parents regaled her with stories about the heyday of the artists—symbolists, impressionists, famous writers, and musicians—like Pablo Picasso, Claude Debussy, and Amadeo Modigliani, who frequented Au Lapin Agile.

I can't believe I'm going to this historical place I used to visit with Maman and Papa.

Raucous laughter and raised voices paired with strumming guitar and cello as they entered. Lulu kept up a steady stream of amusing gossip, her arm linked through Xavier's, as Jenee absorbed her surroundings. If there was a silver lining to time travel, it was seeing the world as it had been. The restaurant was drenched in greenery that matched the green shuttered windows. The rectangular sign above the cottage door depicted a grinning rabbit wearing a top hat, holding a bottle of wine as he leaped out of a saucepan. The sign read: *Au Lapin Agile*, which literally translated to *The Nimble Rabbit*.

A haze of smoke floated in the air, and Jenee blinked back tears, not just from the smoke but from the lovely memories of visiting here with her parents on numerous occasions. Her parents had always been her biggest supporters. Losing them when she was in medical school was a devastating loss, and she'd had to develop a tough hide to get through her pain. It also caused her to bury herself in her work and fight to the top of her field to make them proud. How she missed them.

Oil lamps with red shades dangled from wires around the room, casting a dingy light over the patrons. Posters and paintings hung on the walls, and in the corner, two bearded men in hats played cello and guitar, accompanied by a singer with a birdlike voice, her milk-white breasts barely contained within her striped satin bodice. The bar was crowded with boisterous people hoisting glasses brimming with alcoholic beverages, clearly enjoying their merrymaking. Most astonishing was the menagerie of animals sheltered beneath the sizeable white plaster hearth. White mice vied for space with a monkey, a crow, and a donkey, which, Lulu said laughingly, was named Lolo.

They were greeted by a bearded man who bussed Lulu on both cheeks and shook hands with Xavier. Lulu introduced Jenee to Pere Frédé, the soon-to-be owner, and he pointed to a table against the wall that was being cleared. The unmistakable fragrance of simmering onions and garlic blended with the sweat and perfume of the patrons, creating a riot of smells that played havoc with Jenee's senses. They took their seats, and Lulu insisted they start with the *combine*, a drink particular to the place, made of white wine, cherries, grenadine, and cherry liquor.

Her parents had often enjoyed a glass of *combine*, and Jenee had had a sip or two when she was a kid. She recalled how potent it was and sipped slowly. Even so, on an empty stomach, it didn't take much for the spirits to go to her head. She sat back in her chair, feeling a warmth spread through her limbs.

"Let's order," said Xavier. Jenee had noticed the tension ease in his shoulders since they sat down. She imagined his work was a constant source of stress, and for some reason, watching him relax added to the feeling of contentment and warmth flowing through her. *It must be the wine making me giddy.*

"I suggest the Civet de Lapin. It is the best in the city," Lulu declared, never taking her eyes off what was happening in the small, crowded barroom. Jenee couldn't blame her, because the restaurant was a people-watching paradise. Beautiful women in colorful and provocative costumes danced and laughed with rakish young men who might be aspiring artists and poets. This was the bohemian world of Renoir, Seurat, Modigliani, and so many other famous painters, before they were famous.

Xavier leaned in close to Jenee. "Is that good for you, Jenee?" His expressive blue eyes studied her face, and his voice felt like a caress. Jenee was very aware of how she looked, with her black hair twisted atop her head and the tight-waisted, royal-blue dress with a flowing skirt she wore. She could feel his eyes on her with a growing frequency. She wondered if Lulu regretted choosing the outfit for her.

"Yes, that sounds wonderful. My mother used to prepare a wonderful rabbit stew, but it's not very common in America."

"Do your parents also live in America with you?"

Jenee clenched her hands together, digging her nails into her palm. "No, I'm afraid my parents died about ten years ago—" She cut herself off, hoping he wouldn't ask her how they died. She couldn't tell him her parents were killed in a bombing at a popular Algerian restaurant. Xavier was already suspicious about her sudden appearance unscathed at the boardwalk bombing.

"May I ask how they passed?"

Shit! Think fast. "In a—um, a boating accident. They drowned."

"*Je suis désolé.*" He took her hand and squeezed it.

She bit her lip to hold back more tears. The sadness in Xavier's eyes made lying to him even worse. She sensed something more profound than his empathy for her loss—a loss of his own lay hidden in the depths of his eyes.

A loud laugh from another table rang out, and the moment passed.

The food arrived with a bottle of *vin rouge*, and Xavier filled their glasses. After almost twenty-four hours with nothing to eat and little to drink, a lethargy had seeped into her limbs. The delectable stew made with rabbit, onion, garlic, *ventrèche*, rosemary, and thyme absorbed the headiness of the wine, but she feared if she didn't slow down with the vino, she'd soon be slurring her words.

Lulu leaned over. "*Excusez-moi*, I must say hello to some friends."

Xavier waved her away. "Go, *chérie*."

Jenee had spent the last ten hours with Xavier, but being alone with him now felt different. Even in the crowded bar with so many distractions, she was acutely aware of him. Her eyes wandered to him time and again. He leaned back in his chair, his hat pushed back on his head, freeing his curls to tumble over his forehead. She'd switched to sipping water to help clear her head, so it wasn't the wine making her feel heady now. It was the nearness of Xavier. His scent of clove, citrus, cinnamon, and something else, something sensual and mysterious and oh so appealing, stirred a longing in her she'd never experienced. It enveloped her, making her want to slide closer to him, lean in, and press her nose to his skin.

She took another deep drink of water and looked at anything other than Xavier. Her gaze fell on a nearby table, where a youth verging on manhood stared at her. She nearly spilled the water down the front of her dress. He stared at her with a force that shocked her. Even at this young age, he possessed a Svengali-like magnetism, demanding recognition.

Recognition came to her in a flash. She'd read enough about him in books and magazines and, of course, the numerous films based on his life, art, and volatile private life. Pablo Picasso tossed his head, smoothing back an unruly lock of straight black hair that fell over his forehead, and he smiled at her. She felt her cheeks blaze with color. *OMG, Pablo Picasso is flirting with me.*

Jenee recalled the painting of the dancers at the Metropolitan Museum had been painted in 1900. Picasso was nineteen and newly arrived in Paris. But seeing him sitting close enough to touch, she found it fascinating that he already owned that arrogant aura at such a young age. He exuded a boldness that told the world he was destined for greatness. Beside Picasso sat his best friend and roommate, Carles Casagemas. Seated between them, in a red dress, with her hair knotted atop her head, was Germaine Pichot, a ballerina who, as a sideline, modeled for artists.

Jenee could scarcely believe what she was seeing and would have loved to keep watching them like they were actors on a movie screen. Carles Casagemas was an artist from a wealthy Catalan family who fell head over heels in love with the pretty ballerina. Germaine became his obsession, but she did not return his affections, to his dismay. Most likely, Carles' addiction to alcohol and drugs had exacerbated his downward spiral and led to his rumored impotence and mental instability.

The two friends could not be more different. One was solidly the captain of his ship, while the other was an emotional wreck. In 1901, a year from now, Picasso would convince Carles, who increasingly was losing control and suffering from severe depression, to spend Christmas in Barcelona. Afterward, they traveled to Malaga to celebrate the New Year with Picasso's family. But Carles' mood swings and belligerence caused a rift, and he abruptly left Malaga and returned to Paris. His obsession with Germaine reached a climax. At a farewell dinner at the Hippodrome Café, when Germaine again refused to marry him, he pulled a gun and shot her. She fell to the floor. Thinking he'd killed her, which he had not, he turned the gun on himself and put a bullet through his head.

That tragic end of his best friend would result in some of Picasso's most powerful paintings and inspire the blue period that propelled him to fame. He often painted Germaine, even featuring her in his breakthrough work *Les Demoiselles d'Avignon*. For a time, Germaine would become Picasso's lover and one of the hundreds of women who paraded through his life and art. Their friendship would last until her death in 1948. Perhaps Picasso's most redeeming act was that he cared for Germaine until the end.

All of this went through Jenee's head as she glanced at the trio sitting together. She wished she could warn them of the tragedy coming down the road, but they would simply think her mad. Besides, it would not be wise to try to change the course of history. *Stop looking at them,* she admonished herself. She lifted her glass to her lips and emptied it.

She saw Picasso stand and sensed his approach. Xavier must have been aware of the artist's stare because, in one swift move, he wrapped his arm around her shoulders and pulled her against him. He cast a steely-eyed look at Picasso as if to say, *Bug off, kid,* and then turned her chin toward him and kissed her.

A kaleidoscope of dazzling sensations flooded her senses, and the kiss, which was no doubt meant to ward off the arrogant youth, became the most searing flame that had ever been lit inside her. Jenee's eyelids fluttered closed, and she sank into the perfection of Xavier's soft lips and demanding tongue. Whatever Picasso's reaction was, she would never know. She was lost in the most dizzying and rapturous kiss she'd ever experienced.

When Xavier finally pulled away, her eyes slowly opened, and she gazed into his startling, pale blue eyes. He looked at her differently, as though he was aware of her in a way that he hadn't been before. Jenee's heart pounded in her chest. He was breathing as heavy as she was, as though they'd both sprinted up a steep flight of stairs. His thick black lashes made the blue of his eyes even more striking. *I have clients who spend thousands of dollars a year on permanent eyeliner and lash extensions that don't look this good.*

Was Xavier asserting his protection, or had the heady wine had the same effect on him as it had on her? Either way, Jenee didn't want it to stop. She wanted to stay in this moment for as long as she could. She sensed Xavier felt the same.

She reached up and caressed his face, and he covered her hand, pressing his lips to her palm. "I apologize, but I'm not sorry, Jenee. I saw the Spanish artist ogling you like a starving man would drool over a roast leg of lamb, and I didn't want—" He swallowed. "I don't want any man here to even dare try to stake a claim on you. I know it was selfish of me, but I…" He seemed to search for the right words. "I didn't expect to lose control and be carried away like that."

"I'm not sorry either, Xavier. It was…it was beautiful." She was afraid to say more and let him know just how deeply and strongly his kiss affected her. She knew his confession of losing control and not regretting it was out of character for him. They both had been pretending they weren't attracted to each other. But should she give in to the moment? Should she see where this attraction took them?

The rational doctor in her warned her to tread carefully. She had only just met him, and everything was different despite her having been transported to the city she grew up in. She was a stranger in a strange land. But her emotional side, the passionate side that she protected behind a concrete wall, wanted to break through precisely because she was out of her own time. *What's the worst that could happen? I fall hard and fast and maybe get my heart broken?* But didn't Xavier face that risk too?

Enough with the ping-pong arguments. Just shut up, Jen, and enjoy the moment.

It was like the sun's rays bursting through cloud cover when he smiled. Beams of warmth spread through her body. Xavier glanced over to the musicians, where a few couples were dancing. "Would you dance with me?"

She nodded, her smile matching his. He stood and took her

hand. As she walked to the dance floor, she glanced back over her shoulder, and her eyes met Picasso's. He winked, tipped his hat, and gave a little shrug. She chuckled and then turned her full attention to the handsome man who had captivated her senses from the moment they'd met.

Xavier took her in his arms and pulled her close, and she rested her head on his shoulder. He whispered in her ear, "You should know I never dance, so don't expect too much. It was an excuse to hold you in my arms."

She met his gaze. "You will not hear me complain."

Laughter rumbled deep in his chest.

This carefree, spontaneous side to Xavier was another layer to this attractive, complex man. The walls between them had toppled with their kiss, and oh, how she wanted to confide in him and tell him everything.

"Who are you, Jenee Lazaar?" he asked.

CHAPTER SIX

April 29, 1900
Paris, France

X AVIER COULD SCARCELY keep his thoughts straight. Who was this goddess who made him believe in tomorrow? Jenee's nearness to him worked on his senses like opium.

The carriage ambled toward the Île de la Cité and his apartment. From the moment she'd stepped out of Lulu's bedroom in the stunning blue velvet dress, he'd realized that his attraction to her wasn't something he could ignore. She was mesmerizing, and his power to elucidate his feelings was minimal. He might have controlled his emotions had jealousy not overwhelmed him. But when that brash upstart Picasso continued to ogle her and stood ready to approach, Xavier acted instinctively to keep her by his side. Picasso may be young, but already his reputation was notorious. Xavier told himself it was for Jenee's protection, but that wasn't entirely true. The truth was that he desired her more than he'd ever wanted a woman, and he couldn't stand back and allow another man to steal her from him.

That dance, that provocative dance. Xavier recalled every moment, everywhere their bodies touched, every heated breath. She'd leaned into him, and the road to heaven opened to him. He should have kept a professional distance, and he should not have succumbed to passion.

That kiss, that damnable kiss, sealed his fate. The effect on him had been profound. He'd been speechless afterward, his heart thudding in his chest and his blood roaring in his ears. And all he knew at that moment, as he gazed into her luminous amber eyes, was that Jenee Lazaar had changed his life completely and there was no way he would ever be the same.

His body responded with such a burning fire it was all he could do not to pick her up and carry her out of the café. He wanted her, every part of her, and the thought of being alone in his apartment with her blazed through his veins like a flow of lava to the sea.

Nothing had prepared him for Jenee Lazaar, and the man who'd dedicated his life to police work found himself lost in a dizzying mystical timelessness that knew no beginning and wanted no end.

JENEE SAT NEXT to Xavier in the fiacre, their shoulders bumping just as they had when they'd driven to Montmartre a few hours before. The two journeys were worlds apart, though. After their kiss, her world had shifted on its axis, and Jenee worried nothing would ever be the same.

Whatever Lulu thought about Jenee's dance and kiss with Xavier, she'd kept it to herself. When they returned to Lulu's apartment, she packed Jenee a change of clothes and sleeping attire and bussed her on both cheeks good-naturedly. Before they bade Lulu goodnight, she invited them both to come to see her in a performance of *Around the World in Eighty Days*, a play adapted from Jules Verne's bestselling novel that was playing at the Théâtre du Châtelet. Lulu had a small role in the production. Jenee had accepted the invitation, seeing Xavier's nod of agreement. She could do nothing less, given Lulu's kindness to her. And despite Lulu's affection for Xavier, she had been kind to

Jenee.

That Lulu cared about Xavier and was attracted to him was undeniable, but did she see Jenee as a threat? A woman like Lulu, without financial means, would try to use her beauty and youth to find a protector. Did Xavier fit that bill? Or was she genuinely in love with him? More importantly, did Xavier feel similarly toward Lulu, and was he merely trying to make her jealous?

Jenee couldn't think straight. She'd traveled back to nineteen-effing-hundred, not knowing why other than it had something to do with Allegretto, the red-haired muse, and his paintings. And she had no idea how to help the Renaissance artist, nor how she would get back to him, or if she could even get back home.

A thought flashed in her mind. Could Lulu be the mysterious woman in the painting? Jenee closed her eyes and pictured the mysterious red-haired muse and Lulu. Yes, they both had long red hair, but Lulu was petite, and Allegretto's lover was taller, much taller, and lithe, and the shade of her hair was different.

What a mess! How am I going to get through it? She was exhausted and had indulged in far too much wine. And she still had no idea how Xavier truly felt about Lulu, other than caring about her as a friend. *Besides, who am I to get in their way?*

Lulu's parting words had confused her even more. "I have very good news to share."

"What good news, *ma chérie?*"

"I auditioned for Sarah Bernhardt's company"—Lulu grabbed Xavier's hand—"and I will be joining the company when *Around the World in Eighty Days* closes. It is the opportunity I have hoped for."

"That is good news, Lulu. You know I always wish the best for you."

It was almost like a final attempt to impress Xavier and gain his favor, but no more was said, and he and Jenee left shortly thereafter.

Jenee had watched one too many reality TV shows pitting women against each other as they vied to catch the hot bachelor.

Not to mention the never-ending stream of L.A. socialites who told her about their revolving-door relationships as they sat through a procedure. She smiled, nodded, and offered a few words of advice here and there, but her policy was to be as neutral as Switzerland regarding her clients' love lives. One thing Jenee was not, and that was a kiss-and-tell gal. Nor was she interested in bed hopping. The downside of living in L.A. was that there were as many fake people as fake boobs. Another reason her perspective on love and relationships was so jaded. But did the same apply here? Was she seeing Xavier and Lulu through the cynical celebrity lens of L.A.?

Now, in the intimacy of the fiacre, a silence settled upon them. Jenee and Xavier were alone, but not completely alone, as the streets outside bustled with hansoms and people milling about. Above the clip-clop of the horse, she was sure Xavier could hear her heart pound as they neared his apartment on the Rue des Chantres. They crossed the Pont Notre Dame from the Right Bank of the Seine to the Île de la Cité. From there, they traveled along the Quai de la Corse to the old neighborhood of Quartier des Chanoines. The picturesque quarter, ancient buildings, and narrow streets were original to the medieval and gothic periods. When the fiacre could go no farther because of the street's narrowness, Xavier descended to the cobblestones and handed Jenee down.

He took her elbow and led her down a narrow side street; his broad shoulders grazed the walls as they walked. Moonlight lit their way, and glancing up, Jenee was awed to see the towering spire of the cathedral, and the statuary of the apostles, including St. George slaying the dragon, all poised as if on a ladder descending from heaven onto Notre Dame's rooftop. She almost expected to see Quasimodo, Victor Hugo's deformed hero of *The Hunchback of Notre Dame*, appear behind the spire, carrying the beautiful Gypsy Esmeralda along the parapets to save her from the hangman's noose. As Jenee walked beside her rescuer, she couldn't help but think about the tragic hunchback whose love for the Gypsy girl destroyed him. It crossed her mind that she posed a potential threat to Xavier just as Esmeralda had to Quasimodo. If they were to fall in love and she was snatched away by the fingers of time, she would destroy his heart. *It's a ridiculous comparison.* But the thought of it lingered in her mind.

Xavier stopped at the door and unlocked it. "I'm sorry it's six flights up, but I know you'll understand when you see *la vue est enchanteresse.* Besides, I like not having anyone living above me, and my apartment is very convenient because it is close to the prefecture."

The climb up the narrow stairway was a test of Jenee's will. By the time they reached the top floor, she was panting. "Now I know why you are so fit. Goodness, I can't even imagine dragging bags of fruit, vegetables, cheese, and bread up these stairs." *Perhaps the elevator and not the wheel is the greatest of inventions.* "I'd forgotten why Parisians frequent cafés so often. By the time you heft everything up here, you're ready for bed!"

Xavier chuckled. "Ah, *oui, mais*—think of the feast you could have after a lovely respite under the covers."

She felt her cheeks burn, and not from the climb's exertion. *Mon Dieu!* She just realized she'd said the phrase *ready for bed.*

I hope he doesn't think I'm coming onto him. Then she almost burst out laughing. *You're on your way up to the apartment of a man you met a few hours ago, and you're worried now that he'll think you're loose?*

"Ah, but I think you will make an exception and change your mind about the difficulty of the climb when you hear the bells ring for Angelus at eight a.m. It's as if the voices of angels awaken you to greet the day." He unlocked the door with a flourish. "*Voila.*"

She entered and waited while he lit a lamp, casting away the darkness of night. A window was open, and Jenee shivered and rubbed her arms.

"I apologize for the chill in the air. I like to air the place out, but the evenings are still chilly in Paris in April," Xavier said, closing the window. "I'll get a fire started. Come sit before the hearth. It will be cozy in no time."

He settled her on the sofa before the fireplace and began building a fire. She looked around, getting a sense of his home. The mansard ceiling was trussed with beams, and the wood plank and peg floors were worn and polished smooth from wear. A reproduction Savonnerie carpet partially covered the floor, perhaps a flea market purchase. Mismatched pieces of mahogany furniture were scattered around the cozy room: a carved wooden chest sat on a multicolored oriental carpet in front of a settee, and stacks of paper were organized neatly in piles on a desk in the corner. Next to the desk, a glass-fronted cabinet held leather-bound books. On the walls hung several small, framed paintings. She could see they were scenes of Algerian life and austere desert landscapes. Ticking on the fireplace mantel was a wood-cased clock. It was near midnight. A round table and two chairs were placed with a view through the window. Jenee imagined there was a kitchen, a bedroom, and a bathroom through the two closed doors leading out of the living space. It was as far from Beverly Hills as you could get. She found it utterly charming.

Xavier stood and dusted off his hands, watching the kindling ignite. "It will warm up in a few minutes."

"Your home is very warm and cozy."

"Thank you, but I'm afraid my woeful bachelor's retreat lacks a feminine touch." He retrieved a bottle from the cabinet and poured two glasses of amber liquid. He handed Jenee a glass, and she smiled her thanks.

"You are very kind, Xavier. I don't know what I would have done without your help." She felt her cheeks heat and took a sip, suddenly feeling like a teenager on her first date.

"I think our meeting was fortuitous," he said, setting his brandy glass on the chest.

"How do you mean fortuitous?" She wondered where she would sleep but was too shy to ask.

Xavier removed his coat and tie, hung them on his desk chair, and sat beside her on the sofa. He took a drink of his brandy.

Liquid courage. Jenee lifted her glass, determined to find her own courage. She kept pushing away an image of waking up in his strong arms, her breasts pressed against his muscular chest. At least, she was pretty sure his chest was muscular. She'd certainly felt the hard planes of his chest as she danced with him earlier, not to mention all the bumping around in the carriage.

Their eyes met, and she felt the amatory heat of his gaze. Would it be terrible if she followed her desire and spent a night in bliss? It wasn't as if she were a virgin. Nor did she have any expectations other than those of a sensual nature. One night of pleasure would be more than enough. After all, she was a modern woman. A modern woman stuck at the dawn of the twentieth century.

But after all was said and done, would Xavier think badly of her?

"I have to be honest with you, Jenee."

Honesty is good. She met his gaze, waiting for more.

"I never mix my investigational work with pleasurable pursuits."

Where had she heard that line before? The modern version: *I never mix business with pleasure.* It was what she told her male clients when they asked her out. Better to pass on an unlikely matchup than lose a client. "Wait, when did I become your work?" She took a too-big swig of brandy, spasming into a cough.

Xavier patted her on the back. "Better not to gulp cognac. It's made to be slowly sipped." He hurried down the hall and returned with a glass of water a few moments later. "Here, drink this and clear your throat."

"Thank you." She sipped the cool water, and the burning eased. "You haven't answered my question."

He sat back and regarded her silently for a few moments, his brow furrowed. "You must realize how suspect your story is. Newly arrived in Paris, no luggage, no money, no friends, no hotel. And at the exact moment the walkway collapsed, there you appear, standing amid the destruction, yet you bear not one cut or abrasion. Would you not consider that suspicious if you were in my position?"

He was right, of course. But how could she convince him otherwise? She needed his help. What if Xavier was the only person able to help her solve this Allegretto mystery and get back home? But dare she trust him with the truth?

"I understand why you would jump to that conclusion, but although it might seem suspicious, I swear to you it's the truth." A searing pain shot through her with her realization. He hadn't let his guard down for one moment, not throughout their carriage ride, dance, and kiss. *What a fool I am for thinking he was attracted to me when all he was interested in was figuring out if I was involved in the bombing. And to think I was worried about the possibility of hurting his feelings or giving him the wrong impression.* She gulped down the rest of the drink and held it out to Xavier. *"Un autre, s'il vous plait."*

His brows rose. *"Ma chérie,* you might want to slow down, or I will spend the night holding your head over *les toilettes."*

The nerve! "Will you fill my glass or not?"

He took the glass from her with a bit more force than necessary. She raised her chin triumphantly, knowing she was getting under his skin. He returned, and she took the glass and forced another swallow. *Please don't let me be sick.* He'd undone the first button of his shirt, and a curl of dark hair on his chest enticed her. That damned kiss had utterly shattered her resistance to him.

"If I'm under suspicion and you're contemplating arresting me, why the hell did you bring me to your home?" She held out her wrists. "Perhaps you'd like to handcuff me."

Xavier's face reddened. "You are behaving like a child."

The room felt impossibly hot, and she longed to stick her head out the window and drag in the cold air. She, who meticulously controlled her emotions and carefully planned out every day, right down to what she was having for dinner, found herself not caring what this night brought. Whether Xavier wanted her in his bed because she was a suspect and he thought he could learn her secrets or if he wanted her because he was as attracted to her as she was to him didn't matter. Damned if he didn't have the worst effect on her, and double damned, he held all the cards. She was trapped, with nowhere else to go. What was she going to do? Beg sanctuary from the priests of Notre Dame like Esmeralda?

What she would not do was sit another minute on this sofa with him. She stood on rubbery legs and stumbled to the window. Opening it, she leaned out, closed her eyes, and breathed deeply. After several bracing breaths of fresh air, she opened her eyes and gazed at the magnificent view. The moon balanced on the tip of Notre Dame's spire as though a magician conjured a trick. It looked close enough to touch—an illusion, of course, but she reached out as if she might scoop it up and put it in her pocket.

Large hands grabbed her from behind, pulling her against a brick wall. No, not a brick wall, a very manly chest. Her breath released with a whoosh, and the heady feel of him so close, his arms around her, made her simultaneously giddy and dizzy.

His breath rasped in her ear. "Be careful. You could have fallen." He held her in a vise grip tight against his body. She turned, pressing against his chest to push him away. But once her hands got there, they wanted to stay. *Damn hands!* She wanted him more than her next breath.

Don't give in. She slurred, "I'm fine. You're being *overbraying*—um, *overbearing*—bossy!"

His mouth clamped over hers, silencing her. Her head was spinning, and her knees buckled. He tightened his arms around her, sensing her wobbly state.

But instead of pushing him away, she grabbed hold, feeling only the solidity of hardened muscle. She wanted more, and now she was getting it. His tongue swirled against hers hungrily.

I want him, but I don't trust him. Not one bit! Her feeling went against every rule she'd ever set for herself. Trust was the one component of a relationship that could not be compromised.

What am I doing? Why am I ignoring the warning signs?

Xavier's lips trailed along her jaw, neck, and collarbone, making her sigh with pleasure.

Ah, that's why I'm ignoring the warning signs. His hot breath in her ear sent electrical pulses pinging throughout her body. She quivered like an arrow strung taut in a bow.

"I cannot fight what I'm feeling anymore," he said in a deep, raspy voice. "My desire for you is beyond reason, but I will stop if you wish me to." He spread his hands across her back, pressing her against his chest. The beat of his heart was a seismic percussion matching hers. "Do you not feel the same?"

Her reply was halting, gasped between her struggles to breathe. "I-I do, but it pains me because I have no ulterior reason, unlike you. I am drawn to you like a moth to a flame, but I don't believe you can say the same thing. Your desire is mingled with something else, *n'est-ce pas?*"

He pulled away but remained with his face so close that all she could see were his blue eyes. "I swear on my life I will never hurt you. I want to love you. Let me love you."

The declaration pierced through the last of her armor, disarming her. She cupped Xavier's face and feathered kisses over his mouth. His sigh of relief was as great an electrical charge to her core as his lust. Sweet, delicious kisses gave rise to the wetness between her legs, and purrs of pleasure poured without restraint.

Deftly, he undid the buttons of her dress, kissing every inch of exposed skin. He took his time, relishing the taste of her neck and then kissing one shoulder and then the other as her dress slid lower. He pulled the pins from her hair, releasing a cascade of hair down her back. "Beautiful," he whispered. "So beautiful."

She fumbled with the buttons of his shirt. He watched her as if surprised when she succeeded, and his shirt slid away to the floor. *You are the beautiful one,* she thought. His pectorals hardened into stone like the statue of Hercules she'd seen at the Getty Museum.

With a mind of their own, her lips and hands grazed his skin with kisses and caresses. His groan turned her insides into hot liquid. It was the sweetest of sounds, the sound of a need that only she could satisfy. At this moment, the heady cognac, the uncertainty of what tomorrow would bring, and the beauty and intensity of this man had combined to ignite a feminine power that seemed to pour from her pores, and Xavier drank it up.

Taking command, he spun her around, making quick work of the laces of her corset. It fell away, and he pulled her tight from behind against his body, his hands enfolding her breasts, fondling, and squeezing, while he kissed the pulse points on her neck and his warm breath teased her ear. "You will tell me what pleases you."

"Yes," she breathed, "whatever you want…everything. It seems you already know what pleases me." The intensity of pleasure made her arch against him, and as if drawn like a magnet, she felt his hardness press against the seam of her derriere, the throbbing pulse of his excitement tapping out a secret message meant only for her. She was being carried away, little more than flotsam and jetsam tossed by the swells of the sea, drowning in a need that would not be satisfied until he possessed all of her.

A primal growl of desire erupted from his chest. A baritone chord of sound ripped through her, tearing away her inhibitions, resistance, and ability to survive without his touch.

All her life, had she not wished for this? To be overwhelmed by passion. Xavier awakened every fiber of her being, yet it frightened her. She was afraid to lose herself and trust this man from another time. But Jenee could not stop the desire that flooded her senses any more than she could stop the Earth's orbit around the sun. She sensed that never knowing where this led would be a price too high, and she would be the loser.

Unable to pretend even for an instant that this was not what she wanted, she turned, eager to remove the rest of their clothing. She wasn't a virginal young girl who'd never explored a man's body and didn't know what pleased him, but Xavier somehow turned the world inside out, and what she felt for him made her want to lose complete control. What he awakened in her made her never want this moment to end.

His lips on her sparked frissons of excitement like none she'd ever felt. His lips gave birth to feelings she'd never known possible. Every delicious brush of tender skin, hot, wet, desperate, and demanding, pooled inside her as if it was the first time. Was this some side effect of time travel that changed what had been into what might be? It was insane and would never end well, but whatever he asked of her, she could not deny him, because denying him would be an affront to truth, beauty, and love.

She recalled her feeling of failure when she looked at Allegretto's paintings. She'd scorned herself for living a life too planned, too controlled, never allowing for spontaneity. But tonight, she would be redeemed. No feelings of failure here. Everything was about the here and now and her shared moment of deep desire with this incredible man.

Her body, mind, and soul lived only to please his need. All she wanted was to feel his fullness deep within her, his body thrusting inside her until the intensity exploded, carrying them away on a tide of today, tomorrow, and forever. It made her nearly weep thinking of the years she'd lived without him.

He caressed her face with trembling fingertips, searching her eyes as if questioning if she was feeling the same powerful surges of desire, as though longing to know he was not alone. Her ability to speak had abandoned her, and words were insufficient. Words could never transmit the inexplicable perfection of what he did to her body.

She pressed against the hardness of his life-giving manhood, leaving him covered in her dew. His gasp of breath, held deep in his chest and slowly released, signaled his struggle to hold on to his equilibrium. The heat between them burned hotter than the embers blazing in the hearth and coated her body in a glistening sheen. His sweet lips pressed against hers, and she was lost again, dizzy, spiraling out of control. Her heart beat wildly against his chest like a bird fanning its wings against a cage struggling to be free.

Xavier. She repeated his name over and over in her mind like a mantra. It seemed impossible that her life had changed so dramatically in one day. How had he become the artist and she the clay beneath his fingers in only a few hours? His lips burnished her skin, molding her into whatever he wanted. His long, slender fingers could do to her whatever he wished, so long as he didn't let her go.

She caressed his neck, shoulders, and muscled back, and the delicious slickness of his smooth skin. He held her captive, one hand on the back of her head, fingers entwined in her hair, and the other clasping her buttocks, pinning her against him. Had any man ever felt so hard and hot?

His cock would bring her pleasure, pleasure like no man ever had before. It pulsated against her, beating out its own rhythm, somehow matching her racing heartbeat. His lips slid down the space between her breasts, and he turned his head slightly and locked on to a nipple, teasing it with his clever tongue, sucking while his hand gently squeezed. A charge of electricity sizzled between her legs. As he devilishly cupped both breasts in his hands, his lips slid to the other nipple, grazing her nub with his teeth, sending shivers to the bud between her legs.

She wanted to savor his exquisite lips forever. To feel them on her in the dead of night and at the break of dawn. She would not think about tomorrow, the day after, or the possibility of being denied the feel of his body against her for the rest of her life. No, she would only think about now, tonight, a magical night unlike any other.

His lips released her, and he lifted his head until his beautiful blue eyes searching hers reminded her of the translucent waters of the seashore. She felt his warm breath on her face, sweetened by cognac, making her drunk again. Drunk on him. She closed her eyes.

"Are you all right, Jenee?" His deep baritone sent shivers through her. "It was never my intent for this to happen. I-I—"

Her eyes fluttered open, and her finger on his lips silenced him. "Will you spoil with words the perfection of tonight?"

"I just want you to know this is not something I take lightly. There have been so many firsts for me tonight, and I need you to know."

She barely dared breathe. "Firsts? What kind of firsts?" Could he hear her heart pounding in her chest, feel her fear he might stop himself from going further?

"Jealousy. I can't recall ever feeling it before, but I was jealous of that artist. Jealous that you might choose him over me. I was maddened by my reticence, that I was too much a fool to show you what I'd only just begun to discover. Afraid I might lose you and never know what it felt like to taste, touch, and make love to you."

"The Spaniard is barely a man, and I have no connection to him." She couldn't help but tease him with a smile. "What other firsts?"

"I'm sworn to my work and dedicate myself to nothing else, but"—he shook his head—"I find myself thinking about spending tomorrow, the next day, and the day after with you."

"And..." Her fingers traced his cheek; it was uncanny how alike they were and how in tune.

"I feel changed by you. I've never known such a hunger pang, and I don't want to ruin it by taking you where you're not ready to go. But, *ma chérie*, I have no control when it comes to you. You appeared out of nowhere, and nothing will ever be the same." He took her hand and kissed her palm. The heat of his lips rekindled the embers that had cooled with his confession.

He had no idea how valid his words were. Jenee had appeared out of nowhere, and she might disappear to nowhere, but for now, she was here, and she wanted everything he could give her, and she wanted to give him everything she had.

She didn't know what possessed her, but she ran her hand

down the taut muscles of his chest, tracing the definitive indentations on his stomach to his hardness. He sucked in a ragged breath, but she would not stop. She wanted—no, *needed*—to feel if he ached the way she did. If the deprivation of her touch was as keen for him as for her. She was not disappointed at his groan or his growl. Not disappointed at the blue eyes that glowed with desire. He grabbed her wrist.

"Will you undo me before I please you?"

A flush of heat emblazoned her cheeks. "I want to know all of you, Xavier," she whispered. She pressed her hips against him, and he crushed her to him, burying his tongue in her mouth. Her heart leaped like a gazelle fleeing from a lion. There would be no escape. Only the sweet ecstasy of *la petite mort*. The little death.

He swept her up in his arms and carried her down the hall.

It didn't matter what tomorrow would bring. Tonight was about love. Love was everything, and love would conquer all.

CHAPTER SEVEN

April 30, 1900
Paris, France

"*F*AIS-MOI L'AMOUR. MAKE love to me."

Jenee's words nearly undid him. Xavier held her in his arms. Nothing in the world could dissuade him from losing himself in her. She'd stolen into his hardened soul and disarmed him. He, who had lost so much and trusted no one, was putty in her hands. She drove all his doubts away as if she were the mistral that sent waves tossing in the sea and leaves swirling in the wind. She tasted like fine-aged cognac on his lips, sweet and lingering, overcoming his sense and sensibility. He didn't know precisely how or when her taste had made him drunk. In an instant, she'd fractured and shattered his haunted past. A past that had held him prisoner for far too long.

He'd cared for his wife but had not been in love with her. He'd adored his daughter and would miss her every day of his life. For the first time since the death of his family, he felt the dark shadows in his heart begin to fade. He felt the flow of light warm his soul. And for the first time in his life, he felt a powerful surge coursing through his veins like an electrical current driving him forward. And that was all because of Jenee.

Xavier laid her on his bed. "Let me light a candle and start a fire. You're trembling." He wasn't sure whether anticipation, trepidation, or cold made her shake. He thought about just holding her until she warmed up. But it was too cold, and her comfort was foremost in his thoughts…well, perhaps not foremost.

"Yes, I am feeling a bit cold, but I'm sure you'll warm me up."

"I promise you, I will." He chuckled at her girlish giggle. "But I would prefer your quivering to be from the heat of pleasure and not the snap of cold." He lit the hearth, blowing the embers to life and praying she wouldn't change her mind in the next minutes.

"Oh," was all she said as she watched him, one of the things he liked best about her. She didn't gab about the inconsequential or just to hear herself speak. Jenee was comfortable with the quiet spaces between their words.

The fire roared to life, and the room warmed up with its heat. The glow from the flames and the candles he'd lit cast shadows that danced on the walls.

Her breasts were free of her corset, but she wore her pantalettes. The vision of removing her pantalettes was almost more than Xavier could bear. Her smooth skin, the color of amber honey, begged for his mouth. He imagined she would taste as sweet, or sweeter, than the nectar of the bees. He joined her on the bed, forcing himself to keep a few inches between them to maintain his internal control. He would not rush this. "I never imagined we would be lying on this bed together."

She met his gaze. "Neither did I. Are you regretting that we are?"

"*Mon Dieu, non.* All I want is to be with you. Are you regretting your decision?"

Her smile sent his heart soaring above the rooftops. She turned on her side, ran her hands over his shoulders, and pressed her lips to his. He saw the sparkle of amber eyes tilted upward and the slant of her dark brows that made her always appear amused. Her exotic beauty made him envision her as the heroine of the *Arabian Nights* tales. The clever and beautiful *Scheherazade* who conquered a king's heart. Jenee, like he, was originally from

Algeria, and their backgrounds informed who they were. Neither of them, he was sure, could recall much of their birth land, but for some reason, being with Jenee made him think of the Sahara and the Mediterranean Sea. Her beauty drew him with its promise of homecoming.

Still, there was something unexplainable about his attraction to her. Something mystical about the way she'd appeared from out of nowhere. He thought the rest of his life would be devoted to the memory of his daughter Lila. Lila became the repository of his love, and his ability to love died with her when she perished. He thought he would always carry the guilt because of his loveless marriage with Saad. And he thought he would always carry the agony of losing his parents, daughter, and wife in that apartment fire. Guilt, loss, and work were all that life offered. But everything changed when Jenee appeared amid the rubble, and his dead heart began to beat again.

Xavier's hands came alive from the touch of satiny skin as they explored the hills and valleys of Jenee's curves. His cock strained against his trousers with a piercing need. How Xavier reveled in the ache, knowing it represented the rebirth of desire, which had sadly been missing from his life.

"Embrasse-moi?" she whispered.

"Oui, ma chère fille. All I want is to taste your lips."

Lips, tongue, and hands sought hidden treasures of sighs and moans. Her breasts were small but exquisite, proportionate with her petite figure. Her nipples remained puckered, and it wasn't the cold but her sensuous response to him. Pushing her gently to her back, he suckled both divine buds, watching her eyes close and her teeth press against her lip as she arched into his mouth. Her fingers flicked through his hair, trailed over his shoulders, and down his back, tethering her to him.

He nibbled and kissed his way down the silken hollow between her breasts, the urge to taste her a craving he would not deny himself. And then, in a swift motion, he pulled the pantalettes from her, growling with delight at what he saw. He found her goddess head neatly trimmed and sculpted like a work of art. He'd never seen anything like it, silky black tufts on sweet skin.

He sank his face into the plump, sweet mound that protected her sex. He tongued lightly, probing through her folds, quickly finding her pleasure bud, and suckled. It was daring of him—his wife had found this intimacy displeasing, but an unquenchable need to taste her drove him to explore Jenee's limits.

As he lapped and sucked, using his tongue and teeth to arouse her, her moans grew, becoming louder and breathier.

"Oh, please, Xavier, please don't stop. Don't stop. Please…" she panted breathlessly.

Mon Dieu, her response, her singsong moans, her little shudders, and her sweet, sweet whimpers would be his death. His cock pulsated in its confinement as he struggled to maintain control.

She arched her hips and pressed herself to his mouth as his tongue worked nimbly, bringing her to a crescendo. She shuddered beneath his lips, and a cry of pure elation escaped her, a surge of sensation so primal that his rod jumped to attention, almost tearing through the seam of his trousers.

With delicate precision, he continued to lap her sweetness as he tore away his pants, ending his torturous confinement. The release of his aching arousal awoke a yearning to be implanted in her. It was all he could do not to spread her legs and plunge himself in.

Curbing his impulse, he inhaled, and the fragrance of the sea mixed with the sweetness of honeysuckle affected him like an aphrodisiac. He inserted two fingers inside her, and her warm wetness enticingly drew him deeper. Clenched inside her, his fingers slid in and out with a slow, rhythmic thrust while his tongue and lips continued to worship her.

"Oh, Xavier," she exhaled. Her fingers tore into his scalp, pushing his face deeper.

He breathed, tasted, and touched her; focusing on her glistening pink pearl, he licked and sucked, again bringing her to climax.

She erupted with a cry. *"Oui, mon amour,"* he said.

Had he not held her firmly to the bed, she might have levitated with her climax. His lips drained the last drops of bliss from her. Jenee panted, her nipples swollen and erect, her cheeks flushed red. She looked deliciously wanton, her hair strewn wildly upon his pillow. He kissed his way up her smooth, silky thighs and then over her stomach. Taking his time, he sucked her nipples and was pleased to see them pebble again. He continued up the slender column of her neck, kissing the sweet spot behind her earlobes, and whispered, *"Sa bite était raide."* As if she didn't already know how stiff and aroused his cock was.

Jenee's lashes beat against her cheeks, and she feathered a kiss to his neck. She didn't shy away from what she wanted. *"Baise-moi, s'il vous plait?"*

Hearing her breathlessly say, "Fuck me, please," pumped the blood through his veins. But her hand sliding over his length and the rapture of her touch nearly undid him. He grabbed her chin, delving in with a passionate kiss, and their tongues sparred like two fencers with epees. He rubbed against the silken flower of her sex with his staff. The mysterious transformation of her face from sensuous desire to wanton hunger was a wonderment beyond any he had ever known. The time was ripe. The anticipation of filling her with his cock was all he could think about.

He pushed, and her lips parted, giving him entry. He slid his hands beneath her beautifully curved ass and plunged deep, loving how she clenched tight around him, holding him deeper until he could go no farther. Mad with pleasure, he could no longer control his body from what was instinctual. Unleashed and unbound, he rocked inside her, plunging in and out of her sleek feminine folds. Over and over, he took and took and took. She gave and gave and gave.

He heard her gasp, "Yes, yes, yes." And then his mouth silenced her, his tongue stealing her breath. Her fingers were in his hair, her legs wrapped tight around his waist, and her nails dug into his back. Her wild abandon set his pent-up lust free, and he ravished her. Shifting his position to pleasure her more, he'd do anything to hear her cry out his name. The head of his cock swelled even more, rooting itself inside of her. Her lyrical cries of pleasure blended with his baritone moans of ecstasy in a musical symphony of desire.

Their bodies were slick with sweat and heat. His orgasm was close, and he could feel she was too. When Jenee cried out, "Xavier," he could do nothing but follow her like the tail of a comet. Together, they came and erupted like fireworks in a midnight sky.

He collapsed on top of her, repeating her name on his lips as he continued to undulate inside her. Their joining was the most perfect moment of his life; the release of his seed as she clasped him tightly was beyond his most sensual dreams. He struggled to regain his breath, loving the feel of her hands roaming his back, not wanting to break their precious union.

He'd found paradise, and he never wanted to leave.

CHAPTER EIGHT

April 30, 1900
Paris, France

THE PALE LIGHT of dawn crept through the window and inched its way across the rumpled sheets, and the musical sound of bells ringing filled the silence. The warmth of the sun's rays tickled Jenee's toes, and her eyes fluttered open. Confused for a moment, she looked around. *Where am I?* Her cheek was pressed against a broad back, and when she pulled away, the body stirred, voicing its complaint.

The passionate memories floated into her mind, and her lips curved up in a smile. She did a mental check-in and noted her head ached a bit from all that cherry-red concoction at Au Lapin Agile and then the brandy with Xavier in his living room. She shifted and felt an ache between her thighs. A delicious ache. *No regrets.*

And then reality flooded back. Jenee cut herself some slack—after all, it had been only one day since she'd *arrived*. But the truth was she felt only elation at what she and Xavier had shared. The stirrings of love had not been dispelled by the light of day. Despite the unbelievable circumstances of how they met, what they shared had been beautiful. It hadn't been the most delicious dream of her life. *It was real. What we shared was real.*

She propped herself up on her elbow and peeked over Xavier's shoulder to look at his face. Her heart skipped, and her body flushed with heat as she remembered the way he'd made love to her, passionately, thoroughly, entirely. It was the most fulfilling sex she'd ever experienced. No, it went beyond sex. She couldn't think of enough adjectives to describe their night of lovemaking: incredible, amazing, and erotic were just a few words that played in her mind.

Watching him sleep, she marveled at how much younger he looked, boyish almost. The deep lines in his face had smoothed out in his sleep, tousled curls splayed across his forehead and over the pillow, and a slight smile curved his mouth. Delectable goosebumps rose on her arms, and she pressed her lips to his shoulder. Xavier stirred in his sleep and exhaled a deep sigh of contentment.

Although the thought of waking him with her lips was tempting, Jenee refrained. She was sure he rarely got a chance to sleep in, let alone sleep as peacefully as he was now. It was early, and there would be plenty of time for a repeat performance.

Rising from the bed, she grabbed his bathrobe from the chair. The robe carried his masculine scent within its folds, and she buried her nose in the soft fabric and inhaled the heady aroma. Feeling a heck of a lot better this morning than she had yesterday after her time-traveling crash landing, Jenee grabbed her undergarments from the floor and tiptoed from the room, closing the door behind her with a soft click.

The embers in the hearth had gone cold, and Jenee trembled from the chill in the air. Sunlight streamed through the window, and last night's vision of the moon pierced by Notre Dame's spire seemed like a dream. Xavier was right: the view of the six-hundred-year-old cathedral was as stunning in the day as at night. It was hard to imagine that an inferno would nearly consume the cathedral more than a hundred years later. She'd watched the conflagration on television and recalled the entire world mourning the loss of a treasure representing Paris' soul. It reminded Jenee of how fragile life was and how what you loved and believed were forever could disappear in a second.

She pulled Xavier's robe tighter around her. Even though she felt like a stranger in a strange land, she was determined to make the best of an impossible situation.

The throbbing in her head told her she needed coffee. She padded back down the hall and found a small kitchen. Poking around the cabinets and drawers, she saw only tea. *Not nearly enough caffeine for me.* There was only one solution. Every street corner in Paris had a café, she was sure to find one, and she'd only be gone a few minutes. Not wanting to worry Xavier, she'd leave him a note should he wake and find her gone.

Jenee dressed and went to the tidy desk to search for paper and pen. She opened one of the drawers and, shuffling the contents around, found herself staring at a framed photograph. She hadn't meant to pry but couldn't resist picking it up.

She gasped in dismay, and her eyes became awash with tears. Her world exploded in a sudden blast of deceit that shattered her cocoon of burgeoning love.

The pain couldn't have hurt her more if she'd been stabbed. Tears blurred her vision, and her fingers shook as she touched the photograph. She could tell it was recent because he looked the same age in the photo as he was now. Xavier stood beside a dark-haired woman in the traditional dress of Jewish Algerian women. She wore a headdress called a *chechiya*, and a *djubba*, a dress covered by an open-fronted velvet jacket known as a *ghlila djabadouli*, embroidered with a beautiful silk braid. Xavier was also dressed in traditional garb and held a little girl with a thick, dark braid who looked too much like him not to be his daughter. Jenee was sure she would have seen pale blue eyes if the photograph were in color.

Wait. What if the woman is his sister and the girl his niece?

An envelope that must have been attached to the back of the framed photograph fell to the floor. Jenee picked it up and opened it. She gasped as the last vestiges of hope shriveled up in her heart. The envelope contained a thin gold wedding band, and the truth became irrefutable.

Son of a bitch! He's married!

Xavier was just like every other asshole she'd met in L.A.

But where were his wife and child? Were they visiting relatives, or did he keep them stashed in Algiers? Maybe the wife didn't want to live in Paris and preferred the old country and the companionship and community of family. Jenee studied the photo, searching for clues, but there was none other than the one absolute truth. The smile on Xavier's face told her everything she needed to know.

She racked her brain, trying to recall anything he'd said that might have hinted at such deceit. But not a word came to mind. She did remember an inference from Lulu that Xavier wasn't the man she thought he was. But she'd been blinded by her attraction and was sure that anything Lulu said was colored with her feelings for him.

Xavier had presented himself as a lonely, single man who devoted himself to his police work and protecting society. *Lies, all lies!*

He'd plied her with wine and booze and taken advantage of her!

Stop it! You're not some naïve college coed. What you did, you did willingly. You wanted him as much as he wanted you.

Even though her heart hurt, she didn't regret her night of passion with him. It had been incredible. Besides, even if he hadn't lied, what kind of future could they have? She could be snatched up and hurled back to her own time or, even worse, flung into another place and time far more dangerous than 1900 Paris. Maybe Xavier had been lonely, burning the midnight oil chasing bad guys, far away from his wife and child. Men were the weaker sex, after all. He'd been too ashamed to tell her about them, and he wanted to escape for just one night.

Well, I certainly gave him the night of his life. She sighed in regret and wiped the tears from her eyes. He had given her the night of her life too.

This is probably for the best, anyway. I need to figure out how to help Allegretto and then return to my own time. The sooner, the better.

She searched Xavier's jacket that he'd left on a chair and found his wallet. Taking a wad of francs, she returned to the desk. She pushed the framed photograph and envelope to the back of the drawer, found paper and pen, and wrote him a brief note. She was pissed off by his duplicity, making her believe that what lay between them was so much more. *Good, focus on that anger; it'll get you through the next few days.* She wiped her tears with the sleeve of his robe and ignored the scent of him that had made her giddy earlier. She finished writing, unable to resist a little dig at his duplicity, and reread the note:

Merci, Xavier,

Last night was a lovely beginning and a lovely end. You and I are an impossibility, not at all suited for each other. What happened between us is as much due to the liquor we consumed as anything else. I will admit that I did enjoy our brève aventure, but now that it's over, I'm sure you are equally relieved that I'm gone. It makes things less complicated and less messy. After all, you have a busy and full life dedicated to your work, and I would never want to come between you and your commitments.

I wish you the best of luck with your case. I hope you find the bad guys. I have taken the liberty of borrowing some francs, which I will return to you as soon as possible. I will also see that Lulu's dress is returned to her, clean and pressed.

Avec bien coridalement,
Jenee

She slipped out of the apartment that had been their love nest without looking back. Once off the Île de la Cité, she'd find a café and replenish her lagging spirits with coffee and breakfast. Then she would hire a fiacre and find Constance Shipley.

XAVIER AWOKE WITH a smile on his face. He hadn't slept this well since the fire. Hell, he rarely slept at all, so the idea of sleeping in was as decadent as his night spent with the beautiful Jenee. He yawned and stretched. The rumpled sheets reminded him of a night he would never forget and a night he wanted to repeat.

More importantly, Xavier wanted to spend all day making love to Jenee and, in between, holding her in his arms. Perhaps he would cook something wonderful for their evening meal. He could already picture them sharing bites and kisses. Everything seemed brighter with Jenee in his life, and the newness of hope made him smile. For the first time in a long time, he looked forward to the future. Marriage, children—he envisioned it all with her.

Slow down, or she'll think you're a lovesick fool, or simply a fool.

He jumped out of bed, ready to conquer the day, and saw that his robe was gone. *I'll coax you back to bed,* mon amour. "Jenee," he called. Looking about, he saw none of her clothing on the ground. "Jenee, *ma chérie,* where are you?" He padded down the hall, wondering if she'd risen early, borrowed one of his books to read, and fallen asleep on the settee. But the living room was as empty and cold as the ashes in the hearth.

He rushed back down the hall, checking the kitchen, the bathroom, and even the closet, on the chance that the imp was playing a trick and hiding. But she was nowhere to be found. The excitement that filled his loins dissipated in an instant. The apartment was empty.

He spied the paper on his desk and snatched it up. He read it twice and then crumpled it in his fist. Anger pulsed through his veins, but he had nowhere to vent it. Putting his fist through a wall wasn't an option. He was a civilized man. Besides, strangling her would be much more satisfying.

His first reaction was hurt. Had he done something that displeased her? He picked up the note and read it a third time, wondering if he'd missed something. Some reason to make her vanish and leave this note. How dare she call what they shared a "brief affair," a diversion. It was something he would expect to hear from Lulu, but not Jenee. He had trusted his instincts, but he'd obviously misread her. He was planning their future only a few moments ago, and now, his dreams had been shattered with a few hastily written words.

What a damn fool I am. Jenee is every bit the user that Lulu is. There is no difference between the two except honesty. Lulu is at least honest as to who she is, what she is, and what she wants. Jenee… He couldn't finish the thought; it was too gut-wrenching.

The more he thought about her abrupt departure and the callous note, the more he wondered about her involvement in the bombing. It was entirely possible that she'd been a decoy the entire time. The poor damsel in distress. His complete absorption in her had no doubt allowed her fellow assassins to go into hiding to plan their next attack. His besotted attraction and lust had also given her a perfect escape from questioning and a way to blackmail him if she so chose. His head would roll if his superiors learned of him bedding a suspect.

Yes, she'd played him for a fool, and he deserved it for letting his guard down. But he hadn't risen to the top of his profession for nothing. He could be just as cold and calculating as the lovely Jenee Lazaar. He would track her down and determine what she was planning next.

He walked to the window and looked down the narrow alleyway, half expecting to see her. He rubbed the back of his neck, frustration and anger getting the upper hand. Images of her naked, breathless, sleek with sweat, and the potent scent of their lovemaking flooded his senses. *No! I will not wallow in self-pity.* He needed to funnel his anger into action.

I will find you, Jenee. Mark my words, I will find you.

CHAPTER NINE

April 30, 1900
Paris, France

JENEE PAID THE driver of the fiacre and stepped onto the cobblestoned road in front of the Gare d'Orsay train station. A line of coaches unloaded a steady stream of people, luggage, children, and every dog breed imaginable. She smiled to herself. *No country loves its pets more than the French.* Red-capped stewards helped those who needed assistance, whether the travelers were transferring to a train or staying at the hotel.

Jenee could have stood there all day just watching the world go by. It was also a good distraction from thinking about Xavier. *Xavier.* Whenever she thought of him, she wished she'd confronted him then and there. She wanted to dig her nails into his back, and this time not in the throes of passion. At least then she'd have had the satisfaction of knowing he would have to explain his infidelity to his poor wife. His lone cop persona of a man whose life was devoted to serving and protecting was a ruse. He was a game player, like all the other guys she'd dated in L.A. It made her blood boil.

Hey, chalk it up to an incredible one-night stand. And at least Xavier was good for a few francs so you could make your getaway. She hoped she could prevail upon Constance for help. Jenee was no freeloader; she would offer to work for the wealthy American heiress, be her companion, oversee her healthcare—heck, she'd cook and clean if she had to. But she needed a safe place to stay while she figured out what to do next.

The morning sun was beginning to break through the clouds, and the day promised to be warm and pleasant. Realizing it might be too early to disturb Constance Shipley, she planned to spend an hour visiting one of her favorite places in Paris, the Gare d'Orsay, which she'd visited on school field trips and with her parents many times growing up. She'd confirmed from the driver of the fiacre when he dropped her at the train station that the Rue Odinout was only a twenty-minute walk from here. After she visited the train station, the walk would be invigorating on such a beautiful spring day and give her time to consider her best approach to the woman whose life she'd saved.

Walking was at the top of the list of all the things she missed most about living in Paris. Everyone in Paris walked. It was a city designed for walking. And why not? Was there ever a more beautiful city? Paris in 1900 was an Eden created by the sheer force of wills of Baron Haussmann and Louis-Napoléon Bonaparte. The old, decrepit structures had been torn down through the baron and emperor's urban renewal program, and wide-open boulevards had been constructed, bringing order to the city. A new aqueduct and reservoir had been dug, and pipes were laid to supply the city with fresh water. Beautiful green parks were designed and planted, sewers dug, and gas lines laid, turning Paris into the City of Light. And to top it all off, the magnificent crown jewel of Paris' renovation was the largest theater in the world, the Paris Opera.

Newly opened in time for the exposition, the Gare d'Orsay was the most modern train station in the world. Jenee followed an elegantly dressed family up the steps toward the entrance of the Beaux-Arts architectural masterpiece. A little girl clung to the hand of a woman that Jenee thought must be the nanny. In her other hand, she held a red balloon. The little girl looked up as if sad to be dragged indoors, and the balloon slipped from her fingers, floating up toward the sky as if, with the act of setting it free, the child could set herself free. Most children would have cried or protested, but the girl said nothing. She tilted her head back and watched the balloon rise to the clouds.

Jenee watched with her, and when she glanced at the pretty child with dark braids wrapped in blue ribbons, they shared a smile. She waved goodbye as the family entered the building and the busy lobby. The little girl turned and waved several more times until she disappeared into the main hall.

Jenee felt a wrench in her heart. The beautiful child stirred a yearning within her. A longing for motherhood, and regret that she would probably never experience the joy of birth or nurturing her own child, tugged at her. It was even more profoundly felt now, when she finally had reached a point of opening her heart to the possibility. Xavier had killed that bud of hope, and she would never forgive him. Not that he cared a hoot whether she forgave him or not.

She dashed aside her remorse and self-indulgence. *Well, I don't need Xavier to have a child. I don't need to fall head over heels in love. I can have my own child. And as my parents nurtured me with all their love, so will I share all of mine.* After she solved the Allegretto mystery and figured out how to get back home, she wouldn't waste any more time. It would be full speed ahead. Whether she adopted or used artificial insemination, or a surrogate, she would be a mother on her own terms. And given her success and the savings and investments she'd accrued since launching her practice, she'd have no need for a man's financial support.

Feeling better about her future, she looked around the hall that was filled with light from the glass-domed ceilings. Jenee had many times visited the train station that in 1986 became the world's largest repository of impressionist and post-impressionist art, the Musee d'Orsay. The magnificent building had been saved from the wrecking ball when it was declared a historical monument.

Jenee glanced around the reception lobby and followed the

crowd into the great hall. This was the heart of the building, familiar to her even in its present state of a working train station. She scanned the interior, finding the two giant Roman numeral clocks. The last time she'd seen them was a hundred years in the future, but somehow seeing them now anchored her and linked the future to the present.

She turned in a circle, feeling quite alone amidst the throngs of people arriving and departing. These people knew where they were going, and from where they'd come—they were where they were supposed to be. She was the anomaly; it was she who was lost in time.

She swiped a teardrop away and searched the central aisle to find something familiar, something of permanence. Her gaze alit on the sizeable ornate gold clock hanging on the wall of windows, and she sighed with relief. One hundred and twenty years later, the clock would still be keeping time, and Jenee couldn't help but smile. Some things never changed, and she hoped they never would.

She looked at her watch and gathered her courage. Jenee followed the crowds outside and took a last glance at the magnificent Beaux-Arts façade. Determined to find her way home, she hoped Constance Shipley would help her.

Everywhere she looked in the Faubourg Saint-Germaine neighborhood, she saw tulips blooming. Fancy carriages carrying the surviving nobility and the captains of business and government plied the pristinely cleaned streets. The sun was warm and bright, and the clip-clop of horses' hooves, the twittering of birds, and the occasional *"bonjour"* from people she passed was a delightful soundtrack to her walk.

Twenty minutes later, she stood before the tall black iron gates of 12, Rue Odinout. She drew in a breath and entered an inner courtyard of crushed yellow limestone bordered by flower beds. A fountain gurgled bell-like tones, intermingling with the chirping of birds that sang from a surround of towering trees and greenery. To the rear of the courtyard was the private mansion, styled like a country house. The entrance was beneath a seventeenth-century carved pediment, undoubtedly inspired by the Parthenon.

A liveried servant answered the door.

"I'm here to see Madame Shipley."

"Have you an appointment?" the gray-haired butler asked. He critically took her in from head to toe with a disapproving frown. Her outfit was clearly not up to snuff, and certainly not the kind of clothing worn by someone paying a call on Madame Shipley.

"No, but she asked that I come to see her today. Please tell her that I am the woman who saved her life yesterday at the exposition."

His frown disappeared, and his eyebrows arched up in surprise. An almost-smile appeared on his dour face. "We are all grateful, mademoiselle, that you saved our mistress. Please come in, and I will inform Madame Shipley you are here."

A green and white marble checkerboard floor led to a grand staircase bookended by standing urns decorated with dancing Greek nymphs. The urns contained potted ferns whose green fronds echoed the color of the polished floor. Jenee's gaze traveled up, and she gasped at seeing a magnificent Baccarat chandelier, its teardrop crystals reflecting prisms of light and color that danced on the ceiling and walls.

She followed the servant through a hallway leading to the rear of the villa. A floor-to-ceiling window opened to view a beautifully designed French garden of manicured hedgerows, blossoming flowers, and stately trees. Jenee sat down on a Recamier facing the window and folded her hands in her lap.

"I will announce you to Madame Shipley." The gray-haired doorman, without further ado, shut the doors behind him and disappeared.

A short while later, Constance Shipley entered the room in a whirlwind of energy and with a warm, engaging smile that soothed the fluttering butterflies in Jenee's chest.

"Miss Lazaar, I am so happy to see you." The woman was tall

and statuesque, perhaps forty, with bright hazel eyes communicating intelligence and determination. She was dressed in a high-necked, puffy-sleeved white lace blouse tucked into a flowing ecru skirt, with a black, swirling geometric pattern decorating the front. From what Jenee could see, Constance wore no corset. The older woman spoke with a crisp, upper-crust Boston accent. "May we dispense with formalities? Please call me Constance."

"Jenee."

"Lovely name for a lovely young woman. Now, as we say back in Boston," she said, switching to a definite working-class accent, "I'm famished, and cook makes a wicked good chowdah!" She winked. "You must join me so we can get to know one another." Without taking a breath, she called over her shoulder to the servant who must have been hovering just outside the door. "Olivier, Mademoiselle Lazaar and I will have luncheon in the garden. Please see to it."

She took Jenee's hands and kissed her on both cheeks in the continental manner, as if they were dear friends who hadn't seen each other in some time. "Now, before we become thoroughly engaged in discovering each other's secrets, let me express my profound thanks to you for saving my life. You are my guardian angel, and I am eternally grateful."

"You're most welcome. I'm a doctor, and finding you in need was my only thought. I am just so happy to see you recovered and well."

"A doctor!" Constance's brows rose quizzically. "Here in France?"

Jenee nodded smoothly. Everyone seemed to react similarly when they found out she was a doctor. *My time travel may serve a purpose, if only to dispel the misguided notion that women can't be doctors.*

"I was born here in Paris. However, I went to America to attend medical school, and I attended the USC College of Medicine in Los Angeles." Having attended the Keck Medical School of USC, Jenee knew that the turn-of-the-century incarnation of the school had opened its doors in 1885, and the first graduating class of twelve students, including one woman, graduated in 1888, so she was well within a decent timeline.

"I can't believe you traveled to the wild west to become a doctor. You, my dear, are an admirable young woman." Constance opened the floor-to-ceiling French doors that led to the garden. "Come, I must hear everything about your remarkable life."

She linked her arm through Jenee's and led her outside. They sat on a lovely wrought-iron bench beneath an old beech tree on comfortable cushions covered in a floral pattern and sipped lemonade. Two liveried maids in black and white uniforms dressed the table on the terrace in white linen, china, crystal, sterling, and, of course, flowers.

Jenee told Constance about her parents' deaths and being offered a scholarship at USC, but she omitted that her attendance took place a hundred years in the future. She did try to stay as close to the truth as possible, focusing on her struggle to find her place in a man's profession. Lunch was served in short order, and included *poulet au vinaigre* with a side of long-grain rice and asparagus prepared in a mustard vinaigrette. *So much for the chowdah.* Jenee complimented Constance on the delicious meal.

"Chef is a genius. I plan to bring him home with me to Boston when I return, which I'm loath to do. I'm enjoying myself in Paris and won't consider going home until next spring. Father, of course, would prefer I return sooner."

"You are lucky to have your father. I'm sure he misses you."

Constance laughed. "My dear, my father only misses one thing: his lack of control over everyone and everything in his life. The only time I see him is at dinner, and those are few and far between, since he often dines at his club with various business associates. His life is his company, and I rarely see him. We fight on the same side, but our lives simply don't intersect."

"And what of your mother?"

"My mother died giving birth to me. In truth, I believe she

was the only thing my father ever loved, aside from his cargo ships that traverse the oceans. I will give him credit, though—many men have blamed and detested the child that deprived them of the love of their life. Father had the good grace not to hate me, but he did not make time for me either. I was raised by governesses, tutors, and our beloved housekeeper and butler, which suited me fine."

"I hope you won't think this too forward of me, but you are not married?"

"Oh, good heavens, no, at least not anymore. I married quite young, and not to a gentleman of my father's choosing. I was foolish and naïve in those days. Rebellious as well. When one lacks a parent's steady hand and loving influence, one can get into all sorts of trouble. James Martell was the man I married. Tall, dark, and handsome, as they say. But most definitely a philanderer with no interest in working for my father or earning a living. However, I did my duty and provided my father with an heir. Even lazy as my husband was, I would have stayed married to him if he hadn't been such a louse. Unfortunately, that was not meant to be. And so, I divorced him and took back the far more commanding name of Shipley."

Xavier fit the philanderer side of the equation, Jenee thought, but at least he wasn't out for money. "I'm very sorry."

"Thank you, my dear, but it was a long time ago, and my once-broken heart has healed quite nicely. I caught the rake with his pants down, literally. His latest paramour, a married Broadway showgirl, is quite cheesy, poor dear. But I suppose she satisfied his proclivity for *a menage a trois*, which was exactly how my detective found them: the chauffeur, the showgirl, and the bon vivant *in flagrante delicto*."

"Oh, my."

"The photos were very entertaining."

"I can just imagine."

"The result of being idle and rich is often sordid behavior, and I'm afraid too much time on one's hands can be debilitating.

James also needed to protect his hide from the showgirl's brutal, jealous husband, who would have most likely killed James had he found out. My detective discovered all of this, and I threatened James with exposure if he didn't agree to a divorce. He folded like a cheap suitcase. But not to be cruel, and for our son's sake, I settled enough money on him to keep him in the manner he's grown accustomed to. James Martell will never control my fortune or my father's company, which he had designs on doing all along when he married me. Imagine, never worked a day in his life, and he thought he could steer the family ship."

"You reclaimed your life and protected your son and family," Jenee said. "You are a strong woman."

"Thank you. That was also the one time my father sat me down for a good heart-to-heart talk. His advice was to never lose control of what is mine. I'm sure he must have suffered some guilt over not guiding me through the ups and downs of my youth. Randall, my son, is eighteen and at college, where he will gain the education that will help him in the future when the time comes for him to take over the helm of Shipley Shipping."

"It is hard for me to relate to having your life planned for you. Is Randall happy about his decided future?"

Constance chuckled. "He has always known where his responsibility lies, and he adores his grandfather, who adores him in equal measure. That makes me happy. I know my father wanted a son and had to settle for me. But Randall is the crowned prince in waiting."

"Does that bother you, that you were overlooked because you are a woman?"

"Oh, I suppose it did when I was a girl, but not anymore. I have my charitable works and believe they make a difference, but I live my life the way I choose and not by society's dictates. Money can buy freedom for a woman." She eyed Jenee critically. "Speaking of money, I really must take you shopping. That dress does not do you justice. Paris has the most marvelous designers, Charles Worth, Jacques Doucet, and a new up-and-comer, Paul

Poiret. They are changing the silhouette of women's clothing."

This was the opening Jenee had been waiting for. Her instincts told her that Constance had an open mind and would help her. "The truth is I came to Paris to make a fresh start, and I missed the way of life here more than I realized. When the walkway collapsed, I lost my handbag with all my money and identification. I need to find a position and a place to live until I can get back on my feet. I'd be grateful for any suggestions you can offer." She looked down, not wanting Constance to see the tears that brimmed in her eyes. She also needed a genuine friend, not like Xavier, who'd let her down.

Constance reached across the table and took her hand. "You have no idea how fortuitous this is. You have solved a problem that has been on my mind. I am invited to many social functions and love to attend the opera, but it is dreary to go alone. I have been considering hiring a companion. It is a paid position with many benefits. You would live here in a lovely suite of rooms and accompany me everywhere. Of course, this will require a new wardrobe, as you must look your best. It will be such fun creating you from scratch. I can't help but think that you and I were destined to meet. What do you think, Jenee? Would this not be a perfect solution for both of us?"

A tide of emotion rose in Jenee, making it difficult to speak. "Thank you, Constance. You are a lifesaver. It would be a pleasure for me to be your companion, but even more, the greatest pleasure will be to be your friend."

"Wonderful, then it is decided. It will also be a relief to Violet, as she does not enjoy crowds or like being questioned by strangers."

Jenee's ears perked at the mention of the name Violet. "I'm not sure I understand. Who is Violet?"

"Violet Rousseau is my secretary and sometime companion. She's a wizard with hair and has impeccable taste. She is French, like you. I'm sure you will become fast friends. In fact, I can't wait for you to meet her." Constance reached for Jenee's hand once more. "I always longed for a sister. I now have two, with you and Violet. And it is a bonus that you are both French. I must confess that I am an inveterate Francophile." She looked around, her thick brown brows nearly coming together. "Now, where is our dessert? And I must have some tea. Then you will meet Violet, and she will help you settle in."

CHAPTER TEN

April 30, 1900
Paris, France

SOMETHING ABOUT VIOLET Rousseau was familiar, but Jenee couldn't put her finger on it. She recognized people by their complexions; Violet's was as unblemished and polished as a carved marble bust. Jenee couldn't imagine where she'd seen her before. Constance Shipley's secretary wore wire-framed eyeglasses tinted pink and her dark hair pulled back tight in a bun. If Jenee didn't know better, she'd think the woman did everything possible to make herself look plain and unattractive. Was it because she took her position so seriously that she believed she must look like the unobtrusive yet efficient personal secretary? Or was there something more to it? Perhaps she simply did not care for crowds? Maybe that was why she didn't like attending social events. Or possibly she'd run away from an abusive husband?

Well, not much has changed. Jenee was a board member of a women's foundation that funded shelters for women and children who escaped abuse. She could understand if Violet were in hiding and feared being recognized.

Violet led Jenee up the staircase to the upper floor and what would be her suite. The few words they exchanged were spoken in French, whereas they spoke English when they were with Constance. Violet was amiable but not overly warm. Perhaps she was not as happy as Constance thought she would be that a stranger might usurp her position or undermine her standing in her employer's affections. Jenee was determined to win her over. She hoped her position would be temporary as she figured out how to resolve her dilemma.

"Violet—may I call you Violet? How long have you been working for Madame Shipley?"

"Six months now. I worked for an English family before that in London. *Oui*, the madame favors using given names, and she is *très informel*."

"I like that too. Please call me Jenee." She smiled. "Constance speaks very highly of you." When Violet made no comment, she continued. "May I ask why you left your position in England?"

"I grew homesick for Paris and felt it was time to move on. The people I worked for moved to the countryside, and I enjoy the advantages of city life."

"Constance said you do not care for social events or crowds."

Violet glanced at Jenee over her shoulder, her lips curved in a slight smile. "I don't, but I enjoy the museums and taking solitary walks in the parks. I enjoy seeing people going about their lives but not necessarily interacting with them. As we grow older, the place of our birth can bring comfort."

"Do you have family here?"

"*Non*, my family is no more. And you, Jenee, have you family here?"

"No, my family passed on years ago. It's one of the reasons I stayed in America after I finished my studies. My parents passed away, and it was too painful to live here."

"And yet you have returned."

Think fast, Jen. Violet had a probing way of asking a question without asking it. "Yes. I grew homesick like you, and wanted to see Paris again, and what better time than during the exposition?"

"Yes, and I understand you went through a harrowing experience, as did Constance."

"I lost everything in the bombing: my money, identity papers, and suitcase. I am indebted to Constance for her kindness and generosity."

"Constance is indeed a most generous lady."

"I-I just wanted to say that I'm not here to cause problems or interfere in any way. Once I set things to rights, I'll be out of your hair."

"I'm sure your presence here is not a problem for Constance; it certainly is not for me, Jenee," Violet said. "And you saved her life, which is most commendable. I also admire greatly that you are a doctor."

"Thank you, I appreciate that."

They reached the end of the hallway, and Violet opened the door to rooms overlooking the back garden. *"Voila."*

The room was decorated in white and pale blue shades, with gilded stucco moldings adorning walls and ceiling. The Empire furniture featured a carved wood bed and wood-framed chair upholstered in gold brocade. The windows and French doors, draped in pale blue velvet and tied with gold swags, opened to a balcony with a wrought-iron table and chair. Violet opened the doors, and sweet birdsong serenaded them. Captivated, Jenee closed her eyes and inhaled the lush fragrance from the rose garden below.

"It is a beautiful view, *n'est ce pas?"*

"Yes, just beautiful."

Violet stepped back into the room. "And the suite, it is to your liking?"

Jenee nodded. "It is paradise." Every inch was harmonious. Even the Savonnerie patterned gold rug beneath her feet was a work of art. Jenee's home in Los Angeles was the exact opposite in every way. Sleek and minimalist, with neutral colors and furnishings throughout. She'd hired a top interior designer to envision everything and give her the feel of a modern luxury hotel. But, surrounded by such color and beauty now, she realized that she'd made it so much like a hotel that the décor was devoid of emotional satisfaction. She'd created many such spaces in her life. *I'll have to remedy that when I get back. If I ever get back, that is.*

Jenee let her gaze linger on the satin bedding, her mind overcome by a vision of Xavier, his warm body pressed to hers, their legs entwined, their lips fused together in passion. A sharp pang in her heart made her gasp with sadness, yearning, and regret. "Have you ever been in love, Violet?" she asked.

Violet looked at her curiously. "Yes, I have loved someone more than anything in this world."

"Did you ever doubt his love or his intentions?"

"Never. He is my soul mate and the great love of my life."

Jenee was confused by Violet's use of the present tense. "Please forgive my asking, but what happened? Why aren't you together?"

"That's a story for another time." Violet seemed to transform, glowing with an inner light. Jenee felt tears well in her eyes. It wasn't jealousy that made her cry. It was hope.

A faraway look filled Violet's eyes. "One day, we will be together, and nothing will ever part us again."

TWO WEEKS PASSED in a blink of an eye, and Jenee was so busy with Constance that she had virtually no time to think about Allegretto, the painting, and how she would get back home. Mornings were spent in a flurry of fittings at various fashion houses, and afternoons were spent working with Violet in organizing Constance's whirlwind social calendar.

Finally, the moment had arrived. Constance squeezed Jenee's arm as they entered the Théâtre de l'Opéra to attend a performance of the composer Charles Gounod's opera *Faust*.

"Do not be nervous when all eyes are drawn to you," Constance said. "You are an absolute vision and a new face among the bored Parisienne beau monde. The House of Worth outdid themselves."

Jenee smiled even though her heart fluttered in her chest. It was ridiculous how nervous she was. *For goodness' sake, they'll all be long dead and forgotten before you're even born.*

She couldn't get over the feeling of being a stranger in a strange land. She'd done her best to temper Constance's purchases for her, but to no avail. This dress was obscenely expensive and was just one of many items out of the entire wardrobe Constance had ordered for them, including tea dresses and lingerie garments. Charles Worth, the man who invented haute couture, had only recently died, but his sons had successfully continued his atelier, and Constance was a longtime client. John Philippe Worth had designed the imaginative gown made of ivory satin, cut with a daring heart-shaped bodice and a long train. The showstopping number was intricately sewn with swirling black velvet tendrils that resembled the scrolling gridwork of an Art Nouveau staircase railing. Violet, a wizard with hair, had completed the transformation by twisting Jenee's dark hair into an updo, leaving one long ringlet free to fall across her breast. Jenee barely recognized herself in the mirror.

Now, as the doors opened on a world she'd never seen before, the world of the beau monde, she was left breathless. "Although I'm terribly grateful, I still don't understand why you've gone to such expense or effort for me," she whispered, unable to process the gifts Constance had bestowed upon her.

"True friends, I have very few, money I have plenty. And you have become most dear to me."

"Thank you, I am honored." She smiled, blinking back sudden tears. "I feel the same about you, Constance, and I value your friendship very much."

"Good, that's settled. There will be no more talk about my gifts." Constance flashed her a cheeky grin. "Besides, to see you take Paris by storm tickles me pink. Let us focus on what I believe is the most beautiful building in the world, and then you won't even notice when the world focuses on you."

Constance, of course, was right. It would be hard to imagine a more beautiful building; Jenee had certainly never seen one. The exterior of the Théâtre de l'Académie Royale de Musique was a romantic wonder of Baroque, Renaissance, and classic Greek architectural design. Its edifice was crowned with gilded sculptural groupings of Harmony and Poetry, and the sculptures of Fame holding Pegasus adorned both ends of the roofline. But to arrive amid gilded carriages pulled by elegant teams of horses and see the formally attired men and women step out of them in a swirl of perfume and luxurious fashion was something else altogether.

Jenee had never attended the opera before, and seeing it like this seemed otherworldly. She tried to absorb every detail as they walked up the steps to the entrance. Looking up before passing through the entry, she caught a glimpse of a bronze bust of Beethoven below the carved entablature where a frieze proclaimed *Academie Nationale de Musique*. It would still be years before the opera house was formally renamed Palais Garnier after its designer Charles Garnier.

When they walked through the entrance, Jenee was struck with awe. The grand staircase seemed a stairway to heaven, paved with white Carrera marble and red and green marble balustrades polished to a gleaming sheen. At the bottom of the staircase, two female allegorical statues holding torches greeted them, as if to say welcome to paradise.

The staircase branched off left and right at the top of the landing. The second floor was surrounded by an arcade of marble columns that supported carved and gilded arches, giving view to every arriving guest from the upper floors. A thousand electrical bulbs glowed in chandeliers, candelabra, and sconces, creating a shimmering interior that shone from the gilded columns to the frescoed ceiling. As she walked up the grand staircase, it was nearly impossible to control her trembling knees.

"What do you think?" asked Constance.

"It's glorious." Jenee grasped the balustrade. "But if I don't concentrate, I'll end up on the floor, embarrassing us both."

"Oh, don't be silly. You're as agile as a woodland sprite, and you forget I've seen you running through the garden with the dogs and leaping over low hedgerows." Constance raised a brow.

"Yes, but sprites usually have wings and fly, and they also wear nothing but a flimsy, short dress that does not hinder their every movement. I'm petrified of tripping on this train and doing a face plant."

"Sometimes, you utter the most frightfully clever phrases." She chuckled. "'Face plant.' I've never heard that before. I really don't know where you get them."

Jenee kept forgetting, and she slipped up sometimes and used modern lingo. Constance chalked it up to a quaint eccentricity.

"It's probably better you're so focused on walking and not on the men leaning over the balustrade ogling you."

"What men?" Jenee lifted her head and locked eyes with the last person on Earth she'd expected to see at the opera. She nearly tripped, catching herself before she did indeed take a face plant. *Xavier!* Her heart exploded into a gallop like a horse kicked with spurs. He stood at the top of the stairway, his gaze fixed on her. Formally attired like every other man in attendance, he looked breathtakingly handsome. *What is he doing here?*

"My dear, is something amiss? You look as though you've seen a ghost." Constance followed Jenee's eye line. "Ah, I see. He is very handsome, I must say. Do you know him?"

"Yes, we've met. His name is Xavier Doumaz, a chief inspector with the *Sûreté*." Jenee looked away. "Pay him no mind." She had discovered that Constance was quite the mischief-maker and enjoyed playing the fairy godmother role to the hilt, despite having gone through an unhappy marriage and a scandalous divorce. Jenee purposefully looked away, intent on not showing the slightest interest in Xavier and stirring up Constance's curiosity. Xavier had been a mistake, and their one night together, although incredible, was based on lies.

Constance regarded her with a sharp-eyed look. Jenee knew

she'd have to fess up to her new friend, who would no doubt demand every juicy detail. Even a high-society lady from the early twentieth century was no different than her modern-day friends, Em and Gaby, who would have hounded her until she fessed up every sensual morsel.

"My lips are sealed for now, but later, you will have to satisfy my curiosity about your connection to him." Constance walked ahead, stopping on the landing to chat with friends.

Jenee followed more sedately, gripping her gown so as not to trip. When she reached the landing, Xavier moved quickly to impede her from walking past him, and he grabbed her elbow and spun her to face him.

His coldness hit her like a bucket of ice water. His audacity threatened her composure, and Jenee's ire rose like a tidal wave of fury ready to do battle. She was tempted to have it out with him right then and there.

"It seems you have landed on your feet, but women like you usually do, don't they?" Xavier spat.

"Spare me your insults," she said between clenched teeth. She didn't want to cause a scene that would embarrass Constance. She tried to yank her arm from his steely grasp, thankful for her long evening gloves, grateful she could not feel the warmth of his skin directly on hers. "Let me go." *Bastard!*

"You seem to have found a generous patron for yourself. My wallet would never have been enough for you. Oh, but you know that already, don't you, given that you stole from me. You are far more cunning than Lulu, but at least she never pretended otherwise."

"The money will be returned to you soon, and if you'd spoken to Lulu, you'd know that her things were returned to her. Now, if you will excuse me, I have an important liaison with my generous patron," she spat, trying to pull her arm away. But Xavier held her in an iron grip. "You are hurting me," she said.

"Far less than I would like to hurt you."

"Jenee"—Constance gave Xavier a withering glance—"I have

someone I want to introduce you to."

Xavier released Jenee's elbow.

"Yes, Constance, forgive me. I stopped to speak with an acquaintance. May I present Chief Inspector Xavier Doumaz."

Constance offered her hand imperiously, and Xavier took it and pressed a kiss there.

"The pleasure is mine, madame. Let me not keep you from your friends."

"Thank you. I hope we will meet again, chief inspector." Constance walked away, and Jenee turned to follow her.

Behind her, she heard Xavier say, "We are not done, mademoiselle. There is much more for us to discuss."

Oh, you jerk! First, he insulted and manhandled her; now, he dared to threaten her. Barely turning her head to acknowledge him, she hissed. "How wrong you are, monsieur. We are more than finished. *Occupe-toi de tes oignons!*" It was a French expression that meant "mind your own business!" She joined Constance, who was engaged in conversation with an extremely handsome man with silver-gray hair and eyes black as pitch.

"Jenee, darling, I have met the most charming man. May I introduce the Vicomte de Maurnier?"

The vicomte took her hand and pressed his lips to her glove. "My pleasure, mademoiselle, I am at your service." She had no idea why she felt a shiver spread up her spine. Most likely, she was still suffering from her encounter with Xavier, whose gaze she felt boring into her back.

"Lovely to meet you, Monsieur Vicomte." She hoped she'd addressed him properly with the respect due his title. She'd come across a book on etiquette in Constance's library and read it from cover to cover, hoping it would help her avoid making social missteps.

"I was telling Madame Shipley that tonight is my lucky night."

"And why is that?"

"Why, meeting her, *bien sûr*. I am a widower and quite alone.

Madame Shipley is a breath of fresh air."

He looked adoringly at Constance, whose cheeks flamed red from his compliment. Jenee knew that look—Constance was smitten.

"Please share a glass of champagne with me before the opera begins," he said.

"That sounds lovely, doesn't it, Jenee?"

"*Bien sûr.*" Anything to get away from Xavier. "Please lead the way."

The vicomte looped his arms through both of theirs. He turned his head slightly to add, "I hope that man who accosted you is not a friend. I noticed his behavior and found it most ungentlemanly."

"Oh, no. The man is no friend of mine."

"Men like him should not be allowed in here."

She forced herself not to look back at where she'd left Xavier and turned her attention to the vicomte and Constance. Their eyes seemed to glow with mutual appreciation and attraction. Jenee doubted the vicomte was interested in money. He was most likely well off, considering his fine attire and title. Yet he could be faking. Jenee couldn't put her finger on it, but her "Spidey-senses" had tingled from the moment she met him. But was she on edge because of Xavier or because the vicomte could be a wolf in sheep's clothing?

She cast her worries and fears from her mind and focused on enjoying her night at the opera. For now, she would try to relax and be in the moment. Later, she would analyze everything that had happened and hope it didn't add up to a potential disaster.

CHAPTER ELEVEN

May 13, 1900
Paris, France

H*E IS NOT the one for you. You must not be taken in by him again. Stick to your plan, and then get out of Dodge.*

Jenee enjoyed spending time with Constance, a lovely, generous, kindhearted woman who could have become president had she been living in Jenee's time. Despite her fondness for Constance, Jenee needed to figure out what Allegretto wanted from her. Her instincts told her that once she helped the Renaissance master and his mysterious redheaded muse, she would be able to get back home and back to her life.

Even though it means never seeing Xavier again?

She couldn't answer that question. At least not yet. Seeing Xavier had brought her feelings back in a rush of heat and passion.

Oh, what am I going to do? I've fallen for a liar, a cheating husband. She would not, could not allow herself to give in to her feelings. She forced her thoughts in another direction. She did not want to ruin Constance's evening, or her own, for that matter.

She gazed about her, taking in the Grand Foyer. Paris' elite glittered like the stars in the heavens.

But nothing could upstage the room itself, no matter how beautiful or dazzling the beau monde in their brilliantly colored gowns and jewels, or how titillating their clever conversations. The Second Empire style of Emperor Napoléon III's opera house was opulent and spared no expense in the same manner that its forebearer, the Hall of Mirrors, dazzled. Still, the Grand Foyer at the opera was far more decadent than that monument to monarchy, Versailles. The foyer, nearly the length of a football field, shimmered from the glow of magnificent chandeliers that illuminated what felt like a stage for the elite guests to see each other and be seen. It was such a dramatic space that she wouldn't have been surprised if suddenly everyone in the room broke into song and dance, and the performance took place right then and there.

Jenee felt her skin prickle from attention as she and Constance strolled into the room with the vicomte. It felt as if everyone was looking at them. She breathed a sigh of relief when the vicomte disappeared to arrange their refreshment. She avoided meeting anyone's eye and tilted her head back to admire the beautifully painted vault overhead. The frescoed ceiling framed in gold depicted scenes recounting the history of music and dance. She might have remained fixated on it for the duration of the evening had Constance not interrupted her reverie.

"Please do stop looking at the ceiling. You are making my neck ache."

Jenee giggled. Using her fan as a shield, she commented in a whisper, "I'd rather look at the ceiling than this nosy crowd."

"They are curious about who we are and our relationship with the vicomte. Gossip is the mainstay of the highborn and the wealthy, it's how they amuse themselves, and we have presented them with a juicy morsel and a mystery to be solved."

"Well, it makes me uncomfortable. Distract me. Tell me what you know about the vicomte." She knew Constance was waiting with bated breath to talk about him. And talking about the vicomte meant Constance wouldn't ask her about Xavier.

"At last, you ask! The Vicomte de Maurnier is the most eligible man in the republic. He is wealthy beyond measure and, as you can see, devilishly handsome. Every single and not-so-single woman in Paris vies for his attention. They say he has many lovers. But that could just be rumor and gossip. He certainly has his pick of any woman he chooses. How he has managed to remain single is a miracle. I must admit, I'm very attracted to him."

"Really, I had no idea."

Constance rolled her eyes and gave Jenee a gentle swat on the arm with her fan.

Jenee giggled. "You've been blushing like a schoolgirl from his every gaze and compliment."

"I knew of him by his reputation, of course, but I'd never met him. Then the splendid man approached me and introduced himself. He admitted that he had been hoping to meet me. Well, my heart practically did a somersault in my chest—" Constance suddenly stopped speaking, and Jenee noticed the vicomte approaching. "I'll tell you the rest later," Constance whispered.

The vicomte arrived with a waiter in tow holding a silver tray. "Ladies." He handed them each a flute of bubbling champagne. "Shall we toast our fortuitous meeting?"

They raised their glasses without touching, which was the French way, and sipped.

"We only have a few minutes before the curtain, and I will be deprived of your charming company." His dark eyes regarded Jenee. "Madame Shipley tells me you are a doctor. How remarkable. Are you here for a short visit or a long one?"

"Yes, I am a doctor from America. A set of unusual circumstances has arisen beyond my control, and it seems I must remain here for some time. Constance has kindly asked me to stay with her as her companion." She turned the tables on him in what she knew to be an impertinent question. "And you, my lord, how do you occupy yourself?"

His brows rose. "You are astonishingly direct."

"Is there any other way to be?"

"In truth, there is not. However, women rarely are, and I find it utterly refreshing that I have the pleasure of conversing with two such women this evening." His dark gaze glinted as he regarded her. "As for my occupying myself, I work in service to my country and various other private enterprises. I am not an idle man who rests on the laurels of his title or inheritance, if that is what you are asking."

"My apologies if I gave offense, my Lord."

"No offence taken, mademoiselle. Your family must be very proud. May I congratulate you on your accomplishment."

She pressed her nails into her hand. She had no desire to start blubbering in public because the vicomte mentioned her parents. He could not have known he'd hit a nerve, that her greatest regret was that her parents died before she'd completed medical school. "Thank you, my lord. Sadly, my parents are deceased and did not live to see me realize my goal."

"My deepest sympathy and apologies to have reminded you of your loss."

She inclined her head, as regal as a queen, and sensed he was anything but sympathetic. *There's something about this guy. Something I don't trust.* He reminded her of one of the top real estate magnates in L.A., whom she'd met several times at various parties and events. He was a billionaire many times over, but word had it he had connections to multiple drug cartels and had been able to bribe local officials to get every development greenlit in record time. Despite being handsome and charming, he'd always given Jenee the creeps. The vicomte gave her the same feeling.

"Thank you. You could not have known," she said.

He nodded and turned to Constance. "Madame Shipley and I have discovered we share a common passion; we are both art collectors. It seems we were meant to find one another."

"I believe it's called a confluence of fate. We must celebrate our newfound friendship," rhapsodized Constance.

"I believe we are celebrating it now," Jenee said with a chuck-le. She suspected fate had little to do with the vicomte and

Constance's meeting. Despite his charming nature, Jenee couldn't help but sense an undercurrent of ulterior motives. As a dermatologist, she'd studied faces her entire life, and the tight lines that appeared between his brows and around his lips got her "Spidey-sense" tingling again.

So, how come your Spidey-sense didn't tingle when you met Xavier? She didn't know the answer to that, other than Xavier must be a primo liar.

The vicomte was as hypnotizing as a cobra swaying to a melody from a flute. "Yes, but I have another thought in mind. If you are free, I would be delighted if both of you could join me for the opening of the Olympic Games tomorrow. You might have heard that it is the first time the games have been held outside Greece."

"What an honor for France. You must be very proud, Lord de Maurnier," said Constance.

"It is an inspiring time for our republic to be able to lead the world on so many fronts," said the vicomte, "but we must dispense with the formality of titles. Please call me Albert. I'm afraid I find the use of my title too reminiscent of the days before the Revolution. My family barely survived the reign of terror. I was a child during the Franco-Prussian War when my father lost his life in service to his country. My uncle the vicomte became my guardian, and I his heir. Unfortunately, he died two years ago."

"How difficult for you to lose your father and then your uncle," Constance said.

"Yes, life is never equitable, I'm afraid. But let us think of happier things. You must accompany me tomorrow to the Olympics. I promise you won't regret it."

"We would be delighted, Albert, and please call me Constance." She looked at Jenee, her brow raised inquiringly.

"Yes, of course, I would love to attend as well. And please, do call me Jenee. Is there a particular event we will attend?"

"Fencing, my dear," he replied. "I am an aficionado and an

avid fencer. It is my favorite sport."

Albert seemed exceedingly fit for a man of fortyish, lean and muscled. Jenee imagined he spent much time in exercise. Undoubtedly, he hired the best to train him in all his athletic pursuits. *Money can't buy happiness, but it can sure buy everything else.*

"*Bon*, I will call for you tomorrow at ten."

"Oh, there is no need for a carriage—" Constance began before Albert interrupted in a soft voice.

"Please, I insist. The crowds will be overwhelming, and I have reserved seating for my guests," he added with a smile. "I can predict it will be a delightful outing for all."

Constance echoed his smile. "Then we look forward to it, Albert."

The lights dimmed and brightened, signaling it was time to go to their seats. "Ah, *Faust* will begin momentarily. Your address, Constance, my dear?"

"Twelve, Rue Odinout."

Albert lifted Constance's hand in a daring display and raised it to his lips, pressing a kiss. "Until tomorrow, *ma chérie*. You have made this evening most memorable."

Like the Grand Foyer, the horseshoe-shaped auditorium was designed for the audience to see and be seen. Jenee and Constance sat in their plush red velvet seats and faced an enormous proscenium arch and a painted red and gold-trimmed curtain. The ceiling was crowned with a spectacular bronze and crystal chandelier that would glorify and inspire Gaston Leroux's novel *The Phantom of the Opera* nine years later. The auditorium sat nearly two thousand guests, and the stage could accommodate four hundred and fifty performers.

The orchestra was warming up, and the cacophony of voices lowered to whispers. Jenee relaxed, relieved she hadn't seen Xavier again. What she couldn't understand was his animosity and contempt. He should have been embarrassed and ashamed, given his lies and subterfuge. He was married with a daughter, for crying out loud. Well, he'd certainly missed his calling. He'd given a fine performance of the outraged and spurned lover when she crossed paths with him on the staircase.

"Albert is quite marvelous, isn't he?" Constance remarked as she flipped through the program. "He was so kind to invite us tomorrow to the games."

Jenee regarded her friend, deciding that a neutral tone would be best for now. "Yes, it's fortuitous that he found you this evening in this throng." Then again, Xavier had found her as well, as though he'd been searching for her.

"You don't seem very excited about our outing tomorrow," Constance said.

"I am cautious, as you have come to know in the past few weeks." Jenee smiled.

Constance raised a brow. "Yes, I do know you quite well, my dear. And I understand your caution, but he is a vicomte. With a few discreet inquiries, I'm certain we can learn everything there is to know about Albert. Besides, the event will be in public, in broad daylight, and as Albert mentioned, he has invited several other guests. I see no danger or risk in attending. And besides, the French are not nearly as stuffy as the English when it comes to matters of the heart."

"I'm sure you're right. I apologize for my suspicious nature."

Constance patted her hand. "Nothing to apologize for. I'm sure you're not yourself after dealing with that insufferable man. You must explain what transpired between you and the chief inspector."

"Nothing transpired, but I will explain it all."

"Good. Just as you are protective of me, so am I protective of you."

Jenee echoed Constance's earlier gesture and patted her hand. "If Albert makes you happy, I promise I will embrace him."

Constance flipped open her fan and fanned herself. "It's been a long time since I was attracted to someone, and I find him utterly charming and very handsome. We share so many things in common."

"Yes, my friend, this is all true. I want you to be happy."

"It is something to look forward to." Constance smiled and looked radiant with expectation.

Her hope for the future reminded Jenee of what she'd begun to feel with Xavier. It also reminded her of her precarious situation. As much as she wanted to return to her own time, there was nothing to indicate when that would be or if it would ever happen. *I need to get my butt in gear and figure out what Allegretto needs me to accomplish.* As much as she longed to go home, she was painfully aware she had little to return to besides her medical practice. Yes, she would miss Em and Gaby like crazy, but what could she do? She had to make the best of things. It would be challenging, but she would find a way to practice medicine, even here. She knew Constance would be a supportive ally on that front. She was grateful for the older woman's friendship and guidance.

As for the romance department, Xavier had let her down big time, but there was no reason she couldn't make a life for herself here. The one gift he'd given her awakened her to the possibility of love. She realized that she didn't want to go through life alone. She wanted to live a full life even if she was stranded here forever, and she wanted a husband and children. She wanted a family.

The lights dimmed, and Constance squeezed her hand again. "Let the show begin."

The strains of the orchestra filled the air as the curtain rose to resounding applause. On the stage, the aging scholar Faust sat in his study surrounded by books, regretting the choices he made in his life. His incredible aria expressed his disillusionment as he contemplated killing himself with poison. He attempted to drink the poison three times, but a vision of a beautiful young woman stopped him each time. Mephistopheles appeared, offering him a chance to return to his youth and redress his loveless life. In his deep baritone, Mephistopheles offered to grant him the life and love he missed in exchange for his services in hell upon his death.

Faust readily agreed, not realizing that he'd sold his soul to the devil.

Jenee lost herself in the majesty of the production. She could not help but see the similarity in her own life. She, too, had forsaken life and love for a successful career in the superficial world of the rich and famous in L.A. The shock of being hurled back in time had awakened a longing she'd suppressed her entire life—to fall in love and have a family.

A sudden commotion shook her out of the absorbing opera. Spectators began to shift and grow restless, whipping their heads around for the source of the unrest.

"What is going on?" Constance whispered.

A buzz of whispers echoed her question, and a rising tide of annoyance could be heard rippling throughout the auditorium. The orchestra abruptly ceased playing, and the performers made a hasty exit to the wings.

"I'm not sure, but something must be wrong." Jenee felt the hair on her nape rise.

The curtain dropped, and shouts of outrage could be heard from the upper boxes. When Xavier took the stage, Jenee's heart constricted and began to pound like a fist against her chest. She could not imagine what he was doing, and she trembled, realizing whatever was happening could not be good.

"*Mesdames et messieurs*, the performance is suspended due to unforeseen circumstances. The management of the opera house conveys its sincere apologies and has promised to reschedule the performance for a future date, honoring your tickets. We ask that you please rise and exit the building in a calm and orderly fashion without delay. Thank you."

Shouts of outrage and anger reverberating among the audience were silenced with the arrival of the police, who came down the aisles, forcing the attendees to make their way to the exit. Jenee and Constance held tight to each other's hands as they flowed with the tide of elegantly dressed patrons. There was pushing and shoving as the crowd moved like a surging tide toward the doors. Word of a possible bomb threat by anarchists spread like wildfire. The press of humanity was claustrophobic, and Jenee's fear for herself and Constance made her heart race. She swept up the train of her gown, bunching it in one hand, and held tight to Constance with the other.

They breathed a sigh of relief when they finally made it outside, but all around them was shouting and confusion as patrons pushed to get to their carriages. Fistfights broke out, and the gendarmes struggled to quell the melee. There was no sign of Constance's carriage.

"What are we to do?" asked Constance. "We certainly can't walk."

"We'll just have to be patient," Jenee replied. "I'm sure the coachman is trying to find us."

"I have never seen such chaos. Heaven forbid any damage comes to the opera house."

"Let us pray it is a false alarm."

XAVIER STOOD IN the shadow of a column watching as the crowds exited the opera house. He searched every face, looking for anyone suspicious. If he had his way, he would have interrogated every person as they filed out, but that was impossible, given the sheer number of people.

He had been assigned to oversee security at the opera house after the boardwalk bombing. With his team of officers, they'd had everything under control. That was until headquarters received an anonymous tip that a bomb had been planted. Xavier was rushed into action to oversee the evacuation of the opera house and find the bomb before it went off. With so many officials in attendance, he was forced to halt the performance and call up additional reinforcements to search the opera house from rooftop to cellar.

His heart leaped in his throat as he caught a glimpse of Jenee in the sea of faces exiting the building. His first instinct was to call out to her, to push through the throng and reach for her hand. Then he regained control. His chest constricted. The memory scalded, burning like molten lava in his veins. Desire and pain intertwined as one. She was an opportunist and a liar, yet seeing her again after two weeks of scouring the city for her had almost been his undoing. When he saw her on the staircase, he wanted to sweep her into his arms and kiss her senseless. He'd envisioned carrying her back to his apartment and making love to her until she once again burst into shooting stars in his arms.

But he could do none of those things. All he could do was follow through on his vow to find the evidence he needed to link her to the terrorist ring and bring her to justice.

When he first met her, her clothes had been torn and shredded from the collapse of the walkway, yet her beauty and forthright charm had touched his heart. Then, in Lulu's clothing, Jenee had transformed her beauty, glowing like an artist's muse. In his bed, naked, with her hair streaming about her, she was a siren who called out to his soul. But tonight, dressed in such elegance, she looked like a regal young queen, her beauty outshining the stars in the heavens, and it drove him to distraction that she was as out of reach to him as the stars in the sky.

A few minutes later, as the crowd had begun to thin, he spotted Jenee standing on the sidewalk outside the opera house, clinging to her companion's hand. Her eyes were filled with worry and fear, and he was overwhelmed with guilt. His anger at her perfidy melted like ice beneath the sun's rays.

"Jenee, you and your friend must leave here immediately," Xavier said, approaching her.

She turned toward him, and her look of mistrust pierced like a knife's blade through his chest.

"Please do not concern yourself with us. We will be gone as soon as we locate our driver and carriage. Do you know why this is happening?"

The detective in him always suspected everyone's motives. It troubled him that at both incidents of a suspected bombing, Jenee had been present. Still, he had no proof of her involvement, and she did look genuinely frightened. Was it because she was innocent or because the organization she was in league with had abandoned her?

"We've had another tip of a possible bomb threat," he said. "I apologize for my earlier behavior."

She ignored his apology. He wanted to say more, but her companion prevented him from saying everything on his mind. He addressed the woman whose hand Jenee clung to. "Madame Shipley, I would see you both safely out of here as soon as possible."

"Thank you, chief inspector, for your concern, but as you can see, finding one's carriage is nearly impossible. I meant to ask you earlier, but I'm curious, how did you and Jenee meet?"

"We met the day of her arrival here in Paris at the *Exposition Universelle*." He offered no more, as he had no idea what Jenee had told Constance, who, he surmised from her accent, was also from America.

"I see. A twist of fate brought you together."

"Yes, you could call it that." Xavier found he could not keep his gaze from Jenee, and her nearness stole any pretense or possibility of indifference. He was all too aware that both Constance and Jenee could read him like an open book and see his infatuation.

"Please, Monsieur Doumaz, do not concern yourself with our well-being. I'm sure you have more important things to attend to, given the present circumstances," said Constance.

"Exactly," said an approaching voice. The Vicomte de Maurnier strode to them and possessively snaked his arms through Jenee and Constance's. "Madame is correct, and I'm sure you have far more pressing matters, inspector." The vicomte must have overheard their conversation. "I will see *les dames* home safely."

Xavier heard the disdain that always colored the privileged class when addressing those they considered inferior. He contained his anger. His knowledge of the vicomte was insufficient, but his instincts told him the man was not to be trusted.

"Then I will leave them in your capable hands, my lord." It would do no good to challenge the pompous ass; Xavier already had plenty of enemies among the aristocracy who could cause him grief. Besides, he had no good reason to challenge the vicomte. Jenee was free to choose her friends as she desired.

"Sir, we've concluded the search," a young officer called out from the entrance.

Xavier nodded to the young man, then he turned back to Jenee. *"A bientôt,"* he said before striding away.

CHAPTER TWELVE

May 14, 1900
Paris, France

AS RESISTANT AS Jenee had first felt about attending the Olympic festivities with the vicomte, she now embraced the notion. After last night's debacle at the opera, Constance and she needed a lift.

The vicomte took Constance's hand and bent to kiss it. "How lovely you look, my darling."

A florid blush tinted Constance's cheeks. "Thank you, Albert." Jenee was surprised at how much effort Constance had put into her appearance for today's outing. So much so that she'd called Jenee to her bedroom to consult. In the end, Constance chose a pale blue ruffled silk dress and a straw hat adorned with silk roses in shades of pink, blue, and white, which set off her ivory skin and dark auburn hair, giving her an elegant aura.

Jenee was dressed in cool summer colors that contrasted dramatically with her honey-colored skin and black hair, which Violet had painstakingly piled upon her head in what was known as a Gibson hairdo. The white lace blouse cinched tight by a pink satin belt gave way to a flowing voile ruffled bell skirt that accented her curves. The S-bend corset was the newest trend in fashion and not nearly as uncomfortable as she had thought it would be. She carried a ruffled white parasol to protect herself from the sun and wore a straw hat with matching pink ribbons that streamed down her back.

"A lovelier sight I cannot imagine," Albert said. "You both look enchanting. I'm very much looking forward to sharing this day with you."

"Thank you, Albert, as we are with you," said Constance.

Jenee couldn't help but notice Constance seemed to float above the ground at Albert's florid compliments. But she suspected his devoted attention was not what it seemed when he began throwing ogling looks her way. *Oh, I've got your number, you jerk.* Jenee wanted to whack him with her parasol.

"France is fielding the largest fencing team in the competition, and I am on the team," he said. "I don't expect to medal, as I'm the oldest member, but I hope to make it to the quarterfinals, which would be an honor. The truth is I'm hoping to impress you, Constance."

"You have already done that. I will be cheering you on with great enthusiasm." Constance smiled. "I know nothing about fencing; you will have to educate me on the nuances of your sport."

"With pleasure. There are many things I look forward to educating you on."

Jenee's shoes bit into the yellow limestone, and she stopped in her tracks. "Excuse me, but what exactly did you imply just now to Constance?"

Albert threw up his hands, lips twisted into a wry smile. "You misunderstand me. I thought only of everything Constance and I might learn from one another."

"Perhaps you should be clearer with your sentiments."

He chuckled. "*Touché*, mademoiselle. You are on point. I will be sure to heed your advice."

"Jenee is a devoted friend and only has my best interests at heart," Constance said with a fond smile at Jenee, then directed her gaze to Albert. "And I look forward to the blossoming of our friendship as well."

"You are truly a gracious lady," he said.

Oh, brother! Jenee had to stop herself from an extreme eye roll like a typical Valley girl.

The carriage ride proved uneventful as the vehicle made its way across the Pont Royal toward the Rue de Rivoli, and Jenee sat silently with her hands folded in her lap. Albert sat opposite her, engaged in conversation with Constance, and being ignored left her free to pursue her own thoughts. She didn't trust Albert as far as she could throw him. On the other hand, she had no idea how the dating game worked in this era. Maybe Constance *expected* him to use heavy double entendres. And maybe ogling women was no big deal. This wasn't the kind of stuff she would have learned in high school history class. Besides, it wasn't as though Jenee was a member of the aristocratic class or a wealthy heiress. She was Constance's companion, so maybe that made her fair game in the "Ogling Olympics."

Jenee didn't want to ruin Constance's chances for happiness, and Albert really hadn't done anything wrong. He was accommodating and charming and did seem wholly taken with Constance. Perhaps there was nothing beyond the rest of it. Still, Jenee would stay on alert.

She might have remained quiet as a mouse had a turn in their conversation not taken her completely by surprise.

"I would be delighted if you would be my guest for a dinner party I will host at the end of the month celebrating the *Exposition Universelle*," Constance said.

"I would be honored," Albert said. "In what way is this dinner linked to the exposition?"

"As I previously mentioned, I collect paintings by old masters, and I believe those of us who hold important works of art in private collections are obliged to share that work with the public. Recently I have been fortunate to acquire a masterpiece that was thought lost. *Il Divano* by Marco Allegretto is in transit from Italy as we speak. It occurred to me this was a wonderful opportunity to share my collection with my European friends, and so I've arranged for several of my masterpieces to be shipped from Boston. They will arrive next week on one of my father's cargo ships. The celebration will be held at Restaurant Brébant at the Eiffel Tower, where I will share my treasures in a private viewing with my friends. After the preview, the paintings will be exhibited to the public at the Grand Palais, along with the Allegretto painting. Once I return to Boston with my collection, there won't be another opportunity to see these works for some time, so it gives me great pleasure to do this."

A feeling of lightheadedness overcame Jenee, and she leaned out the window, taking a deep, steadying breath. It couldn't be a coincidence. She was meant to meet Constance that day on the walkway after the explosion. This was what Allegretto had sent her back in time for. But to what end? What did Allegretto want her to do? Steal Constance's artwork?

"I am very familiar with Allegretto's work," Albert said. "He's a genius, and what a *triomphe magnifique* for you, *chérie.*"

Jenee's heart raced in a staccato beat. She'd had no idea about this big to-do that Constance was planning with the paintings, but she couldn't express that here in front of Albert. Instead, she decided on a different approach. "I'd be happy to offer my assistance in any way."

"Oh, do not worry yourself about it, my dear," Constance said with a flick of her wrist. "Violet is handling all of the details. She's been working on this for quite some time. It's what she loves to do, and she was instrumental in assisting me with the acquisition. As I said, the event will be an evening to remember." She returned her gaze to Albert. "I hope you will attend. The guests, I promise, will be eclectic and entertaining."

Jenee's thoughts raced around her head like a dog chasing his tail. *Il Divano* was the painting that had transported her through time and deposited her here. It would be arriving in days. This meant the possibility of her returning home. Now, if only she could figure out what Marco Allegretto wanted her to do. If meeting Constance had not been a coincidence, then the same applied to everyone else she'd met since her arrival, including Albert. Considering how he'd reacted when Constance mentioned the painting, Jenee had a hunch that Albert figured into it too. But in what way? It stood to reason that Xavier, Violet, and possibly Lulu could also figure into this. But how?

Jenee looked up and found Albert regarding her with a hooded expression. *You're up to something, Al, and I will find out what it is.*

Upon their arrival, Jenee followed Constance and Albert, who walked arm in arm to the terraces at the Tuileries Gardens, where the fencing matches were to take place. Behind them, two servants carried large wicker baskets. The sun shone brightly in a cobalt-blue sky dotted with cottony white clouds.

A little girl with golden hair cried out, "*Mamma*, look!" and pointed to the sky. Everyone looked up. From the direction of Vincennes, a suburb of Paris, a flotilla of giant gas balloons in bright red, blue, green, and yellow floated east across the sky. The balloons seemed to be in a race with the clouds, but they were actually racing each other. Jenee had read about this event in the newspaper and looked forward to it. The balloons were piloted by teams competing in an unofficial Olympic race determined in three categories: which balloon would travel the farthest, which would remain in the air the longest, and which would reach the highest elevation. Jenee understood the excitement around her all too well. The world was changing rapidly, and the dream of motorized flight was but a few years away. Helium balloons were the precursors to the age of aviation, and everyone, adults and children alike, watched the spectacle in wonderment.

After the balloons journeyed beyond visibility, Jenee felt buoyant herself. The vicomte led them to a grassy knoll where a large elm tree provided shade. Beneath the tree, a team of servants was busy setting up a table for luncheon as elegant as if they'd been in a formal dining room.

Albert invited Constance to accompany him while he checked

in with his team's coach, and Jenee waved them away. "I'll be fine. Please go do what you have to do. I think I will take a walk through the gardens." Content to be on her own, Jenee wandered the garden paths. Since her arrival, she'd rarely been alone except in her bedroom, and even then, a maid was usually in and out. She missed the solitude of her life back in L.A.—going for a swim every morning in her infinity pool. It had cost a small fortune, but it had been so worth it. On cooler mornings, she'd usually go for a jog on San Vicente Boulevard, near her Brentwood home. On weekends she'd lie on the deck, soak up the sun, and tuck into the next book for her book club.

Jenee blinked back tears as she thought about Em and Gaby. She missed her besties and hoped her having gone missing would not be a burden to them.

Sunshine poured through the leafy cover of trees, illuminating the ground, where light and shadow battled for supremacy. The thought occurred to her that she would be declared dead at some point if she never returned home. She didn't know how many years had to pass for that to kick in. *It's a good thing I updated my will a few months ago.* Aside from various bequests to friends, most of her estate would be donated to her favorite charities. Some of that money would have certainly come in handy here. Unfortunately, her purse had been lost in the bombing aftermath. Not that she could have used her credit cards or bank card in any case.

A chuckle escaped her as she thought about that. Walking into a bank and showing the teller her bank card. She shook her head at the silly thought as she walked along one of the lovely paths.

She passed couples walking arm in arm, children with faces flushed with excitement. They walked, skipped, and ran without care, expressing that simple joy that only a child understands. Some of the people she passed acknowledged her—men tipped their hats, and women nodded and smiled—while to others, she was invisible. *Well, this is Paris, after all.*

She giggled again and continued her walk. She wasn't sure whether it was her distance from the life around her or her affinity to it, but the giddiness of life and all its complexities drove her forward as if she were a ship propelled by billowing sails.

A spectrum of thoughts crossed her mind as she contemplated her future. If she could not return to her own time, could she marry and have children, knowing what she knew about the future? World War I was about fourteen years away. If she had sons, they would be too young to be conscripted, but it didn't matter because there would be a great deal of suffering. Not to mention the Spanish flu epidemic that would follow on the heels of the war. She would need to consider going back to the United States with Constance. She could still make a difference as a doctor, but she did not know if she'd have the courage to remain in Europe by herself, knowing what was around the corner. Could she summon that courage?

I could if Xavier were by my side.

Jenee shook her head as she continued her walk. She would not think about that now. Could not dare think about it. She needed to concentrate on the painting and figure out what Allegretto needed her to do.

She took a deep breath and inhaled the sweet scent of flowers and fertile earth. There was nowhere to hide and no way to delude herself. She resolved to live her best life, even if it meant losing everything. Regardless of the era in which one lived, happiness was fleeting, and misfortune could find anyone. To dance with the angels meant battling with the devil. To love with all one's heart meant to risk losing it. To live meant to die. That was the nature of existence, the circle of life, and the frightening knowledge of what was to come would not stop it from coming.

Where did all this self-examination and contemplation lead her? A ticker tape reeled through her mind, repeating a conversation with Violet that had made no sense to her. Violet had spoken of being in love as though she were talking of the present day and sharing her life with her soul mate. This left Jenee to ponder how that was possible, since, as far as she knew, Violet did not have any gentleman callers, and Constance certainly hadn't mentioned any.

Jenee had asked Violet why she wasn't with the love of her life now, but Violet revealed nothing, promising a future explanation that had not yet been forthcoming. That explanation felt pertinent to Jenee's own situation for some inexplicable reason.

Violet. Constance said that Violet had arranged everything regarding the Allegretto painting. Violet… How much did Jenee really know about her? She was mysterious, yet Jenee's instinct told her she could be trusted. Again, she pondered the coincidences that seemed to be piling up. *Violet,* she'd remarked when she'd met her, *what a lovely name.* The name of a flower…

Iris, the heroine in *The Time Traveler's Lover,* came to mind. Iris had also shared the name of a flower. Jenee gasped as the realization hit her full force.

Of course! Violet! She had to be the connection. That teasing temptation dangled before her like a carrot before a horse. Jenee would not rest until Violet gave up her secrets. If only she had her copy of the book that had disappeared beneath the rubble of the collapsing walkway. She knew the book well, having read it countless times, but to reread it now in the context of having time-traveled might bring revelations that had eluded her in previous readings. *If only I had it in my hand, I might find a window to view what has happened to me and what I'm supposed to do next.*

CHAPTER THIRTEEN

May 14, 1900
Paris, France

XAVIER KEPT HIS distance as he followed Jenee. He hadn't meant to follow her, but when he saw her slip away by herself, he felt compelled. He'd seen her arrive with the Shipley heiress and the detestable vicomte, and seeing Jenee in that snake's company served only to rouse his ire. He'd discovered who the vicomte really was: Albert Archambeau, the estranged nephew of the old Vicomte de Maurnier. The elder vicomte, who'd appeared to be in vigorous health, died suddenly two years ago, and Albert inherited both his title and his estate.

A most convenient death, Xavier thought as he'd read the report he pulled from the closed files. There had been an inquiry into the vicomte's untimely death when one of his servants brought to the attention of the authorities that the nephew Archambeau and the vicomte had engaged in a fierce argument, with the vicomte threatening to disinherit the nephew. The vicomte had died within hours of the confrontation, and suspicions were raised, but in the end, Archambeau's legal team triumphed, and he inherited everything. Given the unusual circumstances, the authorities performed an autopsy, but no traces of poisoning were found. Interestingly, also not found was any physical reason for the vicomte's demise, and his death was ruled to be from unexplainable natural causes. Xavier would have bet his last franc that the new vicomte had hastened his uncle's untimely death, but without proof of any crime, the authorities could do nothing about it, and the case was closed.

Xavier did not work the original case, as it coincided with the worst time of his life, the deaths of his family in the fire. He would have had little interest in the case, but the vicomte appearing in Jenee's orbit and his immediate dislike of the man raised his suspicions. Once Xavier's suspicions were ignited, he became a bulldog. His instincts rarely betrayed him, except perhaps when it came to Jenee. In her case, his desire had blinded him to the truth, but with the vicomte, he believed he was on the trail of someone who'd gotten away with murder. Men like the vicomte were rarely brought to justice, but Xavier decided to do some investigating on his own. He didn't know whether he'd be able to build a credible case against Albert Archambeau, but once a criminal got away with a crime, especially murder, they became emboldened to do it again. Xavier suspected the vicomte was that sort of man. He'd sensed the count's hands were dirty and contacted the authorities in Lyon, where Archambeau lived before moving to Paris. Xavier put in a request with law enforcement in Lyon for any information on Archambeau. He would have those reports in a few days, and then he'd have a better idea of whom he was dealing with.

In the meantime, he would monitor the arrogant aristocrat, and if he stepped out of line, Xavier would bring him down. He didn't want Jenee anywhere near the man, but for the moment, unfortunately, he could do nothing about it.

As far as the first day of the Olympics went, the Prefecture of Police had not received any bomb threats. Still, given the crowds expected at the opening event, Xavier had decided precaution was in order. He'd posted both plain-clothed and uniformed security throughout the Tuileries. His own face was cast in shadow under a bowler hat, and he was far enough behind Jenee not to arouse her suspicions.

If only he could control his heart and body's betrayal when he looked at her.

Jenee walked down the path in dappled sunlight just as she walked through his dreams, seizing his imagination and returning him to the bed where he'd loved her. Even though he realized she wasn't who he'd thought she was, he could not erase her from his memory or purge her from his blood. It was as if she flowed through his veins and had become a part of him, damn her. He tried, but he could no more get her out of his soul than he could cut his heart from his chest. But he had to remain on guard. He had a job to do, and he could not allow his feelings to cloud his judgment.

She abruptly turned around, taking him by surprise. *Merde!* Luckily, she hadn't looked up in his direction, but she would soon enough, and there was nowhere for him to go to avoid a confrontation. The best he could do was keep his head down and hope she was too caught up in her thoughts to recognize him.

When she passed him without a word, Xavier didn't know whether to feel relieved or disappointed. He kept walking along the path, staying as far behind her as he could, trying not to be mesmerized by the beautiful sway of her hips.

"Are you following me?" Jenee called out, stopping suddenly along the path. She turned and regarded him, her eyes wide with surprise and, if he was not mistaken, sadness.

"Miss Lazaar, it is nice to see you enjoying the fine weather and gardens."

"You haven't answered my question," she huffed. The glow of her cheeks, flushed with anger, took his breath away.

"I am here officially, merely walking the grounds to ensure no suspicious characters are lurking about."

Her gaze changed from anger to concern. "Was there another bomb threat?"

"My fellow officers and I are ensuring that everyone in attendance is safe."

She tilted her head and regarded him in silence for a few

moments. "And does that include following me about?"

"As I said, Miss Lazaar, I was merely walking the grounds, as many of my fellow officers are doing. You just haven't noticed them."

Her eyes narrowed. "Why do you keep calling me Miss Lazaar?"

He breathed and relaxed his stance, his hand going to his hip. "I am being respectful of your person. Now that you've risen in the world and have made friends with the wealthy and titled, I expect you wouldn't want your reputation to be smeared with any hint of impropriety."

She looked so hurt, damn her beautiful brown eyes. He was trying to maintain a professional distance when all he wanted to do was pin her against a tree and kiss her until she melted against him. The thought of her softness pressed against him was too much, and he suppressed a growl of impatience. Everything about her reminded him of their night together. His memory of her was so strong that he could taste her in his mouth. All he could think about was everything he wanted to do to her—

"Xavier, are you listening to me? I said, I understand about you calling me Miss Lazaar in public, but it is just you and I here. Hello? Earth to Xavier! Honestly, you look a million miles away."

"My apologies." He cleared his throat, suppressing a smile. She had the most curious expressions; he was hard-pressed to stay angry at her. "How have you been, Miss—er, Jenee? Are you happy?"

"That's rich!" she said, closing her parasol and pointing it at him. "You turn up everywhere I go and confront me at the opera in front of the entire city of Paris, and now you want to know if I'm happy? Are you demented?"

How could being the recipient of her white-hot anger make him feel invigorated? Maybe he *was* demented. *Besotted, more like.* What they said about men must be true. Once their lower extremities became involved, they were incapable of rational thought, and that was where things stood, literally, at this moment. He was thinking with his cock, which pressed with aching dissatisfaction against his trousers. Thank God his jacket offered him some cover. He shifted again, hoping to alleviate his discomfort.

Jenee huffed again and opened her mouth, no doubt to keep scolding him, but he paid no attention because he saw something in his peripheral vision—a rush of movement. He turned his head just in time to see a bicyclist barreling at them. There wasn't time enough to shout a warning. He launched himself at Jenee, grabbing her and twisting his body to cushion her fall. They hit the ground with such force and momentum that they rolled atop each other until they smacked into a tree, with Jenee landing on top of him. His head hit the tree with a whack, and as the world went dark, he smiled, realizing his daydream was made real. *Jenee, in my arms, on top of me...*

A voice—her voice. "Xavier, come back to me." Gentle fingers—*her fingers*—prodded his arms and legs and tenderly caressed his neck. It was like floating in a hot bath, so intense was the pleasure. Repetitive slaps to his face were not nearly as pleasurable. "Xavier, you may have a concussion." *Slap!* "You must stay awake. Do you hear me?" *Slap!*

He opened his eyes and saw tears in hers. *Tears for me?*

His angel asked, "Do you feel any pain anywhere?"

If you kiss me, the pain will go away. Maybe not all the pain, but even that pain you could alleviate. He chuckled.

"What could possibly be funny? Shit! He's delirious from hitting his head."

Whom was she talking to?

"Tell me, what is your name?"

"You know my name."

"Just tell me, you stubborn man!"

"Xavier Doumaz."

"Tell me your address."

"Twenty-seven, Rue des Chantre."

"What year is this?"

"1900."

"Good. Good." Her fingers continued to probe the bruise on his noggin.

"Ouch!"

"Ouch, indeed. You hit that tree hard."

"I was trying to save your life."

"Yes, and I appreciate it very much. Thank you for that."

He grinned, feeling like a schoolboy who'd just impressed his schoolteacher. A vision popped into his mind of Jenee dressed like a prim schoolmistress, holding a ruler, placing her boot on a bench, and slowly lifting up her skirt…

"*Mon Dieu*, your face has gone all flushed and red." Jenee pressed the back of her hand to his cheek.

Of course I'm flushed and red. You're practically on my lap, with your soft hands all over me. Xavier doubted she would be laughing if she knew what he was thinking. That was what she did to him. He had no control over his emotions, words, actions, or body.

"I'm very worried about you, Xavier. I need to examine you properly—"

"I love you," he blurted.

Shit! He closed his eyes, hoping she'd attribute his loosened tongue to delirium.

He squinted his eyes open. She sat back on her haunches and gaped at him.

He couldn't read what she was thinking. But for a moment, he saw a look of happiness flicker in her eyes—or had he imagined it?

"Xavier, you must not say things like this to me."

"Why not?"

"Because… Never mind. You have substantial swelling, a knot from hitting your head, and you're bleeding from your abrasions. We need to get you out of here *tout suite*. Do you think you can walk?"

"Yes, with a little help, if you wouldn't mind."

"Mind? You just saved my life, so the least I can do is see you to safety."

Jenee rose and, bracing herself against the tree, offered her hand to him. With her help, he managed to stand, but he was dizzy, and before he could stop himself, he wrapped his arms around her for support, and they were nose to nose. He could feel her breasts heaving against his chest. His eyes dropped to her lips, and all he wanted to do was close the distance.

She cleared her throat, and he looked down and found her worried gaze. "You are definitely not yourself. Lean on me. I will take you back to Madame Shipley's house, since it is closer than yours."

"You needn't worry about me. Please take me to the Île de la Cité; I can get home alone."

"Absolutely out of the question. I have no intention of leaving you alone for the next twenty-four hours. If you have a concussion, you must stay awake and be monitored, and you cannot be left alone."

Slowly they made their way along the path, Jenee's arms wrapped around his waist, his arm draped around her shoulders. He probably could have walked unassisted, but her body curved against his felt so good that he never wanted it to end.

"What are you going to do, babysit me in my apartment? As I recall, you never slept on the sofa last time. Can I hope for a repeat performance?"

"Aha, your smart-alecky quips are coming back. I'm glad."

"Smart-alecky? Your American phrases are truly *extraordinaire*."

She giggled. "Well, you haven't heard the half of them. But truth be told, that is precisely why I am taking you to Constance's home instead. We have plenty of bedrooms at the villa, and I can keep an eye on you without fear of tarnishing my reputation."

"We wouldn't want that," he grumbled.

A hint of a smile adorned Jenee's luscious lips, and two fine lines curving like parentheses punctuated either side of her mouth. He was back in dream mode, because all he wanted to do was plant feathery kisses on those two curved lines and taste her sweetness on his tongue. And that was just for starters.

"Careful." She held him tighter, her exquisite curves aligning with his. "I need to let Constance know so she doesn't worry about me. I hate leaving her alone with the vicomte, but I'm afraid it can't be helped."

"He's a most detestable man."

"I know he's off-putting because of his extreme arrogance. But is there some Spidey-sense reason why you don't like him?"

"Spidey-sense?"

She giggled. "Sorry, another one of my Americanisms. I mean your instinct and experience as a police officer."

"I don't care for his attitude, that is for certain. Something else bothers me about him, but I'd rather not talk about it right now." In truth, he had nothing to tell her; besides, this time with her was too precious to be wasted on talking about that detestable man.

"He's a member of the French team and competing in the foil event. I wasn't keen on watching it, and now I don't have to."

"There is that to be grateful for." He stumbled again, recovered himself, and pressed her closer to his side.

She chuckled again. "I think hitting your head may have awakened a sense of humor that I didn't detect before."

"Before, I was earnest and serious. Now I have nothing to lose, since I've declared myself to you."

She shook her head. "Please, Xavier, do not make me think twice about caring for you."

He nodded, letting her lead him. At this moment, he would have followed her into the depths of hell if she asked.

Constance and Albert caught sight of them. "Jenee, I was worried sick." Her gaze darted from Jenee to Xavier. She could not fail to notice their arms about each other, nor that Jenee's dress was soiled, her hem torn. "What happened? Should I call the police?"

"I am the police," Xavier said indignantly.

"We had a close encounter with a bicycle." Jenee beamed up at Xavier. "The chief inspector saved my life. It was a hit-and-run. It's difficult to explain, but we collided with a tree, and the chief inspector took the brunt of the impact. He was rendered unconscious, and I believe he has a concussion."

"But you're unharmed?" the vicomte asked Jenee.

"Yes."

"I will have my servants see Monsieur Doumaz to his precinct."

"You will do nothing of the kind." Jenee bristled, and, ignoring the vicomte, she addressed Constance directly. "I am taking him home immediately. He must be monitored for the next twenty-four hours if he has a concussion."

The vicomte was not to be dissuaded. "That is most inappropriate and outrageous. To put a strange man up in your house is ill-advised. I am sure we can find another solution."

"He is not a stranger to me. I will hear no more discussion of this. Xavier saved my life. I'm a doctor, and I will see to him until I am certain he is recovered. Constance, if you would rather the inspector didn't stay in your house, I will take him to his home and care for him there."

"Don't be silly," Constance replied. "My home is your home, and I trust your medical judgment. You must do what you feel is best."

Xavier was not pleased to be discussed as if he wasn't there. "I am fine; you needn't be bothered, Jenee. I have no desire to cause you so much trouble."

"Not a word, Xavier," she reprimanded him, and turned to the vicomte. "I am sorry that I won't be able to watch you compete, but I hope you have much success, monsieur. May I use your carriage to go home and then send it back to you?"

The vicomte waved them away. "Go, if you must. I will see Madame Shipley home."

Xavier's head throbbed, and he was torn. The thought of spending twenty-four hours with Jenee had him dizzy, and not from his concussion. But he didn't want to put her in a precarious situation with Madame Shipley. He could see the genuine warmth between the two women, but the vicomte was another thing entirely, and he was concerned the bastard would stir up trouble.

His doubts were overruled by his anticipation of being ministered to by her gentle hands. And he wouldn't trade that for the world.

CHAPTER FOURTEEN

May 14, 1900
Paris, France

OLIVIER OPENED THE door for Jenee, who carried a tray into the room. "Thank you, Olivier."

The *porte-fenêtre* were open, and a light breeze rustled the white sheers. The sunlight washed the walls in yellow and gold, and birdsong twittered in from the open window.

"You're welcome, mademoiselle. Just ring if you require me." The butler bowed and left, closing the door behind him.

"How do you feel?" Jenee set the tray on the side table and helped Xavier sit up, adding plump pillows behind his back.

"Aside from the throbbing headache, I'll survive."

Jenee nodded and set the tray on his lap, then strode to the window and drew the dark blue drapes over the sheers. The room was too bright, too stimulating for someone with a concussion.

She returned to the bedside, picking up the ice pack from the tray. "Lean forward, and I'll place this behind your head."

He did as she asked, and she parted his thick curls and gently examined the bump on his head.

"You have quite a knot back here. You could have been killed." Without applying too much pressure, she held the ice to the lump, causing him to wince. She was so close to him that she could feel his warm breath on her neck, which sped her heart into a gallop. She sat on the edge of the bed to keep the ice pack in place as she spoke to him.

His striking eyes reminded her of the shallow waters of the Caribbean Sea. They were more dilated than she liked, which confirmed her diagnosis that he had a concussion. She was relieved he had no bleeding from his nose or ears, as that would have indicated a brain bleed. She'd sent one of the servants to the apothecary to obtain acetylsalicylic acid, an aspirin powder used for pain in the early twentieth century. The bottle sat on the nightstand.

"Yes, I could have been killed, but I wasn't. Such is the risk of a police officer every single day." He reached for her hand and kissed the palm. "*Chérie*, I couldn't have better care if Florence Nightingale herself were looking after me. While I am certain that a kiss from Miss Nightingale would be akin to a kiss from a *grand-mère*, considering she is probably at least eighty years old, I think a kiss from you would be far more pleasurable."

"Oh! You!" she exclaimed in a huff. "When you speak like this, I can only think your brain has been damaged by smashing into the tree. Here, hold your own ice pack." She lifted one of his hands to the back of his head. "It will keep your hands occupied while I prepare the tea."

"Perhaps I am suffering from brain damage." He sighed. "Because I can't find any reason not to tell you what I'm thinking and feeling."

Jenee avoided his intense blue gaze as she poured a steaming cup of tea from the pot on the side table. She added the aspirin. "Cream and sugar?"

"Just two lumps of sugar, please."

His free hand covered hers as she held the cup to his mouth, and she had to bite her lip to keep her hands steady. His words may have traveled to her heart, but the heat from his touch traveled to her core.

By the twitch of his lips, she knew he saw the effect he had on her, and it made her want to wipe the smirk he made no effort to hide off his lips. She felt dangerously close to losing control and kissing him to within an inch of his life. But it was her medical knowledge that stayed her desire. The most important treatment for a concussion was zero stimulation. He needed to be calm and rest, and she would never risk his life for a kiss.

Just keep reminding yourself that he's married with a daughter. Even if he was telling the truth, concussion or not, that he was in love with her. She was no homewrecker, and his wife and daughter deserved better than that. *And so do I.* She'd known many a woman who succumbed to the lure of a married man who made promises he couldn't keep. If Xavier did indeed love her, then he'd have to be honest with her and come clean to his wife. Legally divorce her and be a good father to his daughter. Then and only then would Jenee let him back in my bed.

Don't you owe him the truth about who you are as well?

Shame washed over her. She was just as guilty of lying as Xavier. She, too, would have to be completely honest with him, or they would have no chance at a decent future.

And what happened if she solved the Allegretto mystery? Would she stay here or go home?

Xavier once more brought her hand to his lips.

"If you don't behave, I will leave this room and arrange for Olivier to be your nursemaid," she said.

His eyes widened. "If you do, I can assure you I will escape out the window, climb down the trellis, and find a way back to the Île de la Cité, taking with me my broken heart."

"It's not your heart that's broken, it's your head, and you will remain in this bed until I say otherwise."

He smiled like the Cheshire Cat from *Alice in Wonderland.* "So long as you administer to me, I do not want to leave. In fact, no power on Earth could cause me to vacate your bed." He chuckled.

"You are becoming quite incorrigible. It's not my bed."

"Close enough and quite comfortable." He raised his brows

flirtatiously.

"I don't know why I am even bothering with you."

"I did risk life and limb for you."

"How can I forget when you keep reminding me?" She proceeded with her examination, taking his pulse, then placing her ear to his chest, wishing she had a stethoscope.

"I suspect my heart is beating faster now, considering your soft cheek is pressed to it."

"However do you come up with such nonsense?" She lifted his eyelids and examined his eyes. "How's your vision? Do you have any blurriness, haze, or fog?"

"I can see the specks of gold in your beautiful amber eyes, and I can also see the truth."

"And what truth is that?" She avoided his gaze as she removed the ice pack from behind his head.

"That you are as much in love with me as I am with you."

She didn't want to upset him because of his injury, but she had no choice. How could she tell him the truth about being a time traveler? Where would she even begin? Besides, she would not allow herself to ruin a family because of her selfishness.

"How wrong you are. I lied when I told you I didn't care about wealth." She spread her arms wide. "See my beautiful clothes, this beautiful house, the jewels, the paintings, the carriages and horses, the servants, all of it—this is what I desire. Can you give me this?"

"I see," he said in a stiff voice, the teasing sparkle in his eyes fading away. "Perhaps you say that now, but none of this"—his eyes roamed the room—"will bring true happiness to your life, Jenee."

"Perhaps, but illicit love affairs can't bring happiness either," she replied softly.

"Illicit?"

"Please, Xavier, it has been a most tiring day, and you need your rest. Let us argue no more about it."

"Very well. I have suddenly grown weary and would like to

be alone." His eyes narrowed as he regarded her. "I will be gone in the morning, and you can get on with your life."

She'd expected him to put up more resistance, and she felt bereft that he hadn't. "You should rest. I will sit and read."

"Do as you wish." He closed his eyes, and the warmth left the room with their closing.

She'd wounded him. Even worse, she'd insulted him. She felt dirty and cheap, but it was for the best. She did him a favor by sending him back to his wife and daughter. She'd send him on his way tomorrow, and he'd be fine in a day or two, forgetting her completely.

So why did she feel so terrible? *Because, you fool, you know you're in love with him, and you can't imagine you'll ever love anyone else.* Tears ran down her face, and she was glad Xavier's eyes were closed. She would never be able to explain why she was crying, and she didn't want to confuse him even more.

JENEE SHOOK HER head, clearing her vision. She must have fallen asleep while reading. The sounds of gravel crunching and the clip-clop of horses' hooves drifted through the window. She jumped up and ran to the window, parting the drapes. The vicomte's carriage stopped, and he and Constance climbed out laughing.

"It's been such a wonderful day, and I don't want it to end. Please stay, Albert, and I'll have tea served. We can check on Jenee and see how the chief inspector is faring. I want you to meet Violet, since you were curious about her."

Jenee looked back to the bed where Xavier slept, and she checked on him. His breaths were even, and his color was good. He would be fine for a few minutes without her.

She slipped out of the room. Hurrying down the hallway, she could hear Constance telling Olivier to please call Violet. When Jenee was nearly at the stairs, she saw Violet hiding behind a column at the edge of the upper balustrade. She clearly didn't want to be seen. Violet frowned and bit her lip.

Jenee kept her voice low. "Don't worry, Violet, I'll be with you when you meet the big, bad vicomte." She knew Violet was uncomfortable meeting unfamiliar people, but she had never seen her this unwilling.

"You don't understand. I cannot be seen by him."

"But why? To be sure, he is arrogant and entitled, but he is not a monster."

Violet glared at her. "You know nothing about him. He is worse than a monster!"

"But—"

"*Non!* Tell madame I've taken to my bed. That I have *un terrible mal de tête.*"

"How do you know this man, and what has he done to you?"

"Come to my room when you are done. It is time you knew the truth."

Time I knew the truth? "But—"

"Please, if you value my life and yours, you will do as I ask." Violet turned and strode to her bedroom, closing the door and locking it.

Why, suddenly, do I feel like I've landed in a James Bond movie? Jenee had no choice but to relay to Constance Violet's excuse. Her mind spun in a million directions as she descended the stairs. What had the vicomte done to Violet? How did she know him? Whatever it was must be horrific for her to call him a monster.

Dear Lord, it made Jenee weak in her knees to think of Constance becoming involved with such a man. She knew she would have to tread lightly because Constance was falling fast and hard for the vicomte. Nevertheless, if he were a danger to Constance, she would step in and bear the risk of her condemnation.

"There you are, Jenee." Constance glowed with the radiance of a woman at the threshold of love. "How is your inspector feeling?"

Jenee smiled in greeting. "He's resting, and I think I will be satisfied he is on the mend by tomorrow."

"That's good news. Why don't you join the vicomte and me for some tea in the library?" Constance glanced toward the staircase. "And where is Violet?"

"Violet is in her room resting. She has a terrible headache. She sends her apologies."

"Oh, dear. Should I go up and see how she is?"

"No, I think it's probably best for her to rest."

"I'm sure you're right. I'm completely useless when the *malaise* comes. Will you join us for tea, darling?"

"Forgive me if I beg off. I don't want to leave Inspector Doumaz for too long in case he should wake up."

"All right, my dear, will I see you for dinner?"

"I've already told Olivier I will have dinner with Monsieur Doumaz in the blue bedroom."

"Of course."

Jenee could hear the disappointment in Constance's voice. She hated lying to her.

Heck, I've been lying since I got here. What's one more?

Constance turned to the vicomte. "I guess it's just you and me, Albert. You will join me, won't you?"

"I'm afraid I have some business to attend to, but I received an invitation for tomorrow evening if you are free. I have tickets for *L'Aiglon* starring the Divine Sarah herself at her Théâtre Sarah Bernhardt. Afterward, there is to be a small soirée, and Miss Bernhardt's gatherings are always eventful. I would be honored if you would accompany me, along with you, Mademoiselle Lazaar." He smiled at Jenee. "It should prove to be a very entertaining evening."

Constance clapped her hands. "Oh, what a treat. She plays Napoleon II in that play, does she not?"

"*Oui*, she has received great acclaim for her portrayals of men. Her performance as Hamlet was spellbinding, and she is again taking the critics by storm and receiving their praise for her Napoleon."

"I saw her some years ago in *La Tosca*, and she was unforgettable. You will come, Jenee?"

Jenee loved theater, and to meet such an icon was an experience not to be missed. "I would love to attend. Enjoy your tea, and thank you, Albert, for allowing me to use your carriage. Oh, I forgot to ask, how was your match?"

"Thank you for asking. Both my opponent and I advanced."

"I thought only the winner advances in a competition."

"The foil is the most demanding of the three fencing disciplines and requires the most precise technique and strategy. In this first part of the competition, the judges look for both style and discipline, and both my opponent and I displayed enough to move us forward."

"Congratulations." Jenee could only think that his sword-fighting ability made him more dangerous, which worried her. She had to find out what Violet knew about this man, and fast.

CHAPTER FIFTEEN

May 14, 1900
Paris, France

XAVIER WAS STILL asleep when Jenee returned to the guest room. He looked peaceful, the lines of his face so smooth in repose that she couldn't resist brushing back an errant curl that fell over his forehead. She wanted to snuggle up in bed beside him, fall asleep and wake him in the morning with one soft kiss, then another, and another until she ignited his passion to a white-hot frenzy and then lost herself in the consuming blaze.

Get a hold of yourself. She needed to learn what Violet knew about the vicomte. Exhaling a deep sigh, she quietly left the room and hurried down the hallway. She knocked softly on the door. "Violet, it's me. May I come in?"

Violet opened the door, and Jenee entered a room decorated in shades of lavender. The French doors were open, and snatches of conversation wafted up from the garden. The voices of the vicomte and Constance sharing tea were discernible, and Jenee wondered if Violet had been listening to their conversation.

Violet closed the French doors, took Jenee's hand, and led her to a settee, inviting her to take a seat. A silver tray of tea and scones awaited on a table in front of the settee. "Come, we'll have tea. I have much to tell you, and you will need refreshment to overcome your disbelief."

Jenee was puzzled; she couldn't imagine what Violet meant. "What I must know is what danger the vicomte poses. What did he do to you?"

"All in good time, *mon amie*." Violet filled two cups of tea and served them scones with healthy dollops of clotted cream and preserves. "The cream is a habit I picked up in England when I lived there, and it tastes delicious with the scone." She served Jenee and then sipped her tea before setting the cup and saucer down.

Her sigh seemed significant, as if what she was about to impart was too much of a burden. From her pocket, she pulled a book and handed it to Jenee.

Jenee read the title and gasped. "*Mon Dieu*, it isn't possible." Her hand trembled as she reread the title. With shaking hands, she flipped it over and read the back. The title *L'amant du Voyageur Temporel* was the French version of *The Time Traveler's Lover*.

Jenee covered her mouth with her hand, unable to tear her eyes away. This was insane. How could Violet possess a book written in the future and published more than a hundred years from now? The manuscript wasn't even found until long after World War II. Yet here she sat in the Paris of 1900, holding the book in her hand.

She could scarcely breathe as she watched Violet remove the tinted glasses she always wore. Her eyes were a beautiful emerald green. Jenee looked closely at Violet's face, high cheekbones, dimpled chin, and mouth. Jenee had a memory for faces, and now, with the disguise lifted, she could see that Violet possessed the face immortalized in Allegretto's paintings. The only difference was her hair color, which could easily be dyed.

Her voice shook when she said, "You are Iris Bellerose. And you are the anonymous author of this book."

"*Oui.*"

"And it's a true story?"

Violet nodded.

"Of course it is. And you are also Allegretto's muse and lover, *oui?*"

Violet reached over and took Jenee's hand. *"Oui, mon amie.* I am Iris Bellerose, the heroine of the book and Marco Allegretto's lover and the subject of his fascination in *The Three Stages of Love* paintings."

Jenee felt as if she might faint. "You are a time traveler, and that's why you spoke of the man you loved in the present tense. You hope to return to him, don't you?"

"With your help." Iris nodded again.

"You know that I am a time traveler too." Jenee squeezed Iris' hand, her pulse quickening. "Can you help me get back to my life in the twenty-first century?"

"We can help each other—that is, if you want to leave."

"What do you mean if I want to leave?" Even as she said it, she knew the answer.

"Mon dieu, you've let slip many clues to your feelings for Monsieur Doumaz. You are in love with the gallant inspector, are you not?"

"I'm—I'm…" She couldn't deny the truth to Iris. Her shoulders shook as her emotions overwhelmed her. Tears stabbed her eyes, blurring her vision. "What does it matter if I'm in love with him? I can't remain here, and even if I could, he's married and has a child. There is no future for us." A sob escaped her, and she pressed her hands to her mouth.

"I'm sorry, but you know in your heart that love is worth fighting for. Why would you allow any obstacle to stand in your way?"

"Because I could never live with myself for destroying his marriage, and in this case, it would be two lives. There is a child, a daughter."

"Chérie, trust me when I say that a man such as Monsieur Doumaz does not fall in love easily. And I think he truly does love you. Have you spoken to him of your feelings? Or asked him about his wife and daughter?"

Jenee shook her head. "I found a framed photograph in a drawer in his flat that he had hidden away."

"Jenee, I do not know the truth of the inspector, but you must ask him. Perhaps there is a reason why he keeps the photograph in his drawer. People marry for all sorts of reasons. And from what you know of him, do you really believe he is the kind of man who would abandon his own daughter? You cannot assume the worst until you hear the truth from his lips."

Jenee wiped her tears with a napkin. "I will consider your advice. But right now, I need to know how I can help you. Who is the vicomte, and why did you call him worse than a monster?"

At the mention of his name, Iris' expression darkened. "He is a murderer, a serial killer, and, unfortunately, he is also a time traveler."

Jenee felt her temples throb. Again with the time travel? "How many time travelers do you know?"

Iris chuckled, and the lines of tension eased from her face. "I have only come across a few others, and none are as evil as the Vicomte de Maurnier. He wishes to destroy me and will stop at nothing if he gets the chance."

"But why?"

"Power, money, and eternal life."

"But how does destroying you give him that?"

"The paintings are the key. The paintings have been cursed, and until all three are reunited, Marco and I can never be together. I will be doomed to travel through time for the rest of my life, possibly forever. The vicomte is an evil time bandit. This noble title is merely a persona he has assumed in this life. He becomes a different person in every era he travels to. He is always searching for *The Three Stages of Love*, which would allow him to time-travel at will, leaving him free to murder and steal without restraint. In his last incarnation, he was a duke, a rapist, and a killer of women. He is a master of disguise and transfigures into the host he chooses. He picks the wealthy and titled, kills them, then takes over as their heir so he can have money and power at his disposal in his evil quest for the paintings."

"What does he need the paintings for?" Jenee asked.

"The paintings are portals. Marco pulled you through the portal of *Il Divano* so you could help me. The last time I was helped was in London. A young woman named Emily Christie helped me, and we foiled that bastard's plans. I made it through the portal and took *La Sedia* with me, but he followed me at the last second through the portal and escaped murder charges and arrest in London. Now he is after *Il Divano*. After a brief reunion with Marco, I was swept through time again and ended up here in Paris. I must escape through the portal again and bring *Il Divano* back to Marco. Then, unfortunately, I will once again be hurled to another time to find the last painting, *Il Letto*. The portals must be closed, or the cycle of death and destruction will never end. Nor will I ever be able to remain with the man I love."

Jenee barely heard what Iris said after she heard Emily's name. When she heard Iris say *Emily Christie*, she was sure she'd been pulled through the looking glass. It wasn't possible, was it? "Did you say the woman who helped you was Emily Christie?"

Iris looked long and hard at her as if deciding whether to explain. "Marco brought a young woman named Emily Christie through the portal to help me."

Jenee was speechless as she tried to wrap her head around what Iris was saying. "Did Emily return to the future? Did she find her way back to the Metropolitan Museum?"

"*Non*. She chose to stay in the past. She married the Marquess of Danbury in 1892 and lives happily on an estate in Eastbourne, England."

"How do you know all this?" Jenee was sure she had become a permanent resident of the Twilight Zone.

"I am in correspondence with her, and we write regularly to each other. She has become a dear friend."

"I just can't believe this. Emily is also my dear friend. We were at the museum together, and our traveling through time could not have been more than a few minutes apart. How could she be married? How could she have abandoned her life?"

"*Mon amie*, as Moliere wrote, *Vivre sans amir n'est pas proprement vivre.*"

Jenee repeated in a whisper, as a tear slipped down her cheek, "To live without love is to not live."

"*Exactement!* The choice is yours."

"Emily landed in 1892, only eight years earlier than I did. That means I could see her again. Would you give me her address so that I might write to her? I would so like to correspond with her."

"*Oui*, of course. I am sure it will bring you great comfort to hear from her. Emily will counsel you wisely."

"Thank you." Jenee took Iris' hands and squeezed them. "How can I help you return to Marco?"

"We must steal the second painting in the series and make sure that the vicomte does not get his hands on it. *Il Divano* is the key to both of our futures."

CHAPTER SIXTEEN

May 14, 1900
Paris, France

JENEE RETURNED TO find Xavier still sleeping. She made sure he was breathing evenly and then settled herself into a chair and pulled *The Time Traveler's Lover* from her pocket. To have the book in her hand gave her courage and hope. Now that she knew the truth about Iris, she saw the book in an entirely different light.

She glanced at Xavier, and Iris' words replayed in her mind. *To live without love is to not live.* She was completely torn in two by her feelings. She never would have believed in love at first sight if it hadn't happened to her. Yes, she did love Xavier, and she would have to tell him the truth at some point and demand the truth from him. Even if he divorced his wife and they could reassure his daughter that she would not lose her father, could Jenee make her life here, in a time she wasn't born into, as Emily had done? And what about Gaby? Was she also transported back to another time to help Iris retrieve the third painting? And if so, where and when?

She opened the book and flipped through the pages. Although the love scenes between Marco and Iris were tempting to lose herself in, they would only stimulate her, and she might do something foolish like crawl into bed with Xavier. Now was not the time for that. She wasn't sure they would ever share that magic of passion again until she made her decision. Better to make sense of the paintings and what happened to them.

She found the page she was looking for and began to read.

October 17, 1503

Tuscany, Italy

The carriage jostled over the rutted road that led from Florence to Montalcino. Marco held Iris' hand. Occasionally he lifted it and kissed it as though to reassure himself that she was still beside him. His usual playful exuberance was muted. Iris could not assuage his worries, nor could she assure him that they would make it safely to his family's farm and vineyards outside the hilltop town. There was always danger on the roads, bandits, mercenaries, and other malcontents. The Italian peninsula's constant internecine warfare meant his coachmen were armed, as was Marco. His house in Florence had been locked up, and his paintings packed and stored in the carriage he'd hired to take them to Montalcino. They'd left just after dawn, determined to reach the Allegretto estate before dusk.

"You haven't told me why we left Florence in such haste, Marco."

"Amore mio, I want my family to meet the woman I love. We must be married as soon as possible, and our issue must be recognized as legitimate." He eyed her adoringly, with the hint of lust that never left his gaze when he looked at her. "You might be with child even now, or you will soon be."

"I'm not with child."

She wasn't even sure if she could get pregnant so long as she was a time traveler. In the back of her mind, she worried that Marco would one day abandon her if she didn't bear him children. He longed to be a father, and she sometimes feared their love was doomed.

"Your parents are never going to approve of me, Marco. A woman with no family, penniless—thank God they don't know I'm a Jew."

"I have told you before, none of that matters to me. When my family meets you, they will fall in love with you just as I

have."

Iris shook her head. There was no getting through to him when he'd made up his mind. She wanted to believe him, but she knew nothing went as planned. Her own life was a perfect example. She'd seen her parents gunned down before her very eyes, witnessed unspeakable murders, was catapulted to different eras, and then was ripped through time to the Renaissance, where she found love with an artist. Not just any artist, but an artist who would be recognized as a master on an equal footing with Michelangelo, Leonardo da Vinci, Raphael, and Titian. How strange was this life she'd been given?

"And you still insist that the attack had nothing to do with the contessa? We'd be dead if we weren't on the terrace when the assassin plunged his sword into our bed. Thank God there was no moon, and he couldn't see us."

"Thank God Dominic came quickly when he heard my shouts and made quick work of the bastardo. *The assassin was an amateur."*

Dominic was Marco's friend and bodyguard, who'd been with him since he was a boy. The faithful retainer would willingly give his life for Marco in the service of his protection. He was born mute and reminded Iris of a ninja, coming and going without a sound. It had taken some time for her to get used to him and he to her. Neither had trusted the other at first, but their mutual love for Marco had bonded them over time, and now she knew the silent man would give his life not only in defense of Marco but also for her.

"My presence puts you in danger. The contessa will never rest until you are punished for forsaking her, and I am dead." Iris wiped a tear that slipped down her cheek. Would they ever know peace from the wicked Contessa Catarina di Farnese? Iris had only seen the contessa once, at a gala at the Hall of Five Hundred, and was shocked by the malevolence emanating from her. Even Leonardo da Vinci had noticed and commented on the enmity directed at her and Marco: "That is a woman I will never paint, not for all the gold in Florence."

The maestro was wise; she wished Marco had not been

duped into involving himself with the widow. The well-connected contessa had commissioned a portrait from him, and like a spider, she'd lured him in, getting him drunk and seducing him. From his inability to recall much about the encounter, Iris also believed she'd drugged him. Whatever the case, Caterina had become obsessed with Marco, determined to control and possess him. Marco would have none of it; he returned her deposit and canceled the commissioned portrait after meeting Iris in the Mercato Vecchio.

It had been love at first sight for both of them, and Iris had lost her heart and soul to Marco, becoming his lover and muse. But Caterina was not a woman to be scorned, and she swore vengeance. Since then, she'd smeared his name and publicly belittled his talent. Her power and influence were vast, and his commissions had dried up. But her attempts to destroy his career had had no impact on Marco or his mindset.

But somehow Caterina had blackmailed Agostina, the trusted midwife and soothsayer who had attended Marco's birth. The woman who'd predicted Marco's rise to fame as a great painter had been forced by Caterina to curse his greatest works of art, The Three Stages of Love, *and transform them into portals. On her deathbed, the midwife summoned Marco to her and begged his forgiveness. To redeem herself, she placed an incantation that amended her spell. She gave Marco the key to closing the portals and ending the curse, but to do that, they must destroy Contessa Caterina di Farnese and the evil time bandit who served her.*

"Tesoro mio, we will beat her, I promise you," Marco said.

"But how? She has become a powerful sorceress and has unlimited means to buy the services of powerful sorcerers, mercenaries, and murderers. That bastard Nazi who murdered my parents and tried to murder me is doing her bidding. If she gets her hands on all three paintings, we are doomed, and he will be free to roam through time and satisfy his blood lust for killing."

"This time-bandit murderer that you call a Nazi will not win. I will kill him."

"You can't kill him when he has the power of time travel, and if Caterina has the paintings, he will be able to travel through time forever," Iris said.

"She does not have the paintings. We do. Once we reach my family's property, the paintings will be safe. We will be safe." Marco cupped her cheeks and kissed her. "I love you, il tesoro. You must not allow your fears to overwhelm you. Believe in us, believe in our love, and believe I will keep you safe." The sweetness of his lips on hers made her believe everything he promised. His undying love made her believe they really could defeat the contessa and her Nazi cohort.

The lurch of the carriage as it came to a sudden stop, accompanied by shouts and the horses neighing their protest, threw them apart and ended their kiss. Marco pushed her down so that she could not be seen through the window, nor could she see out. She tried to move forward and look out, but he held her firm. "I want you out of sight!"

"What is it, Marco? What is happening?" Her heart raced at a dizzying pace from her terror. "If anything happens to you, I don't want to live." Her fear of losing him was so great that she wasn't thinking straight. Her rational mind should have remembered that the artist Marco Allegretto was not murdered on a dirt road, and he was destined for a long life and would produce many works of art not yet dreamed of. But all Iris could think about was the possibility that a person with access to time travel could, in fact, alter or change the future.

"Stay in the carriage." He was already half out the door.

She grabbed his arm, and he looked back at her. "Be careful, mon amour. Remember, you are my heart."

Despite Marco's warning, Iris sat in a crouch on the floor of the carriage, just high enough to peek through the window.

A gang of masked bandits with swords drawn surrounded the carriage. Dominic was in a standoff with one of the villains. His blade glinted in the sun. Iris knew he would not stand down, even when outnumbered. He would fight to the death.

"Signore, I would suggest you order your friend to put his

sword down, or I will have my men run you both through," said their ringleader.

Iris could not see his face, as he wore a mask and a hat with a wide brim.

"I have no desire to shed your blood, but I will if need be. All we want is your valuables, and then we will be on our way."

"This is outrageous," Marco shouted.

"What is outrageous is that you have not yet complied. I believe I spotted a red-haired beauty in your carriage. My men would happily take turns with her after we've tied up you and your friend. I would also take great pleasure in partaking in the sport, if only to see the look on your face."

Marco dropped his sword and said, "If you touch a hair on her head, I will hunt you down and eviscerate you." He nodded toward Dominic. "Do as the bastardo says, Dominic—drop your sword."

Reluctantly, the swarthy bodyguard let go of his sword, and it hit the dirt with a great clatter. His black eyes flashed with anger.

Iris knew Marco and Dominic would launch themselves at the bandits should they come near her. Hidden beneath their pantaloons strapped to their legs were knives that both men would send flying in the blink of an eye. Dominic could hit an object dead center at sixteen braccio. If the bastards tried anything, many of them would die.

Marco kept his eyes on the leader. Iris also knew that Marco would attack at the exact same moment as Dominic and slash the thief's throat. It was always best to cut off the head of the snake. The rest of the gang would run for their lives once their leader was dead.

"A wise decision, gentiluomini." Two of the thieves were busily grabbing everything out of the luggage boot of the carriage. They loaded everything into a cart and drove off with the plunder, getting a head start. "Do not try to follow us, or we will kill you. Now hand over your money."

Marco pulled a purse from his tunic and threw the bag at

the gang leader, who caught it and pocketed it in his saddlebag.

"There is nothing of great value in our belongings. Who hired you to rob us?" snarled Marco.

"That is for me to know, signore, and for you to wonder."

"Tell her I swear she will pay for this!"

"You have made a dangerous enemy, signore, and I suggest you don't make things worse. Be happy I have no stomach for killing." The leader spurred his horse and galloped off with the rest of his men, leaving a trail of dust behind.

Do you want me to tail them and find out who their master is? Dominic signed.

"No, it can only be her. They took everything to make it look like they were common thieves, but it was the paintings they came for, and now she has them."

Iris leaped out of the carriage and ran to Marco. He enfolded her in his arms, and she looked up at him, eyes filled with panic. "What are we to do? She will use the paintings to destroy us."

Without letting go of Iris, Marco slipped a ring out of a pocket inside his shirt and put it on his left hand. A large ruby set in a gold band with ancient symbols etched into the gold caught the sunlight. "A magical parting gift from Agostina with as much power as anything the Contessa Farnese can conjure. With it, we will know what our enemy plans. Like a child seeking its mother's breast, the portals seek the ring's power. They belong to the ring and wish only to return to it. The mirrored paintings were never meant to open and must be destroyed. Once we destroy the fakes, the portals will close, and the curse will end. Remember, tesoro, knowledge is power. We have the tools to destroy this evil and the evildoers..."

A gentle rap on the door roused Jenee from her reading. She closed the book and laid it on the table next to her. "Come in."

The door opened, and Estelle, one of the maids, poked her head in. "Madame requests you join her in the library."

"Yes, of course. Please run ahead and tell madame I will be

with her momentarily."

A cool evening breeze ruffled the curtains, and Jenee peeked out. The vicomte was bent over Constance's hand, obviously taking his leave. Jenee would wait until he departed.

His words wafted up to her. "I will escort you and Jenee to the Théâtre Sarah Bernhardt and the dinner party to follow. I will send you word as to what time I will call for you."

Constance smiled. "We look forward to it."

Jenee was hesitant to attend, but she would never let Constance go anywhere with that monster alone. Besides, it would be an excellent opportunity to keep an eye on him and report back to Iris, and a part of her was looking forward to meeting Sarah Bernhardt.

Jenee closed the French doors, went to Xavier, and placed her lips on his forehead. He had no fever, and for that, she was grateful. She was tempted to brush his lips with hers but stopped herself. One day soon, they would need to talk, and she would have to tell him the truth. But for now, she and Iris would follow their plan. The swish of her silk skirt whispered as she gently closed the door.

CHAPTER SEVENTEEN

May 14, 1900
Paris, France

Xavier opened his eyes and sat up. He'd pretended to be asleep when Jenee was in the room. To say he was frustrated was an understatement. He knew she cared about him, maybe even loved him, yet she persisted in ignoring her feelings. If he thought it would do any good, he'd get down on his knees and beg her to give them a chance, but that might only push her away even more. He'd finally found the one woman who ignited his passion, and she was as stubborn as a mule. He'd turn her over his knee and give her a good spanking if he could.

The thought of her perfect derriere splayed across his lap only kindled his desire. He envisioned kissing and delivering love bites to that most perfect derriere, which only swelled his manhood. *Damned if I don't and damned if I do.*

He sat up and got dressed, trying to ignore the throbbing in his head, which was far preferable to the throbbing in his trousers. He glanced out the open French doors and saw the vicomte's carriage leaving. *Good riddance.* How he detested the arrogant man.

He rubbed the tender spot on his head. The swelling had gone down thanks to the ice Jenee had administered. She was the most capable woman he had ever known, and his heart ached to hold her in his arms.

Needing a distraction, he looked around the room. His gaze settled on the book she'd left on the table. He absent-mindedly picked it up, opened it, and flipped through the pages.

His breath caught in his chest. It had to be a typographical error. He stared at the publishing date and shook his head. Was he hallucinating? Perhaps his injury was worse than he thought. The date of publication was over a hundred years in the future.

He read the title, which only confused him even more. *It's not possible.* Was this a practical joke, intentionally printed incorrectly to match the fantastical plot device of time travel? Even as he tried to find a reason for the publishing date, his instinct told him it was not a joke.

The idea of time travel was not new to Xavier. He had stumbled upon *The Lifted Veil* by George Eliot, a story about a man who could see into the future, which led him to discover one of his favorite authors, H. G. Wells. Wells' novella, *The Time Machine*, was the story of a scientist who invented a machine that transported him to the future.

Intrigued by the title of Jenee's book and thinking the publishing date was a gag in line with the book's theme, he sat in the armchair by the French doors and began to read.

Page after page flew by as he soaked up the story as fast as he could. After the first few chapters, he looked up, his thoughts churning. The memory of Jenee appearing as though by magic amid the falling concrete of the walkway flashed through his mind. He pictured her peculiar clothing, like none he'd ever seen before. The many pieces of her story that didn't add up, and her not knowing anyone in Paris. He recalled how she'd choked on her tea when she heard what year it was, and her unique turns of phrase that he doubted had come from years of living abroad in America. He'd met many American officials and tourists in his work, and he'd never come across Jenee's particular way of speaking.

In addition, there was her lack of familiarity with the city she grew up in. And the final oddity was her medical abilities, namely, the breathing resuscitation procedure she'd performed with such assurance on Constance Shipley. He knew of no other doctor who could perform this new method.

One after another, the incongruities added up, and now he could clearly see the whole picture, rather than just the individual parts. None of it should make sense, and yet it did.

From the moment he met her, his instincts had been right on target, but he'd been wrong about the reason. She wasn't an anarchist or a revolutionary. Jenee, like Iris in the book, was a time traveler! It was hard for him to believe, but it was the only explanation. She had rejected him not because she was a revolutionary, afraid of falling in love with the enemy, or because she was an opportunist, as she'd claimed. *Mon Dieu*, the woman was a caring doctor who'd saved Constance's life and his own. No, the truth was staring him in the face: Jenee could not allow herself to fall in love with him because she feared she could be sucked up in another time-travel vortex and they would never see each other again.

Voices in the hallway reached his ears, and he returned the book to the table and jumped back in bed just as the door opened. Jenee entered, followed by Olivier pushing a cart with silver-domed cloche servers. The aromatic scents of saffron and garlic infused the air, and Xavier's stomach rumbled with anticipation. He hadn't paid any attention up until now to his stomach's protests, but he was starving.

"I'm so glad you're awake, Xavier. How are you feeling?" Jenee asked.

"Much better, *merci*. What is that marvelous aroma?"

She smiled. "Thank you, Olivier. I'll take over from here."

The butler nodded and left the room.

"I requested the chef prepare one of my favorite meals. I'm famished, and I expect you are too, as we haven't had a bite to eat all day."

He chuckled, happy that the tension between them had

eased. But, of course, the simple act of eating together would mend most ills. His approach would change now that he was almost positive about what stood between them.

"And what, *ma adorable fille*, are we to dine on?"

"Come sit, and you'll see." She eyed him curiously.

He eased himself up to a sitting position and groaned for good measure, determined to wring the most sympathy he could from her.

"Are you all right? Here, let me help you to the table." She wrapped her slender arm around his waist and helped to steady him as they made their way to the small, round dining table in the center of the room. He marveled at how slender she was and yet how strong as well.

Jenee unfurled his napkin and set it on his lap. "*Voila!*" With a flourish, she lifted the silver dome. A delicious, steamy aroma of garlic, onion, and saffron imbued the air. He lifted his cloche and inhaled deeply. "It's bourride," she said, removing a white cloth napkin and revealing a basket of toasted baguette slices. She poured him a glass of lemonade and a glass of wine for herself. "I'm afraid no wine for you until tomorrow."

"I think one glass will not kill me."

"I'm sure you are right, but just one." She filled his glass. "I have such a wonderful memory of my parents taking me to Marseilles for a vacation where I had fish stew for the first time. I loved it so much I begged them to let me have it for breakfast, lunch, and dinner." She thickly spread aioli on a slice of baguette, dipped it in the golden fish broth, took a bite, and hummed with pleasure.

"The east coast of France is beautiful," Xavier said. "What a charming recollection. Tell me, do they have bourride in America?"

"Um, no, food is not on a level equal to our French cuisine."

"Then we should celebrate our special meal together. By the way, I make a very fine bourride."

"I didn't know you could cook."

"There are a lot of things you don't know about me, and I suppose there is much I don't know about you. Perhaps you will allow me to cook for you some time?"

She hesitated, and he held his breath.

Then a slight smile hovered over her lips, and he exhaled with relief.

"I-I would enjoy that very much," she said.

He poured himself a glass of white wine and raised his glass. "To friendship, *ma chérie*."

"*À votre santé!*" They brought their glasses close, nearly touching, and sipped.

Xavier ate a spoonful of the stew and nodded his approval. "Delicious." He took another spoonful and gestured with his spoon to Jenee's book on the table. "I see you are reading a book. Is it a story I might enjoy?"

Jenee looked toward the table, and her eyes widened. "I…uh… I don't think it is something you would be interested in, a romance written with a woman in mind."

"Oh, but I love romantic tales. They take my mind off my troubling caseload. What is the title?"

"It's a silly book. I don't even know why I'm reading it."

"I see. Surely you can tell me the title. You haven't gotten your hands on some *pornographie*, mademoiselle, and are too embarrassed to say, are you?" He winked at her, and she turned red as a beet.

"No, of course not. It's called *The Time Traveler's Lover*. Hardly pornography. If you wish something to read tonight, Constance has an extensive library, and I'm certain we can find you something better suited to your interests. If you like, I can take you to the library after our meal and help you find something that stirs your imagination."

"Yes, that will be fine. Or perhaps you could read to me; that might be less tiring for my eyes." Xavier rubbed the bump on his head and gave a dramatic wince.

She dropped her spoon with a clatter and ran to him. She

probed the back of his head with gentle fingers. "I think we should apply another ice pack."

As she examined him, her bosom was at eye level, and it was all he could do to restrain himself from burying his face against the soft, smooth globes straining against the lacy V of her gown. He remembered wrapping his lips around her protuberant nipples and the delight she'd expressed when he suckled them.

"Your gentle ministrations are so soothing that my pain is already subsiding," he said. "I trust you completely to see to my well-being." Her face was only inches away when he looked up. With ease, he could have brought her lips to his.

Before he lost himself in the moment, she stepped back, tilting her head as if questioning his sincerity. "That is something new. As I recall, you didn't trust me in the least. In fact, you suspected my involvement in the bombing on the boardwalk and the bomb threats at the opera house." She returned to her chair, folded her napkin in her lap, and took a hearty sip of wine.

Perhaps I'm not the only one fighting my desire.

"I ask for your forgiveness in suspecting you. As I explained to you previously, the facts supported my inquiry's direction. I promise you that I do not suspect you of anything nefarious. I do, however, suspect you do not trust me." Instead of meeting his gaze, she looked away. "Aha, the truth. You don't believe me, nor do you trust me."

"I need time, Xavier. There are other matters on my mind and other factors at play that I must consider."

"Yes, I can well imagine your hesitancy. Time is a fickle foe, it does play tricks on us, but we can learn much from the passage of time and where it takes us."

She looked uncomfortable at his use of the word *time* but said nothing. He desperately wanted to pick the book up, open it, point to the publishing date, and insist she explain, but he would not push her, at least not yet.

His first reaction to the concept of time travel had been disbelief, but the more he thought about her strange appearance out of thin air, the more he was inclined to give credence to the notion. He wanted to help her. Hell, he wanted to be part of everything in her life, good or bad. He refused to think about the reason for Jenee's avoidance of any emotional attachment to him. He refused to acknowledge that lying on the fringes of his thoughts was the unknown of how he would cope if she were torn away from him today, tomorrow, or five years from now. In that apartment fire, he'd lost his entire family, his wife, daughter, and his parents. *Mon Dieu*, could he cope with the possibility of losing Jenee?

But even if she hadn't been a time traveler, even if she was someone from his time, he knew the universe could deal cruel blows. As a police inspector, he knew murderers lurked around every corner, waiting to pounce on their next victim. He knew that accidents, fires, and natural disasters were a part of everyday life and could take a loved one in a matter of moments. He knew he could never protect Jenee from the bad things out there twenty-four hours a day, 365 days a year. Nor was Jenee likely the kind of woman who would be happy to hide away from the big, cruel world. She was a doctor, for goodness' sake, a woman from the future. She possessed knowledge the likes of which not even his favorite author H. G. Wells could fathom.

If only he could get through to Jenee and have an open and honest discussion. He wanted to tell her about his past, and he wanted her to trust him enough to confide hers to him. Ultimately, he'd rather take a chance on even a short burst of happiness with Jenee than live the rest of his life with regrets for never having tried.

They finished their meal in companionable silence. It wasn't a standoff per se, but it gave him time to think, and Jenee was undoubtedly doing the same. Xavier focused on a way forward. He couldn't say what she focused on, but he was determined to do everything in his power to keep her. It wasn't his nature to back away or back off, and he had no intention of giving up.

"Would you allow me to cook for you tomorrow evening?"

he asked.

"Oh!" Her hand trembled as she poured them each a glass of lemonade. "I-I can't. Constance and I have accepted an engagement already."

Xavier felt his heart deflate a little that Jenee didn't mention what that engagement was.

"What about Thursday? I could take a day off from work. Given my injury, I think they can manage one day without me. We could spend the day together, go to the market, and then go to my place. You could be my sous chef."

She took a sip from her glass and then set it down. "Xavier, do you think it is a good idea for you and me to dine alone at your home?"

"I am a gentleman, Jenee. I'm offering stew, not seduction."

She laughed. "As I recall, the last time we were alone in your *pied-à-terre*, we didn't eat a thing, and you promised I would wake up in the morning the same as when I went to sleep. I think we can both agree that is not what happened."

"I do not regret it, but I promise to be on my best behavior and follow your lead."

She shook her head. "The problem is I'm not sure I can trust my inclinations."

Xavier felt his heart swell along with his trousers. He was thankful that he was seated, and the linen tablecloth gave him cover. "Then I suppose I will have to be strong enough for both of us." *I will need more than just one ice pack to do that!*

Jenee doubled over with laughter. "You? You, who professed your undying love earlier, will be able to restrain your passions?"

"Stew is all you are going to get." He joined Jenee's laughter, envisioning himself fighting off her advances. God help him, but he adored her. Adored her sense of humor, adored her stubborn streak, adored every inch of her delectable body. If fish stew was the way to her heart, he would cook and serve it to her morning, noon, and night, preferably in bed.

"And you expect me to believe that?"

"*Absolument!* On my honor." He touched his chest with his

right hand. *Well, now you've gone and done it. Given your word of honor, you imbecile.* So be it. But if Jenee changed her mind, to hell with honor.

She held up her own hands. "Well, as they say, don't write a check your ass can't cash."

There she goes again! He burst out laughing at her outrageous comment. "What an unusual American saying. What does it mean exactly?"

"It means don't make a promise you can't keep."

"I see. Would you care to place a wager on that?"

"Are you a betting man, Xavier?"

"I do play poker with the boys at the precinct from time to time."

"Well, perhaps I'll take your wager."

"Perhaps one day, I can teach you how to play poker."

"What makes you think I don't already know how to play?"

He grinned. "*Touché, ma belle.* We'll save poker for another time. But what do you say about dinner?"

She inclined her head with a smile. "I will consider it." She cleared the dishes and placed a domed platter on the table. She lifted the cloche to reveal a colorful assortment of macaron cookies and the *pièce de resistance*, two slices of an amandine tart. "Constance has become quite addicted to this decadent delicacy. She discovered the patisserie on Rue Bourdaloue. Their pastry chef created the Bourdaloue tart. Wait until you taste it."

"It seems your Constance is an aficionado of all things French, including you, *mon amour.* I cannot fault her taste."

She served a slice of tart and macarons on a plate and set it before him. "Eat, Xavier, before you get into trouble. I think we are safer filling ourselves with dessert rather than words."

"Whatever you say, my darling, but any trouble I encounter with you is always a pleasure."

"Oh, Xavier, the things you say."

It is the things we have yet to say, mon amour, *that will determine our future.* He smiled as he reached for a macaron and popped it in his mouth, feeling better than he had in weeks.

CHAPTER EIGHTEEN

May 15, 1900
Paris, France

THE WARMTH OF morning sunlight on her face woke her. Her first thought was of Xavier, but he was not in bed. Then she realized he would have things to attend to. Besides, she would see him tomorrow. She was still worried about his injury, but more than twenty hours had passed, and she'd kept a close eye on him.

Jenee ran a hand over the indentation in the bed where he'd lain, hoping to feel the warmth of his body, but it was cool to the touch. He must have risen early. She felt quite bereft that she hadn't been awake when he left. She picked up the pillow and held it to her nose, breathing his scent in. How remarkable that his essence could stir a response in her mind and body. Nothing untoward had occurred during the night. How could it have when she'd slept in a chair? But, reflecting on the feelings he stirred in her, she almost wished it had.

Glancing around the room, she saw a note sticking out of *The Time Machine*, the book she'd been reading to him when they both fell asleep. The hastily written note said, *I will be waiting for you at 11:00 a.m. at the Fontaine des Fleuves at the Place de la Concorde on Wednesday. Until then, take care of yourself and know that my thoughts are always with you. Yours for all of time, Xavier.*

She was slightly taken aback by his parting valediction. It was a strange way to end his message, "yours for all of time." Perhaps it had to do with the book she'd been reading to him. Xavier had said H. G. Wells was one of his favorite authors, and *The Time Machine* was one of his favorite books. When they found a copy in the library, he'd asked if she would read it to him. He said he found the idea of time travel very alluring, but Jenee had professed that time travel was a bit too fantastical for her taste.

But she did find it curious that he was so taken with the idea of traveling through time. It made her think of *The Time Traveler's Lover*, and she wondered if he'd looked at it when she was out of the room. It made her hopeful that he would believe her when she told him she was a time traveler, but did she dare trust him with the truth? She desperately wanted to trust him, to have his support. It would be such a relief to have a confidant.

She made up her mind to take the risk. She had never said she would meet him on Wednesday, but the more she thought of him, the more she realized she would be a fool not to. To pour her heart out and trust him with her secret would be a relief. The worst that could happen was he wouldn't believe her, and then…then it would be over.

She went to her room, performed her morning ablutions, and dressed. Then she sat down at her desk and wrote Emily a letter. To delay was unthinkable because she could not wait to hear back from her friend. To know Emily was so near and that she might see her was more than Jenee could hope for.

She sealed the envelope and gave it to Olivier to post as soon as possible. Then, feeling as if all things were possible, she joined Constance and Violet, who were having breakfast in the dining room.

"Good morning, dear," Constance said. Violet was busily taking notes while Constance dictated a list of what needed to get done. Constance made lists for everything—she was meticulously organized, and she and Violet worked seamlessly together.

"Good morning, Constance, Violet," Jenee greeted them, and then went directly to the sideboard and filled a bowl with muesli, yogurt, and blueberries. Constance sat at the head of the table, and Jenee took her seat next to her and opposite Violet. She poured a cup of coffee from the *cafetière.*

"I see your inspector is recovered. Olivier was up and made fresh coffee for him before he left. I imagine he needed to get to the prefecture early. Your evening was uneventful, I presume." There was a twinkle in Constance's eyes, and Jenee knew she suspected there was much more to her relationship with the handsome inspector.

"He napped on and off, and I kept watch over him. Thanks to your chef, we had a lovely meal, and then I read to him."

Constance's brows rose with curiosity. "What did you read to him?"

"*The Time Machine.*"

"Really! I must admit Mr. Wells does have a vivid imagination. Time travel sounds like an unforgettable adventure, but to be thrown into a world you know nothing about would never be for me." She picked up her coffee cup and sipped. "And that is all?"

Jenee exchanged a look with Violet. "Yes, Constance, we were quite circumspect."

Constance frowned. "How disappointing. I was sure… Never mind."

Jenee sipped her coffee, hiding her smile. She knew Constance suspected there was something brewing between Xavier and her.

"Madame, a telegram has just arrived for you," Olivier announced, handing Constance an envelope.

"Thank you, Olivier." She tore open the envelope and read. "My father's ship arrived in Marseilles two days ago. It seems they sent an earlier telegram, but somehow it was waylaid. The crates containing the paintings should arrive today." Constance looked up, and her eyes gleamed with anticipation.

"How exciting," said Jenee. "I can't wait to see them."

Her heart fluttered in her chest. She stole a glance at Violet to see her reaction. Violet's face remained impassive, but Jenee could see a slight rigidity in her posture, as if she were preparing for battle. Violet hadn't given Jenee any details about her plan other than that she needed help stealing the painting. Jenee would address it with her as soon as they were alone.

Once they got their hands on the Allegretto, would she be swept back to her own time? *Will I suddenly appear at the Metropolitan Museum, and everything that has happened to me will seem like a dream?* If so, why had she been transported to the past in the first place? Violet seemed more than capable of carrying out her plan of action. But then again, Emily had been very involved in helping Violet in London. Whatever this madness was, it involved Emily, Jenee, and most likely Gabriella. Emily had met the man of her dreams, fallen in love, and chosen to stay in the past.

Xavier was at the back of Jenee's mind, and the possibility of never seeing him again overwhelmed her with sadness. Could she do what Emily had done? Choose to stay here, in the past with Xavier?

"I am on pins and needles, and I haven't seen the Allegretto painting yet," Constance said with excitement. "Stefano, my art procurer, had it delivered from Italy to Marseilles so that it would arrive together with the other paintings. Olivier?"

The efficient butler must have been standing outside the door, because he entered immediately after hearing his mistress' summons. "Yes, madame."

"Olivier, send a message to the vicomte to visit this afternoon. Tell him that the paintings have arrived."

"I will see to it, madame." With a nod, Olivier was gone.

"Violet, how are the arrangements coming for the Restaurant Brébant dinner? Now that the paintings are here, we should send out the invitations immediately."

"I have been waiting for confirmation of the arrival of the paintings," Violet replied. "The invitations will go out today. Everything else is ordered and scheduled. I will need your final decision on the menu and the flowers, but other than that, we are ready. I will let the officials at the exposition know they should expect the painting the day after the dinner."

"Perfect. Let's finalize the menu later today." Constance was like a general organizing his troops. "Jenee, you should wear the royal-blue gown with the shorter train to the theater tonight. Albert will be here at seven to pick us up. And remember, no hat—Madame Bernhardt forbids them in the theater because they make it difficult for the audience to see the stage."

"Aye aye, captain," Jenee teased, saluting.

Constance chuckled. "I forget myself. Forgive me. I'm afraid I'm becoming my father, always ordering everyone about."

Jenee took Constance's hand and held it to her cheek. "My dear Constance, your intentions are always on point, and we are all grateful for your exactitude and generosity."

➤➤➤✦◄◄◄

A FEW HOURS later, Jenee waited by the door to the library while the vicomte studied *Il Divano*, a small Titian, and a Rembrandt self-portrait. She still couldn't believe she was looking at the painting she'd sat before at the Metropolitan Museum, the same painting that had dragged her back in time.

Iris was nowhere to be seen during the vicomte's visit for obvious reasons.

Despite Iris' supreme unflappability, Jenee had seen her distress when she gazed at the painting. Her years of medical training told her that not even Iris could be unaffected by the painting that could very well be her salvation or her destruction. When Olivier announced the vicomte's arrival, Iris had excused herself to "get back to work" planning the upcoming dinner.

Jenee went to check on Iris, leaving the vicomte and Constance to their mutual lovefest over the painting. She brought Iris a cup of chamomile tea.

Iris thanked her and promptly burst into tears. "When I look at the painting, I relive every sweet moment of our love affair, and it breaks my heart." She grabbed Jenee's hand. "What if we fail and I never see him again? How will I live?"

Jenee had never seen Iris lose control, and such vulnerability brought out her protective nature. She did what good friends often did: they were there for you not only in the best of times, but in the worst of times. "We will not fail. We simply cannot."

Iris wiped her eyes. "You're right. We will not fail." Beneath the glistening tears on her face, she smiled. "I will tell you a secret that was not in the book."

"I would love that." Jenee took Iris' hand and held it between hers.

"At first, I was too shy to pose nude for Marco, and it was a running argument between us. I didn't want the world to see me naked and exposed forever, and it bothered me that Marco would share our intimacy so publicly. But Marco would not be dissuaded because his belief was that our joining was the culmination of love and, *bien sûr*, the point of the series. It wasn't until he began the third painting, *Il Letto*, that we came to a compromise, and he agreed to the red scarf, and I was spared being forever immortalized completely nude. Given everything that followed, I think I was foolish to question his vision, but perhaps the painting is more powerful this way, leaving more to the viewer's imagination."

Jenee couldn't agree more, and she assured Iris that it made the painting more of a collaboration of artist and muse, adding that art historians would kill for a tidbit such as this.

When she returned to the library, she found Constance with her hands clasped together, waiting for Albert's reaction. Jenee studied his face as he studied the painting. Maybe it was her imagination, but Jenee was sure she saw a flash of pure malevolence in his eyes. *No wonder my Spidey-senses have been on alert around this fraud from the moment I met him.* Iris had only confirmed what Jenee's instincts had already warned of.

"I cannot bear another minute of waiting. What do you think, Albert?" Constance asked.

"It is exquisite," Albert replied. "I cannot draw my eyes away. How did you ever procure it?"

"My dealer in Florence is always on the hunt for me. He knows my love of Renaissance art. He's very wily and keeps his sources secret, and I never pry too much. I'm just thrilled that he was able to acquire it for me."

"Perhaps you will share this excellent agent's name with me."

"What, and have you competing with me?" Constance teased.

He laughed. "I promise to not bid on any painting of interest to you."

Jenee had learned from Constance that the dealer was also highly cautious and suggested that Constance have copies made of all the paintings she purchased. Listening to his advice, Constance had commissioned an exact replica of *Il Divano*, which was what they were looking at. The original had been transferred to Constance's vault at Crédit Lyonnais, and it would remain in the bank until the Restaurant Brébant dinner.

The clever Italian art dealer had also suggested Constance exhibit the copy at the restaurant, but she would not hear of it. On the night of the dinner, the original would be delivered to Restaurant Brébant, and afterward, it would be transferred and displayed at the Grand Palais. Although this worked in favor of Iris and Jenee's plan to steal the painting, because it wouldn't do them any good to steal the fake, it would also put the artwork at risk from the murderous vicomte, and Jenee fretted that he might get to the painting first. To keep the masterpiece safe, Jenee had convinced Constance to hire security for the event, and she begged Constance not to confide anything about the duplicate painting to the vicomte. She did not want him to know that a copy of *Il Divano* had been made.

Constance had waved off her worries. "Jenee, you can't possibly think Albert is an art thief. For heaven's sake, he is rich as Croesus."

"There is no need for anyone to know. Besides," said Violet, "would it not be amusing with all the art aficionados in attendance to see if any of them question the authenticity of the painting?"

Constance's lips curved up in a cheeky smile. "You make a valid point, Violet."

"And you can tell the vicomte later as your own secret joke. I am certain he will be most amused," Jenee added.

"I am certain he would find it hilarious. He has such a good sense of humor. And he's forever teasing me about my daring American ways." Constance winked.

Jenee had later asked Iris how she planned to disappear with the painting.

"It will have to be at the dinner at the Eiffel Tower," Iris said.

"In front of everyone? What are you going to do? Hurl yourself into the painting and disappear while the vicomte is chatting with Constance?"

"I believe you said you wanted to return to the future, so that means we will both be hurling, as you say. Unless you've changed your mind about leaving."

Jenee couldn't answer because she didn't know what she wanted anymore. Her feelings for Xavier had not diminished. If anything, they had grown stronger. He'd acted so gallantly, saving her from that speeding cyclist on the opening day of the Olympics. And spending the day with him as he recovered from his concussion had only deepened her feelings toward him. It was madness—or was it? If Emily could find happiness in the past, perhaps Jenee could too. If only Xavier wasn't married and hadn't lied to her. It certainly complicated everything.

Jenee's introspection must have been readily readable on her face, judging from the shrewd look Iris gave her.

"As I suspected," said Iris, arching a delicate brow. "You are in love with the handsome police inspector."

Jenee breathed and plunked down on the armchair in Iris' room.

"*Mon amie*, please heed my advice. If you decide to leave, there will be no turning back, and once your decision is made, your choice will be irrevocable. You cannot change your mind and click your ruby-red heels and say there's no place like Paris in 1900."

"Movie or book version?"

Iris laughed. "The book will be released in America two days from now," said the savvy time traveler.

"Is there nothing you don't know?"

"I do not know how any of this will end," Iris said softly, blinking back tears. "I pray that with your help, I will be able to return the second painting to Marco, and then, God willing, locate the third, and then it will be finished at last. The curse and the evil Contessa Farnese will no longer exist, and I will be able to remain with Marco until the end of our lives."

Jenee went to her friend and wrapped her arms around her slender shoulders. "I will do everything in my power to help you."

"*Merci, mon amie.* Together we will find a way to carry out this feat. You must meet Xavier tomorrow and confide the truth to him. And you must give him the chance to confide his truth to you."

"And what of his wife and child?"

"Love will find a way."

CHAPTER NINETEEN

May 15, 1900
Paris, France

THE THÉÂTRE SARAH Bernhardt dazzled like a treasure box filled with gems. The Place du Châtelet was illuminated by thousands of electric light bulbs that cast a radiant glow on the gentlemen, who were all finely dressed in formal tailcoats and top hats, escorting exquisitely dressed women in vibrant silks and velvets. Bejeweled in sparkling tiaras, glittering earrings, and glistening ropes of pearls and diamonds, the ladies sparkled like sunlight on the sea.

These women would put all the Met Gala glitterati to shame. Jenee couldn't help but marvel at the elegance and glamour of Paris in the early twentieth century. She grinned, thoroughly enjoying the endless parade of fashion, wishing she was attending with Xavier instead of being the third wheel to Constance and the vicomte. She was grateful for everything Constance had done for her and every opportunity she'd been gifted, but it would have been so much fun to trade quips with Xavier about the fashionable and the outrageous.

She remembered watching a documentary about the heyday of Las Vegas. It wasn't so many years ago when people went out for a night on the town to see Frank Sinatra, Dean Martin, Sammy Davis Jr., or Lena Horne dressed up as elegantly as the stars on the stage. That glamorous ambiance made everyone feel unique and special. Those days were gone, and what you saw for the most part in Sin City today was athleisurewear more appropriate for a jog through the park rather than a night on the town. *Maybe I was born in the wrong era,* she thought, smiling.

Her smile faded as she thought about the important decision she'd have to make soon. Very soon.

Feeling a knot of nerves in her chest, Jenee refocused her attention on the theater and its magnificent architecture. After being built by Baron Haussmann in 1862, the original building was set on fire by the Paris Commune and burned to the ground. It was rebuilt following the same architectural plans of the original building in 1874 and went through several incarnations before Sarah Bernhardt bought it and remodeled it to its present state. Situated on the banks of the Seine, the neoclassical structure was nearly as elegant as the opera house, with a colonnaded façade of arched windows that reflected the blue of the sky and the waters of the Seine. The playhouse featured plays starring the Divine Sarah and enjoyed resounding acclaim, showcasing her in sellout performances.

Strolling through the lobby, Jenee, Constance, and the vicomte paused to admire the life-size portraits of Sarah by the eccentric artist Louise Abbéma, who'd captured the famous actress in various poses. There were also paintings by one of Sarah's many lovers, and her official portraitist, George Clarins, whose oils showed her off in far more sensual poses. In one of those paintings, she reclined in a chair with a borzoi hound at her feet. She was sinuously posed as if in motion.

Jenee was utterly taken by Alphonse Mucha's colorful Art Nouveau posters of Sarah that were the inspiration for the classic posters from the 1960s celebrating Jimi Hendrix, Janis Joplin, and Jefferson Airplane at venues like the Filmore East in Manhattan and the Filmore West in San Francisco.

Jenee took her seat on one side of Constance, with the vicomte on the other. Her eyes roamed the elegant interior, and then she froze at what she saw. Coming down the left aisle of the auditorium were Xavier and Lulu. All the joy she'd held inside of her died as she watched them take their seats.

What the hell is going on? Xavier never mentioned he had plans with Lulu. She assumed when he'd left before she woke up the day after his concussion that he would go home and rest. Perhaps they had an arrangement and there was more to their relationship than what he'd professed. But now the seeds of doubt had been planted, and Jenee worried he could not be trusted.

The lights dimmed, and she cast any thoughts of Xavier aside. She would not allow his perfidious behavior to ruin her evening. The curtain rose to resounding applause for Edmond Rostand's six-act play, *L'Aiglon, The Eaglet.*

She'd read the program and knew "the eaglet" was the nickname of Napoleon II, the son of Emperor Napoleon Bonaparte and Empress Marie Louise, an Austrian Hapsburg archduchess. Rostand had written the play for Sarah to star in, and it had recently premiered in March, winning critical praise.

When Sarah made her entrance on stage, Jenee found it impossible to look away from the venerable actress. Her presence was spellbinding, and she mesmerized the entire theater with her brilliant performance. It was no wonder Victor Hugo had called her his "adorable queen with the golden voice." The supporting cast were all talented accouterments that enhanced her stature, and they circled like planets revolving around the sun, caught in her orbit and reflecting her glory.

After the performance, the vicomte led them backstage to Sarah's dressing room, an elaborate suite of five rooms decorated in the Empire style. Arranged about the room were velvet and brocade upholstered divans and sofas, and beautifully carved furniture fashioned with delicate veneers and rare woods, neoclassical designs that paid tribute to the glories of ancient Greece and Rome. A fire blazed in the hearth of the marble fireplace and cast a golden glow over the salon. Everything was arranged to provide intimate conversation areas where Sarah could entertain after her performances. Everything Sarah Bernhardt did was on a grand scale. She lived in the moment and spent lavishly like there was no tomorrow. When the money ran low, she would replenish it by going on tour.

The vicomte introduced Constance and Jenee to Sarah's dear friend, the impressionist painter Louise Abbéma, who was expected to receive a medal of honor at the Universal Exposition. The eccentric artist had spent her life ignoring societal conventions, and dressed at times like a man. That evening she was attired in a blue pinstriped suit with a knotted tie. She had observant brown eyes and wore her hair in a no-fuss blunt cut with a fringe of bangs.

As they made their way to the other side of the room to meet two men in conversation, the vicomte whispered, "Rumor has it that Louise and Sarah shared a sapphist relationship at one time. They have remained dear friends even after *le feu de la passion* burned out."

Constance whispered back, "How scandalous yet fascinating. My curiosity is piqued. Louise does dress in a very manly way."

Jenee laughed, thinking about how normal and acceptable same-sex relationships would become in her time. "I am not offended by any person's sexual preference, and whatever makes them happy so long as they don't harm others is fine with me."

"How libertarian of you," the vicomte responded with the slightest edge of a sneer.

Jenee ignored his barb. What she found interesting was that Louise reminded her of Pablo Picasso. Something about their features was so similar that they could have passed for siblings. "As to her attire, I suppose that when competing in a man's world, displaying her masculine side gives her more gravitas and credibility. The art world, like all the other worlds, is not welcoming to women, and it is absurd, to say the least."

"You are right, of course," said Constance.

They approached two men having a lively conversation. One of the men was exceedingly handsome, with a mustache that was waxed and curled upward. He looked to be not much older than Jenee. He had the most expressive eyes, and she was not surprised to learn that he was Edmond Rostand, the playwright, and a favorite of Sarah's.

The vicomte made the introductions. "Monsieur Rostand not only wrote tonight's dramatic tragedy for Sarah, but he also authored the acclaimed play *Cyrano de Bergerac*."

Rostand could not take his eyes off Jenee as he took her hand and kissed it. "Have you ever thought of taking to the stage, Mademoiselle Lazaar? Your unique beauty would beguile audiences everywhere. With the public's fascination for all things *exotique*, you would find yourself offered many roles."

"Actually, I'm a doctor, and I have no talent for the stage."

"Beauty and intelligence—I thought only our Divine Sarah possessed both these attributes," he said with a chuckle.

The other man rolled his languorous eyes. "You are flirting, Edmond." The dark-haired man took Jenee's hand and kissed it. "Marcel Proust, mademoiselle. *Enchantée*."

"*Je vous en prie*, Monsieur Proust." In the presence of such towering icons, Jenee found it hard to project nonchalance. The man kissing her hand and professing his pleasure at meeting her would one day be acclaimed as one of the twentieth century's greatest authors. Proust hadn't yet begun his most famous work, *Remembrance of Things Past*, a seven-volume tour de force that would consume him until the end of his life. Jenee had been enthralled by it when she read it in university. The story, told by a narrator whose identity was never revealed, was a series of recollections provoked by sensory memories of the changes and upheavals in the wake of World War I and the industrial revolution. The book would recount the end of an age and a way of life.

Proust's saga of love and loss would begin with a plate of madeleines. *No sooner had the warm liquid mixed with the crumbs touched my palate than a shudder ran through me, and I stopped, intent upon the extraordinary thing happening to me.*

Jenee could not help but think about what was coming. If she remained in the past, she would have to live through the conflagration of war and the cataclysms to come. She still held out hope that what she and Xavier shared would stand the test of time, and she prayed there was a perfectly good explanation for his attending the theater with Lulu.

If she remained in the past, would the wars on the horizon be bearable so long as Xavier was at her side? As much as she knew about the future, her own future was up in the air. There were no guarantees that if she decided to stay, her relationship with Xavier would lead to marriage and the kind of happy ending that Emily had. Hopefully, Emily's reply to her letter would arrive soon, and her salient advice would help Jenee find a way through the murky waters she found herself in.

"My friends call me Marcel," Proust said. "I will be pleased if you would do the same."

Jenee could see the telltale signs of fragile health in the young man. It was evident that he suffered from severe asthma, given the dark shadows under his eyes and the ever-present shortness of breath.

"Beauty wherever found in life should never be ignored," Edmond said to his friend. "And why shouldn't I speak aloud my impression when it is the truth?"

"Truth—now there is a subject we could discourse for hours," Marcel said. "Truth is often framed within the parameters of what is of benefit to us personally, and it can be swayed and embellished until what is left is distortion, or the farthest thing from the truth. Are you rhapsodizing on the truth or your own attraction?"

"Are you jealous, my friend, to see my attentions elsewhere?" Edmond ribbed Marcel, whose sexual predilection was no secret to his friends.

"Of course I am, you gorilla. I'm not happy if I'm not the center of attention, except when Sarah is present, because she is even greedier for the spotlight than I am. But if you continue with your love-struck basset hound behavior, you will make Mademoiselle Lazaar uncomfortable, and we will be unable to eat our supper. And as you can see, I am forever trying to put on some weight." Marcel patted his scrawny chest and fell into hilarious laughter, which he often did. Proust's good nature was so contagious that everyone joined in.

As quickly as it had begun, the laughter died when a couple entered the room and drew everyone's attention.

"Now that is a beautiful couple," said Edmond.

Jenee turned to look and sucked in her breath, startled. Marcel chuckled at her reaction. "I do wholeheartedly agree. He is most handsome."

It hadn't occurred to Jenee that Lulu and Xavier would be invited to Sarah's dressing room for dinner. Now she would have to endure seeing the two of them together. The best she could do was to pretend indifference.

The other men were all transfixed by Lulu, radiant in a satiny cornflower-blue gown with a ruched bodice that clung to her body in all the right places. Her dimples were on full display, and her red hair spilled enticingly from her loose chignon down her back.

Jenee glanced at the vicomte and glimpsed a momentary lapse in his composure. He looked rapaciously at Lulu, as if she were a canary in a cage with the door open and he a cat about to pounce. Any second, Jenee expected him to lick his lips in expectation of a future meal. His gaze met Jenee's, and his expression suddenly shuttered and became unreadable.

Constance did not catch any of this, as she had turned to Jenee. "What a surprise—it's your inspector, Jenee. I wonder who his beautiful companion is?"

"She's an actress," said Jenee. How could she have forgotten Lulu's parting announcement to Xavier when they were in Montmartre that she had been accepted into Sarah Bernhardt's theatrical troupe? Seeing Lulu here made sense—it was Xavier she was shocked to see. Were Lulu and he more than just friends? She could not stop her vivid imagination or excise her doubts from her mind.

"You know her?" asked the vicomte, the interest in his voice not well concealed.

"I've met her," Jenee said as the striking couple approached. Her heart drummed in her chest, and she had to fight to keep her voice steady when she made the introductions. Jenee's heart wrenched as she watched Lulu press her breasts against Xavier's side. Her flirtatious giggles seemed directed at all the men present, but there was a particular familiarity and affection in her gaze when she looked at Xavier.

Lulu lifted the conversation into merriment when asked about her relationship with Sarah. "I feel so honored that Madame Sarah has taken an interest in me. To be nurtured by the greatest actress in the world is beyond any expectation I may have had."

As Lulu charmed everyone, Jenee noticed that Xavier said very little and appeared as uncomfortable as she was. *Are you feeling guilty for your duplicity?*

There wasn't long to ponder the complexity of Xavier and Lulu's relationship. The conversation shifted to the excitement of Paris being the host city for the Universal Exposition and the nearly fifty million people flowing into the city. Everyone shared their amazement at the wonders that were showcased in the pavilions, including the largest refracting telescope and the largest aquarium in the world.

A waiter holding a silver tray offered glasses of champagne, and another waiter held a tray of toast points and pâté.

"Finally," said Marcel, "I was beginning to feel faint from hunger." Everyone laughed and dug in to the goose liver spread.

With no less drama than would be expected from the stage's reigning star, Sarah Bernhardt swept into the room, wearing a pale green gown composed of a satin underdress with a sheer overlay of printed chiffon and a ruffled neckline that displayed her slender neck and décolletage. The gown floated as she moved gracefully about the room, her lithe form capturing everyone's attention. Her face had been scrubbed of heavy stage makeup, and a more subtle application of foundation and powder gave her a youthful glow.

Her melodious voice embraced all in attendance as she greeted her guests. "Ah, *mes amis*, welcome." She waved her hand dramatically. "Lulu—come to me, *ma chérie*; do not hide in the corner." Sarah tweaked Lulu's chin affectionately. "*Ma jolie*, such a pleasing face, and those dimples—*magnifique*, don't you think?" she asked no one in particular. "Lulu has joined my troupe, and I see a bright future for her on the stage."

The vicomte, who appeared friendly with Sarah, introduced Constance and Jenee to her.

"I have heard marvelous things about you, Constance," Sarah said. "What did you think of the play?" She leaned in and said in a stage whisper, "Be careful. I believe the playwright is in the room." She kissed Edmond's cheek, and he rolled his eyes, amused.

"I thoroughly enjoyed it," Constance replied. "Monsieur Rostand, your plays are brilliant, whether comedic or tragic. And Sarah, I believe my fellow countryman Mark Twain stated it best: 'There are five kinds of actresses. Bad actresses, fair actresses, good actresses, great actresses, and then there is Sarah Bernhardt.' I am a devoted fan of yours. I saw you at the Lyceum Theatre in London in *Tosca*, and I shall never forget it."

"What a lovely compliment. I do believe we are going to become good friends, Constance. The vicomte tells me you will be exhibiting a painting at the *Exposition Universelle* at the Grand Palais."

"*Oui*, I'm excited to share my latest acquisition. I shall be hosting a preview of the painting for my friends at Restaurant Brébant, and I'd like you to attend. In fact, I'd like all of you to attend."

"It sounds delightful," Sarah said.

"What is the painting that you are exhibiting?" asked Marcel.

"Marco Allegretto's *Il Divano*. It is the second painting in his series *The Three Stages of Love*."

"My, that will be something to see," said Marcel. "The title would make an irresistible series of novels. Although, if I were to write it, it would probably be called *The Three Stages of Falling Out of Love*. I will accompany you, Sarah."

"We all will," said Edmond. "It sounds like an utterly unforgettable evening."

Constance looked pleased. "Jenee darling, before we leave, will you get calling cards from everyone so we can send them a formal dinner invitation?"

"Of course, I will see to it."

Jenee noticed the vicomte slip away from the group and lure Lulu into a private conversation. They stood at the opposite side of the room, their heads together, with Lulu's occasional giggle ringing out in response to something the vicomte said. Fortunately, Constance was so engaged in conversation with Sarah that she failed to notice Lulu and the vicomte together. But Jenee knew Lulu was an aspiring *demimonde*, and she would quickly surmise the vicomte was a man who could well afford to keep a courtesan. Jenee knew she must warn Lulu away from him. Iris had told her the man was a time traveler, a deviant, and a murderer. The question was how to dissuade Lulu without making any disparaging accusations against the snake.

"This is what life is about, sharing and expanding one's horizons. Risking everything for what you want, for what you believe." Sarah pulled a linen handkerchief from her pocket and showed them the embroidered words, *Quand même*. "This is my motto," she said.

"In spite of everything," Jenee read.

Sarah's dark eyes glittered like ebony. "*Exactement!* Consequences be damned. It has directed my life's course."

It made Jenee think about her feelings for Xavier. Their eyes met. The way he looked at her sent a thrill up her spine, and she felt heat rise to her cheeks. *Don't believe it, he's a serial philanderer.*

Yet, in that instant, she learned something important about Sarah Bernhardt. The actress would never let anything get in the way of her desires. Iris had encouraged another motto that Jenee recalled: "To live without love is to not live." Dare she take a chance on Xavier when he confused her so?

She was immediately distracted when they were joined by a late arrival to the dinner party. "Constant, *mon cher*," rhapsodized Sarah, "there you are. Oh, my! Now we must contend with a dilemma that champagne will make more difficult. We must address Constance and Constant and not stumble over our tongues." She giggled, as the latecomer took her hands. "You were brilliant tonight, as always."

"As were you, divine one," he said. Constant Coquelin was Sarah's co-star in *L'Aiglon* and the most famous and beloved actor in all of France.

Sarah turned to everyone. "You all know my co-actor Constant Coquelin. Constant premiered the role of Cyrano in our dear Rostand's *Cyrano de Bergerac*." She coquettishly laid her head on Constant's shoulder. "Constant will leave with me for a tour of North America in November, and I will play Roxanne to his brilliant Cyrano, and we will conquer the hearts of America."

"There is no doubt of that," said Marcel.

"America, how wonderful," Constance said. "Sarah, you must visit me in Boston when you tour, and I will arrange a reception and dinner party for you."

Sarah clapped her hands. "Is life not grand?"

CHAPTER TWENTY

May 15, 1900
Paris, France

JENEE WANTED TO pinch herself. She still couldn't believe where she was, surrounded by so much talent: famous French actors, writers, playwrights, and artists.

Time travel had afforded Jenee a perspective no one else at the party could possibly envision, and she was careful not to reveal anything of what she knew was in the future. When she slipped up and mentioned to the gathering that the world might find itself at war, she received a gentle rebuff from Constant, which Jenee gladly accepted, realizing she'd gone too far. While the others laughed off her prediction, she found the vicomte glaring at her and Xavier studying her with serious intent. She was equally upset by their attention and excused herself from the table.

In the powder room, she found Lulu combing her hair. "I'm happy to see you have landed on your feet and are doing so well. Your position as a companion to Madame Shipley benefits you, *n'est-ce pas?*"

"Constance has become a dear friend, and I am lucky to have found her."

This was the truth indeed. Jenee would miss Constance terribly if she found a way back to her own time. For that was what she would most likely do. Despite Xavier's declaration of love to her, he'd arrived here with Lulu on his arm and scarcely looked her way the entire night. Jenee even tried to convince herself it was because he was there not solely as Lulu's escort but on duty, making sure there were no threats to Madame Bernhardt. But as the night progressed, Jenee could not help but notice how he only had eyes for Lulu.

"I'm delighted to see you and Xavier doing so well."

Lulu laughed. "I am doing very well, but I'm afraid our Xavier is not. He suffers, poor man."

Jenee's chest clenched in sudden alarm. Was it the concussion? Had he indeed suffered internal bleeding? "In what way?"

Lulu seemed to ignore Jenee's question and applied rouge to her lips.

"Please, Lulu. What is wrong with Xavier? Tell me."

Lulu glared at her in the mirror. "You're what's wrong with him."

"Me?"

"Oh, are you so foolish you fail to see what is staring you in the face? Xavier is head over heels in love with you." She dabbed at her eyes with her handkerchief.

"He is also married and has a daughter. I refuse to be the cause of their suffering."

Lulu gasped and turned to Jenee, wide-eyed. "What are you talking about?"

"I saw the framed picture of his wife and daughter in one of the drawers in his home. I was looking for writing paper and saw the frame hidden in the drawer."

Lulu shook her head. "You poor dear. How misguided you are. Did you ask him about it?"

"No. I was so upset I wrote him a note and left."

"Jenee, for someone so intelligent, you are completely off."

"What are you talking about?" Jenee was even more worried now.

"You are suffering under a misconception." Lulu expelled a

deep sigh. "I care about Xavier. In fact, I am in love with him, as I am sure you have correctly surmised. But what you did not surmise correctly is that Xavier is not married. He is a widower and a father who has suffered greatly from a terrible loss."

Jenee's head was spinning. "What are you talking about, Lulu?"

"Xavier did have a wife and child, but they died with his parents in a terrible apartment house fire two years ago. He blames himself for not being there and has been tormented ever since. When Xavier met you, I saw him come back to life. Believe me, I wish it was me who affected him so deeply. Unfortunately, Xavier does not return my feelings." Lulu wiped her tears. "Now I implore you, you must either let him go or grab hold with your heart and both hands and love him in the manner he deserves. I refuse to stand by and watch him tortured so heartlessly."

Jenee was reeling from Lulu's revelation and could hardly speak. To have lost his entire family in a fire was devastating. But for her to have jumped to that conclusion without seeking the truth… Oh, she'd acted like a silly teenager.

"I-I had no idea. I'm such a fool. I just assumed—It doesn't matter. I will make it right." She grabbed Lulu's hand. "Thank you, Lulu. You are truly a devoted friend. If at any time I misjudged you, please forgive me."

AFTER DINNER, EVERYONE settled onto sofas and chairs in the salon. When Jenee saw Xavier excuse himself from the settee where he'd been conversing with Sarah and Louise, she followed him to the buffet, where he was refreshing his drink. She asked him to pour her a glass of cognac.

He poured, and they stood a moment in silence, waiting for the other to speak.

"I didn't expect to see you here," he said, breaking their silence. The longing in his gaze sent currents of excitement through her.

"In the note you left for me, you gave me a time and place to meet you tomorrow."

"I left it hoping you would show up. You never committed one way or another," he said before sipping his cognac slowly.

"Xavier, I have so much to confess to you. I don't know where to begin."

"Confess? Should I be worried that I've fallen in love with a criminal?"

"Don't be silly. Do you love me even after everything I've done to you?"

"Do you want me to?" he asked, staring into his drink.

"What a question. You haven't hit your head again, have you?"

"My head is fine. I am feeling a bit of déjà vu. I believe we've had this conversation before. You do this to me, make me act like a boy giddy from being in the presence of his first love. The thought of kissing you or holding you makes me want to pick you up and disappear with you to where you belong, in my bed." He took another swig of the cognac. She sensed he was preparing himself for the worst.

Her words and tears spilled together like water breaching a dam. She was about to plead for his forgiveness but clammed up when she saw Sarah walking toward them.

"Forgive me for intruding, but my sixth sense tells me love lies in the balance, and you need a bit of privacy. I think my study will do nicely," said Sarah.

"But—" Jenee started.

"She is right, *mon cher*," Xavier said. "We must settle this once and for all."

They followed Sarah to a door. *"Voila!"* She held out her hand, inviting them in. Then, with a smile, she said, "Do not return to us until you resolve this," and shut the door behind her.

Jenee couldn't hold back her tears or her words. "Xavier, I-I didn't know about… I saw the photo, and I thought you were just another cheat, a womanizer. Because of the intimacy we shared, I was hurt, upset, angry. I wrote that nasty note to you and ran away from you. I never wanted to see you again, but you kept showing up in my dreams, and then, it seemed, everywhere I went. I tried to hate you, but I couldn't. Ironically, Lulu made me see the light, and now I feel awful. I misjudged her, and I misjudged you. I can't blame you if you want nothing to do with me. Rather than talking to you, as Violet suggested several times, I chose to believe the worst and not even consider the possibility of another explanation."

"Slow down, *ma cher*." He grabbed her hands in his. "What is all of this about a photo?"

She dropped her eyes, not wanting to hurt him or remind him of his loss. "I found a photo of you, your wife, and your daughter in your desk."

Understanding lit his eyes. "Why did you search my desk?"

"I was looking for coffee to make, and I couldn't find any."

He shook his head and chuckled. "And you thought I keep coffee in my desk?"

She couldn't help but smile. "No, silly, I thought there might be a café nearby, and I didn't want you to worry, so I decided to write you a note. When I opened the drawer looking for pen and paper, I saw the photograph and wrote a very different note than the one I had originally intended to write. I'm so sorry, Xavier."

He ran his fingers through his hair. "It happened two years ago, and the pain still tears my heart to pieces. I lost my wife, my child, and my parents in a fire. I've spent the last two years blaming myself for their loss. You can't imagine how often I've berated myself for not being there with them…protecting them."

He looked at her, his eyes brimming with tears, and cleared his throat. "It's difficult for me to speak of it even now. I wasn't a good husband, and I wasn't there enough as a father. It was an arranged marriage, and I never loved her. It wasn't her fault that we were wrong for each other, but she tried. My frustration with my lack of feelings for her surely contributed to losing myself in my work. When our daughter Lila was born, all the love I should have shared with Saad, I gave to Lila. And then the fire took them from me. Until I met you, I thought I was dead. My heart must have been hibernating, because it started beating again when you emerged from the dust after the bridge collapsed."

Jenee wiped her face, which was wet from her tears. "I'm so sorry, Xavier. Can you ever forgive me?"

"If you had just asked me, trusted me, none of this would have happened, Jenee. I would have told you that until I met you, I didn't believe I would ever find happiness again. Everything changed in a moment when I thought of losing you to that wretched artist, Picasso."

Jenee bit back a smile, wondering what Xavier would say if she told him *that wretched artist* would become one of the most famous and prolific artists the world had ever known.

As if reading her mind, Xavier asked, "But this isn't everything you wanted to tell me, is it?"

"*Non.* There is more, but I would rather speak about it tomorrow. We will be missed soon, and I don't want Constance to worry about me."

He pulled her close, and his breath tickled her ear. "Then we have agreed to give what we both feel a chance to grow and not let anything or anyone get in the way."

"*Oui.*" Her voice sounded breathless to her ears as she felt a rush of desire, longing, and yearning for him.

Xavier's lips tilted upward knowingly. He caressed her cheek. "*Mon amour,* you are everything to me."

The most beautiful blue eyes in the world looked at her with such adoration that she almost swooned. *I want to feel his lips again on my lips, my shoulders, my thighs.* The memory of his head between her legs, his ravishing her with his tongue and lips, his pale blue eyes watching her, had her clenching her knees together to assuage the aching throb.

She closed her eyes, wishing they were alone at his loft in the shadow of Notre Dame. *Tomorrow cannot come soon enough.*

When they returned to the party, the first thing Jenee noticed was Lulu and the vicomte sitting on a settee, their heads together, laughing. Lulu flirted with the vicomte, and he was more than receptive, given the ravenous gleam in his eyes. The passionate vision of her and Xavier dissolved in an instant. The vicomte was handsome, wealthy, and titled, a lure that Lulu could not possibly ignore. Jenee was sure Lulu saw the vicomte as her patron.

She sought out Constance and could read her reaction. Her friend had been talking with Sarah and Louise, but her gaze was now fixed on the vicomte and Lulu. Jenee saw the hurt in Constance's eyes, and her heart went out to the woman. Jenee had disliked the vicomte from the beginning. She believed what Iris had told her about his being a monster. She did not wish him on anyone, including Lulu.

"Excuse me, Xavier, I must have a word with Lulu," Jenee said before heading to the settee.

"Lulu, *mon amie*, excuse me for interrupting, but can we speak privately for a moment?" Jenee hoped her winsome smile would placate the vicomte, who glared at her for interrupting their conversation.

Lulu looked at her with as much annoyance as the vicomte, but she demurred. "Of course." She rose and smoothed her gown. "We can powder our noses." With a dimpled smile, she turned to the vicomte. "I shall return in a moment, my lord."

"Hurry back, my dear."

They headed to the powder room, and Lulu closed the door. "What is this about, Jenee?"

Jenee suddenly felt at a loss for words. How to warn Lulu without appearing ridiculous? "Lulu, I must warn you that I have heard rumors that the vicomte is not a man to be trusted. I can see you falling into his trap, and I'm afraid for you."

"*Balivernes!* You are making this up! Is it not enough that you have stolen Xavier's heart? Now you must ruin my chances with a man that could secure my future?"

"I am not speaking nonsense and only want the best for you. The vicomte is not who you think he is."

"I cannot believe I am hearing this. I told you less than an hour ago the truth about Xavier, encouraging you to go to him, and you have the gall to warn me off the vicomte? You are just jealous; I will not hear another word against Albert. I did you a favor tonight. Please stay out of my business. I will forget you ever brought any of this up. If you're smart, you will focus on Xavier. He should be your only concern." Lulu applied a final pat of powder to her nose and was gone before Jenee could reply.

Jenee stood there alone in the powder room, feeling sick. She'd failed miserably in warning Lulu off the vicomte and hoped she would be more successful helping Constance through her own heartache over that horrible man.

When she returned to the salon, Xavier told her the vicomte and Lulu had made a quick exit after a brief goodbye to Sarah. Constance had stood by in stoic silence as the vicomte whispered some excuse to her before taking Lulu's hand and leaving.

"This will not turn out well, Xavier. I truly fear for Lulu."

"Come, *ma chérie*, you did your best. Lulu is very resourceful. She will be fine. Do not worry. I will see you and Constance home." Xavier took her hand and kissed it.

Tomorrow I will confide everything to Xavier. He has no idea what a monster the vicomte is. Together we will figure out a way to stop Lulu's misguided flirtation with him before something terrible happens.

CHAPTER TWENTY-ONE

May 16, 1900
Paris, France

I T WAS NOT the sunny day Jenee had hoped for when she set out for the Place de la Concorde. She had awakened to a persistent drizzle that showed no sign of abating. The sky was a ghostly sheet of white particular to Paris skies, and it did nothing to lift her spirits. At times it seemed Mother Nature did all she could to disrupt the beauty of Paris by stealing her vibrant color and reducing her to a gray palette.

Jenee was nervous and worried about her meeting with Xavier. She kept trying to put herself in his shoes. What would she think if he were to tell her that *he* was a time traveler from the future? Would she believe him? Probably not. She'd probably run as fast as she could to escape him.

But just when she lost all courage to confide in him, she remembered Xavier wasn't like her. He was an investigator and a detective. He would most likely consider everything she said, compare it to everything he knew about her, and then realize that what she claimed made perfect sense. In fact, it was probably the only explanation for her sudden appearance amid a bomb explosion and falling concrete.

Moreover, her nerves were frayed. She'd spent a harrowing night with Constance, who'd been devastated by the vicomte's treatment. Constance could not understand how Albert could have abandoned them and disappeared with Lulu. Jenee, of course, understood the vicomte's lascivious behavior both from her impression of him and Iris' warning about his diabolical nature.

Although she said nothing, she was delighted that Constance had been dropped by him like a hot potato, but the poor woman was devastated and brought low by his unkind treatment. Jenee and Iris had to hold her hand until the wee hours of the morning. They'd drunk innumerable glasses of cognac until they were all quite tipsy. Finally, holding each other up, they stumbled to their beds.

The dark shadows under Jenee's eyes now were a testament to her ordeal. Her head throbbed, and she hoped she could explain her time traveling to Xavier without sounding like a bumbling fool.

She felt guilty for leaving Constance for the day, but Iris had assured her that she should keep her rendezvous with Xavier. Iris would take good care of Constance, and Jenee should not be worried. "If you decide to stay the night, I will cover for you."

"But I couldn't possibly do that. What would Constance think?"

"Constance is a grown woman who understands the needs of those in love. So long as you are discreet, she will never say a word of condemnation. Constance is not a prude; she has confided in me that she has a lover in Boston. He is younger than her and completely inappropriate, but he *satisfait ses besoins sexuels*. We are all entitled to our needs."

"I don't believe it. Constance having sex with a man young enough to be her son?" Jenee waved her hand to cool her heated face. "*Mon Dieu!*"

Iris shrugged and chuckled. "And to think it is you who comes from the future, where sex is as freely given as business cards."

Iris had nearly shoved Jenee out the door, and now she found herself amid a parade of gray and black umbrellas at the Place de la Concorde. She turned in a circle, holding her umbrella as she waited for Xavier at the Fontaine des Fleuves.

About twenty minutes later, a strong arm encircled her waist from behind. She turned and looked up into his pale blue eyes. She loved the crinkly lines that appeared when he smiled.

"Ma chérie, I'm sorry I am late. I had to report to the prefecture and excuse myself from duty." He kissed the tip of her nose. "Then I did the shopping for our dinner, which will be *magnifique.*" He held two fingers to his lips and sent a kiss to the sky. His happiness was infectious, and she found her nervousness slipping away.

"And what do you propose we do on such an inclement day?" she asked.

The gleam in his eyes made her pulse quicken. She could read his mind. "I know what I'd love to do, but I'm not sure you would approve," he whispered, sending a delightful shiver up her spine.

She leaned into his lips pressed to her ear, wondering what people thought as they walked by. Then she remembered she was in Paris and romantic couples were part of the landscape. After all, this was not only the City of Light, but it was also known as the City of Love.

"We've wasted too much time already in misunderstandings," she said. "The only thing I want is to be alone with you." The world narrowed to a pinhole when he was near her, and nothing mattered but him.

As a physician, she knew that the attraction between people was a mystery, unexplainable, and impossible to fight or ignore. It was as much a chemical reaction that expressed itself in physical desire. Jenee had studied the science of attraction when the body released oxytocin. Oxytocin was a neurotransmitter that sent messages to the body's nerve cells. Those nerve cells controlled the pleasure we felt, and there was no denying that between Xavier and her, their oxytocin raged to the point of insensibility.

She wanted to touch him, feel his hands on her, and feel him inside of her until no space existed between them. It wasn't anything she'd yearned for with any man she'd ever known. It exposed her to emotions she'd never explored, let alone allowed.

He kept his arm about her waist, and they began to walk. "When I'm near you," he said, "I cannot bear not touching you. You become the very air I breathe, and it's a need I find difficult to explain or even to understand."

She leaned her head against his shoulder. "I've been fighting what I feel for you since we met," she admitted.

"You should be embracing this gift. We both should. Instead, we've done everything possible to deny its existence, which must stop now."

"Yes." She looked up at his handsome face and saw the determined set of his jaw. A warmth filled her, and she thought how foolish she'd been these past few weeks.

The next thing she knew, they were in a fiacre moving toward the Île de la Cité, and he was kissing her. Her heart sang with joy from the press of his lips, and she contoured her body to the hardened muscles of his solid frame. She was almost sorry when they arrived at Rue des Chantre, and he let go of her to pay the driver.

The rain was coming down heavily, and great gusts of wind swirled around them. They ran down the narrow street to Xavier's building, their laughter ringing like children's. By the time they got inside, they were both drenched and shivering. The climb up the six flights of stairs seemed to take forever.

When they finally got inside Xavier's apartment, he shut the door and pushed her against it, hungrily kissing her neck, face, and lips. His leg pressed between her thighs, rubbing against the delicious throbbing building inside her. She could feel the hardness of his erection pressing against her, and she ached to be filled by him.

Warm breath filled her ear. *"J'ai envie de toi."*

"I want you too," she breathed. Waves of desire overwhelmed her, and it was all she could do not to lift her skirt and satisfy the yearning that threatened to drive her mad.

His baritone voice grew gravelly, and he nibbled her earlobe. *"Je veux te baiser."*

I want to fuck you. Jenee's breaths quickened at his blunt, erotic tone. She was wet, but this wetness was not from the rain. Her pulse raced, and her heart thundered, trying to keep up. The ache intensified to where she only wanted to wrap her legs around him. But she also wanted the pleasure to go on and build.

"But what about the dinner you promised?" she teased, trying to prolong the divine sensations that bubbled inside her.

He caressed her through her dress, cupping her, rubbing his thumb lightly in circles through the fabric. She could scarcely breathe as intense excitement puckered her nipples, and she arched her back. She could feel her clitoris throb, and she pressed into his thumb, but he pulled it back, circling lightly, teasingly, until she was sure she would go mad if he did not give her more.

He teased back, "I think we can manage both, don't you think?" He spoke low, and the vibrations from his baritone voice made her quiver as his warm breath and tongue played with her ear. "Besides, we need to get out of these wet clothes. I don't want you to catch a chill. And then the appetizer. I am hungering for it."

"And what is the appetizer?"

"Can you not guess? It's you."

His sexy words, combined with the touch of his long, beautiful fingers, stoked her fire, igniting an intense passion. A vision of his lips on her sex made her melt with anticipation.

"Then I am yours." She needed to touch his skin. Her fingers trembled as she fumbled with the buttons on his suit coat. He shrugged it off, and before she knew what had happened, he spun her around so that she faced the door as he undid the buttons of her dress and stays. He pressed against her backside, his hands roaming over her breasts. She moaned as her nipples rose to peaks between his nimble fingers as if live wires connected her to his hands. The sweet ache was unlike any other feeling. He turned her around, cupping her breasts, and opened his mouth, taking in her swollen peak, sucking, pulling until a moan escaped her parted lips. As if obeying his command, her dress slid to the ground, and he picked her up and carried her to the bedroom.

He set her on the coverlet, bent to remove her shoes, and then rolled down her black silk stockings. He kissed her ankles and slowly kissed his way upward, nibbling and kissing the tender flesh inside her thigh the way she'd dreamed he would. He whispered, and his hot breath tickled Jenee, making her tremble.

"So soft and silken." He continued leisurely, sucking, licking, nibbling on her flesh until he reached her *chatte*, stroked her seam with his lips, and then gently bit her tender flesh. She gasped as his wicked tongue found her clitoris, bringing unimaginable pleasure to her. He was playful and teasing, coaxing and patient. His tongue circled her sensitive nugget, driving her to greater heights as his hums of delight reverberated inside her as if she were his instrument, and he plucked her strings, composing an erotic melody.

She wanted to give to him the same way he gave to her, but the intensity was building so rapidly that all she could think about was satisfying the ache that knew no end. Her brain had shut down, but her nerve endings were alive and sizzling, demanding on a primal level that the emptiness inside her be filled with his glorious cock.

"*Mon amour. J'adore le goût de toi.* I could eat you forever," he said.

How was it possible that his words alone could elicit such a physical reaction? She trembled and tingled, hot and wet. If his moans of pleasure were any indication, she was sure that he could eat her forever, and the thought of it caused her insides to clench.

She combed her fingers through his dark curls, pulling him closer, arching her back. He was her dark angel, and she was being carried away on his wings. She fell apart, shuddering, wanton cries of rapture escaping her as her climax carried her up, up, so high she thought she'd soar forever.

All the while, Xavier nurtured her, kissing her in that sweetest of spots as she made her way back down to Earth. "Mademoiselle *es content?*"

"I would say content is putting it mildly," she said. "But I want to make monsieur just as content."

He stood, showing his full erection, and heat surged through her body from the tips of her toes to her face. She reached out and delicately explored his length with her fingers, making him shiver. She gripped him tighter, sliding her fingers from base to tip, and felt him grow harder in her hand. She leaned in and took his fullness into her mouth. A deep moan escaped him, and a wave of sensual power washed over her.

He gripped her wrist, and she looked up to see his pupils dilated with lust. "If I spill, it will not be outside you, *ma tendre.*"

She sat up, wrapped her arms around his waist, and ran her lips over the defined oblique muscles of his abdomen. "I just want to pleasure you the way you have pleasured me."

"Do you not know how much you please me?" He sat beside her and took her face in his hands, tracing his thumbs gently over her cheekbones and jaw. "For the first time in a long time, I can see the future, and it is bright because of you."

He lowered his lips to hers, taking her in a sensual yet tender kiss. They fell back into the bed together, and a fire ignited in them. They were like teenagers experiencing the joys of sexual discovery and first love.

He rolled on top of her, pulling her arms above her head and twining her fingers with his. "I want to make this moment last forever. The way you look." He kissed her cheek. "The way you feel against me." He kissed the pulse point behind her ear. "I've never felt anything like this before, and I want to savor this feeling of discovery. This is so much different than the first time. Because now we know the truth between us. There is nothing to stand in our way."

His words shot her with a dose of reality. *There might be some-*

thing standing in our way. The truth of who I am and where I come from. She would have to tell him everything tonight.

But right now, she wanted to lose herself in loving him. She wanted to give him everything: her body, heart, and soul. It scared her how happy she felt. She loved the feel of his body on top of her. The way her breasts pressed against the wiry hair of his naked chest. His manhood pressed firm, molding itself against her sex, and her arousal came in an urgent surge of need. The way he looked at her melted whatever doubts she might have had.

"*Je te veau en moi,*" she said.

"Say that again." He rubbed against her seam, and she parted her legs, needing him.

"I want you inside of me," she repeated breathily.

His shaft quivered against her vaginal lips, and he groaned. "I need you, *mon amour.*"

Her breath caught as he pushed slowly into her wetness. He settled deeply, and his mouth sought hers in a passionate kiss. He began to move inside her, and she matched him in perfect rhythm. His thrusts grew more robust, more profound, faster. Her nipples throbbed from rubbing against his chest hair. He controlled her every response, and she gave herself willingly, arching into him, loving how he filled her. His large hands slid beneath her derriere, fitting her tighter against him as he thrust harder and deeper. The angle had him sliding against her swollen sex dead on, sending scintillating quivers to the heat of her core.

She dug her fingers into his back, anchoring him to her. "Now, my darling, now," she said breathlessly.

Thrust after thrust built into a crescendo of need as he took her higher and higher until she cried out in ecstasy, reaching a pinnacle of pleasure that seized her, sending her out of her body and into the heavens.

A sensual roar escaped him, and he joined her moments later, pouring his seed inside her.

Afterward, he gazed into her eyes, his forehead pressed to

hers, his movement inside her languid but steady. It was the most arousing lovemaking she'd ever experienced.

"*Je t'aime.*"

She wanted to say *I love you too*, but stopped herself. She needed to tell him the truth about who she was and where she came from first.

XAVIER WAS TREADING on ground he'd never walked before. He didn't know it was possible to feel such rapture, such oneness with someone. He loved her, and that was all that mattered. He would do anything to please her and anything to keep her. Was it love? It was heat, desire, passion, and, yes, love. Love on the lowest physical level and love on the highest spiritual plane. If it went on forever, it would never be enough. He knew and accepted that truth.

Jenee lay wrapped in his arms, and a sigh escaped her lips. The afterglow of their lovemaking made him smile. He wished he was a poet and could express what he felt with her heart beating against his chest and the satisfaction that filled him listening to her breaths return to normalcy.

Xavier might have lain in a dreamy state forever if not for the sudden growl of her stomach. Her eyes popped open, and she bit her lip.

"Oh dear, what could be less sexy than a grumbling belly?" she asked.

"I can think of several things, and none are related to you in any way." He laughed and kissed her on the tip of her nose.

"I'm glad you're amused, but it's your fault that my stomach is acting out. You did promise to cook for me."

"I did, and I'm a man of my word, but I couldn't help but take a moment to revel in what was for me a cathartic experience."

Jenee's lips quirked a smile. "So, I take it I pleased you."

Instead of a reply, he pulled her in and delivered sweet kisses to her eyes, nose, forehead, and lips. He was still inside of her, and kissing her stimulated him to where he could feel his member thickening. If he continued, they would be heading for another tour de force lovemaking session, and Jenee would surely starve to death.

He was tempted to risk her life, but her stomach did not collaborate and went into full revolt. A growl resembling an unhappy bear searching for food rumbled forth. They both looked down at the space between them and burst into laughter.

"It seems my desire will have to be put on hold." He rolled over onto his back with a heavy sigh.

Jenee leaned over and whispered in his ear, "Not forever, my love. Your desire is simply being sublimated to my essential need."

He sat up and, taking her hand, pulled her from the bed. She bent to retrieve her pantaloons to dress. "Wait," he said. Then he went to the small closet and brought her one of his shirts. "No need to dress. The chef would prefer you to be comfortable and accessible to his desire. Besides, we need to hang up our clothes and let them dry." He handed her the shirt, and she took it.

"*Merci beaucoup.*"

CHAPTER TWENTY-TWO

May 16, 1900
Paris, France

JENEE REMEMBERED SEEING a TV talk show once and watching a discussion about how many times you should date someone before you cooked dinner for them. To a panelist, they all got it wrong, as far as she was concerned. Xavier's cooking for her was the most romantic, comforting, bonding, and sexy experience she'd ever shared with a man. If anything could predict the future of a relationship, it was a candlelit meal alone without other diners or outside interruptions. Being alone together and being the only focus of each other was enthralling.

The bourride was the best she'd ever had, and that was saying something. They ate wearing only Xavier's shirts, playing footsie. At times Jenee forgot that it was the year 1900. Romance was romance in any era, and the courtship dance between two people in love would never change. Sitting across from her handsome lover and sharing a delicious meal was as sensual and beautiful an experience as their lovemaking.

They sipped and toasted each other with goblets of Haute Medoc from the Bordeaux region and discussed their hopes for the future. Xavier's retelling of a funny incident when he'd met the famous French chef Prosper Montagné had her tearing up with laughter. Xavier had been searching for the cause of a guest's demise at the Grand Hôtel of Paris and dared to enter the famous chef's kitchen. After quite the standoff, Prosper, wielding a meat cleaver, and Xavier, brandishing a wheel of cheese in defense, had reached a détente. The master of haute cuisine, who'd written the classic encyclopedia considered the bible of French cooking, *Larousse Gastronomique*, and the young inspector became friends. The kitchen was cleared of wrongdoing, and it was agreed that the guest died of dyspepsia brought on by overindulging in three bottles of wine, an entire *gateau chocolat*, and a dozen profiteroles filled with whipped cream and custard. Although there was nothing light about the gentleman, it also came to light that he suffered from gout. In gratitude, Prosper gave Xavier a treasured memento, a copy of the recipe for the bourride they dined on now.

A French meal couldn't end on anything other than a sweet note, and the *tarte Tatin* was as sweet and satisfying as the delectable kisses that preceded and followed each bite. After the meal was finished and the dishes washed, dried, and put away, they stood at the window, watching the rain patter off the rooftops of nearby buildings. A flash of lightning hit Notre Dame's spire, and the rooftop sculptures of the apostles for a moment came to life. The boom of thunder that followed made her gasp, and Xavier tightened his arms around her, dipping his lips to her neck and delivering a warm kiss.

"It's okay, my love. The new spire has stood for forty-six years, and I'm sure it will stand for another hundred."

She didn't tell him that Notre Dame's spire would be destroyed in the fire. It was time to confide in Xavier and tell him the truth, but she didn't know where to begin.

"You can trust me, Jenee. I know that you are carrying a burden about yourself, that you are afraid to share with me."

She looked up at him. "But how?"

He turned her around and took her hands, kissing each palm. "Let's sit, and I will pour us a cognac; it will help."

She nodded and took a deep breath, letting it out slowly.

"This will take some time."

"For you, I have all the time in the world."

They sat on the sofa in his living room. Jenee curled against him as she contemplated the amber liquid in her glass. She took a sip of the cognac, and it burned down her throat, spreading heat throughout her body.

He swallowed a hearty sip, apparently needing his own dose of courage, and set his glass and hers on the table. Xavier took Jenee's hand and clasped it between both of his. "Let me be the first to confess. I saw the book you were reading, *L'amant du Voyageur Temporel*, and the inexplicable publishing date of one hundred years in the future."

She looked down at their hands and whispered, "You may find your feelings for me will change when I explain everything. But the worst part is that I can't explain it because I know so little about how or why it happened."

"Tell me, and perhaps I can help you understand."

She looked at him through tear-filled eyes. "I'm not from here, Xavier."

"You're not from Paris."

"No, I am from Paris, just not your version of Paris. I was born at the end of the twentieth century."

She hesitated at his sharp intake of breath, but he nodded for her to continue.

"Much of what I told you is true. My parents were immigrants from Algeria, and they did die, but it was in a terrorist bombing here in Paris. It's hard to explain, but in the future, bombing will become a favorite weapon of malcontents. My parents were academics and loved their adopted country. Their death was devastating to me, but I had been accepted to medical school, and I got through it. I'll tell you more about my wonderful mom and dad later, but for now, I need to tell you how I came to be here."

Xavier cupped her cheeks with his hands and gave her a gentle kiss. "I'm so sorry, *mon amour*. I will listen without interrupting you."

"After medical school and my internship and residency, I became a doctor. Eventually, I opened my own practice and built a very successful career. I never married because I never found the right man until you. But I found my two best girlfriends in a book club, and we bonded over *The Time Traveler's Lover*, the book you saw me reading, *L'amant du Voyageur Temporel*. I traveled to New York to visit Emily and Gabriella and to attend an exhibition of the artist Marco Allegretto's paintings at the Metropolitan Museum of Art.

"Somehow, I was swept through a time-travel portal and transported to the past. The only way I can explain it is to liken it to a tear in the fabric of time that created a passage that allows someone to travel through. Fortunately, or unfortunately for me, I was someone who did. One minute I was standing in a museum in modern-day New York City, and the next minute I was standing on the collapsed walkway amid falling concrete in 1900 Paris.

"I was with Emily and my other best friend Gabriella at the museum when I was swept through the painting. Emily was also taken through the portal in the painting *La Sedia* to the year 1892, and she helped Iris flee through *La Sedia*'s portal when she returned the painting to Marco Allegretto. Emily fell in love with the Marquess of Danbury and chose to remain in the past. Iris told me she married him, and they live in Eastbourne, England. I've written to Emily, and I hope to receive a reply soon."

"And you're sure about all of this? Do you believe this Iris? *Merde*, my head is swimming."

"With all of my heart." She shuddered, remembering the disembodied feeling of being sucked into the vortex. "I sat before Marco Allegretto's painting at the museum, and as if in a dream, he reached out from the painting and took my hand. Without thinking, I took his hand, and the hands of time swept me up, and the next thing I knew, I was here," she breathlessly blurted. "Minutes before, I was with my two best friends in New York.

Now I know that Emily is in England. I don't know about Gaby, but I assume she has been taken through a portal. Marco Allegretto had the power to take us, and he has the power to return us. The paintings are powerful."

Xavier let go of her hand and scrubbed his fingers through his hair as if to wake himself up or, more likely, to better deal with what she was telling him. "But how is this possible?"

"I don't know. Violet says it has to do with the three paintings by Allegretto and a magical curse."

"Violet? What does Violet have to do with all of this?"

"Violet is also a time traveler. She's the time traveler in the book, she wrote the book, and the paintings by Allegretto are of her. She is Iris. Her real name is Iris Bellerose."

His hands fell, and he looked at her. "And Violet told you everything about her time travel?"

"Yes. Well, I'm not sure about everything. Violet, but I think it's best to call her Iris, traveled to many places before she landed in a Florentine market in 1503 and met Marco. I expect she could write several more books based on all her travels. But now you can see why I was so reluctant to tell you about any of this. And my fears about being with you, spending my life with you. I still worry that it's not even possible, but Iris assures me it is. My friend Emily chose to stay and marry, and Iris assures me it is possible I could do the same." A sob escaped her, and her shoulders shook. It sounded unbelievable to her, let alone him, no matter how many H. G. Wells books he'd read.

"*Mon amour*, please don't cry."

"But don't you see, Xavier? My life isn't here. It's in the future."

"Do you—" He hesitated. "Do you want to go back?"

"When I found the picture of your wife and daughter, everything changed, and I did not think we could have a future together. Even after you had your concussion and we became closer, I still worried about it. But now I know that you weren't a two-timing jerk."

"I'm relieved to hear it." He grinned. "How I love your modern turns of phrase."

She giggled and took his face between her hands, kissing his mouth tenderly. "I've never felt about anyone in my life how I feel about you. You're all I think about, and I know if I lose you, I will lose my only chance at true love."

"Are you saying you love me?" The hopefulness in Xavier's voice brought fresh tears to her eyes.

"Of course that's what I'm saying. Besides, who else has promised me bourride for breakfast, lunch, and dinner?"

He threw back his head and laughed. "Then that means you would stay here with me if you were given a choice and if you knew for certain that you wouldn't be flung back into the future or another era, as Iris was."

"It's the unknown that scared me, but Iris assured me that I would be able to stay and make a life here as my friend Emily did in England with the man she fell in love with."

"Then let go of your fears, *mon amour*." He pulled her into his strong arms and showered her face with butterfly kisses. "It's settled; you must stay with the only man who can make you happy."

Jenee kissed him back with a dozen sweet kisses. For a moment, they were two ordinary people deeply in love with a bright and happy future waiting for them. He rested his chin on her head, and she relaxed in his strong embrace. She didn't want to break the spell, but there was much more to tell him.

"Xavier?"

"Mm-hmm."

"We need to help Iris so she and Marco can be together."

"What do we need to do to help her?"

"Constance's painting that she just bought is one of Marco's. It's also a portal, and Iris needs to pass through the portal and take the painting with her."

He looked at her and his brows knitted together, etching a deep groove in the space between them. "That means she will have to steal the painting."

Jenee ran her fingers across his brow, smoothing the lines of his perplexment.

"The painting is hers and Marco's. That's not stealing. But there is a problem." She knew that this was a tough pill to swallow for a man who lived his life by the law. It amazed her that with all the phonies and con artists she'd met over her dating years, she'd had to travel to another era to find a man of true integrity, honesty, and loyalty.

"I should say so. Perhaps more than one problem."

"It's the vicomte."

"The vicomte? What does that bastard have to do with this?"

"The vicomte is also a time traveler. He needs the painting to continue his ageless life through time. He's also a violent man. Evil. He's a murderer, in fact, a serial killer. Iris stands in the way of his plans, and I'm afraid he will kill her. I will not let that happen."

"A serial killer! How do you know this?" Xavier stood and began to pace.

"Iris told me the vicomte murdered several women in London. Vile, gruesome murders. There is so much more to explain that I can scarcely understand it all myself. I want you to come with me to speak to Violet—er, Iris, and she can tell you her side of things. I believe what she told me about the vicomte. I was so worried about Constance being wooed by him, but when I saw Lulu leave with him at Sarah Bernhardt's soiree, my worry is now for Lulu. When I warned her about him, she became very angry with me. We must ensure she is all right and stays away from him."

"I agree. We must act quickly, then."

"Yes, there is much to do and plan. We need your help."

"I will do everything in my power to make certain Iris succeeds in her quest. But I also want to make sure that you truly want to stay here and make a life with me. Perhaps you need to think on this for a few more days."

"But Xavier—"

"Hush," he said, placing a finger on her lips. "I want you, Jenee, more than anything in this world, but it is a lot to ask of you. A tremendous sacrifice for you. You would have to settle for the inconveniences of this world, which for you must be inadequate, given your knowledge of what the future holds."

"None of that matters as long as we are together. There are things I know coming in the future that will make life difficult, but being with you will make it all bearable."

"What kinds of things?"

"War—or rather, wars."

"There are always wars."

"Not like these. There will be two world wars, and France will be fighting with the Allied nations against Germany and her allies. There will be much suffering, millions will die, and unspeakable acts of evil will occur."

"*Mon Dieu*. We must stop this from happening."

"We cannot stop it. But we can help as much as possible and ensure our loved ones are safe."

He wrapped his arms around her. "Together, we can weather any storm."

"We will need to be very strong to weather these."

A blinding light lit the room, followed by a crash of thunder that shook the roof's timbers. Jenee thought again of Notre Dame Cathedral's fate and the wars ahead. One never knew what the future held, at least not typically. Her heart sank as it dawned on her that if she and Xavier had a son, he would be one of the young men called to fight in World War I. All the happiness she found in Xavier's promise of love and devotion was blunted by fears of what the future brought. How could she be happy knowing of this impending doom? Could she just live her life with Xavier pretending the future did not exist? She wished she had the counsel of Emily and Gabriella, or were they too floundering amid a sea of what-ifs and battling the same fears?

A reply to her letter from Emily couldn't come too soon.

CHAPTER TWENTY-THREE

May 17, 1900
Paris, France

XAVIER ROUSED SLOWLY, not wanting to be pulled from his erotic dream. His arms and body were wrapped around the source of that dream, and he smiled, remembering the treasured hours spent loving her. In the years of his marriage, he had never slept nude with his wife, nor did they embrace in slumber.

He should not dwell on the past, nor on his late wife. She had been a good woman and a loving mother, but she was not in love with him, nor he with her, and she lacked the kind of passion he'd found with Jenee.

Jenee's lips were pressed to his chest, and his first sensible thought was a desire to make love to her again. He pressed a kiss to her forehead, inhaling the delicious scent of her. His stiffening cock urged him to greet the day by nestling inside her.

An unfortunate, persistent pounding invaded his thoughts from somewhere outside of his blissful dream. It quashed his desire and shrank his shaft, which exacerbated his annoyance.

His eyes popped open. How long had that infernal knocking been going on? He untangled his legs and arms from Jenee, careful not to wake her. Slipping from the bed, he donned his robe and closed the bedroom door. After taking a quick scan of the main room to make sure Jenee and his clothes weren't scattered about tellingly, he opened the door.

His deputy, Jacque LeFevre, was still huffing and puffing from his climb.

"What the devil is this about, LeFevre?" Xavier asked. "Can you not live without me for a day?"

LeFevre stood stiffly, the jest passing right over him. "Sir, there has been a break-in and a robbery."

"*Mon ami*, there are always break-ins and robberies. What is so special about this one that I must address it today when I am still recovering from a concussion?"

"The robbery took place in Faubourg Saint-Germain?"

The hair at the back of his neck stood on end. Constance's home was in the seventh arrondissement.

"The facts, LeFevre. Give me the who, what, where, and when, *s'il vous refe.*"

"*Oui*, monsieur." The younger man glanced at his notes. "A painting was stolen from 12, Rue Odinout in Faubourg Saint-Germain. It is reported that the robbery occurred sometime between the hours of one and five this morning, when the household slept. The painting is owned by an American heiress, Constance Shipley, who leases the house. Her secretary Violet Rousseau requested you to investigate and that you should arrive as soon as possible." LeFevre looked up. "I've taken the liberty to order a fiacre for you. The driver awaits you at the end of the street."

"Was anyone injured?"

"I do not believe so, sir."

"That is good news. Who has preceded me to the crime scene?"

"Inspector Henri Chauvet, who worked in *le septième.*"

"Of course, I know him well." Xavier ran his fingers through his hair. His problem was not compromising Jenee, who undoubtedly would want to rush to Constance in her time of need. "Very well, here's what I want you to do. Gather the team and meet me at the *maison.* I will want to thoroughly investigate.

Dust for fingerprints and shoe prints, etcetera. When you arrive, inform Madame Shipley and Mademoiselle Rosseau that I am on my way. I need a bit of time to gather myself. Have the fiacre wait."

"Consider it done, sir."

Xavier shut the door and listened until he heard LeFevre's footsteps fade on the stairs. He went to the kitchen and made coffee while contemplating the problem before him. There was no sense in causing tongues to wag among his men or Madame Shipley's servants. It would be better for Jenee to not be seen arriving with him.

He carried the coffee into the bedroom, set it on the table next to the bed, and sat. Forgetting the outside world that called to them, he took a moment and found contentment watching Jenee in slumber. Her midnight hair was splayed across the pillow, her long, dark lashes rested on her high cheekbones, and her sweet lips were slightly parted, tempting him to steal a kiss. Her arms were raised above her head, and her fingers curled, an innocent gesture reminding him of a child in slumber.

His heart ached with love. He wanted to keep her safe and devote the rest of his life to making her happy. Realizing that he'd been sleepwalking through his life made her even more precious.

She shifted, and the light sheet covering her slid down, revealing her lovely breasts, and her nipples beckoned his mouth. He wanted to slip beneath the covers and wake her with a thousand kisses. But he knew how tired she was. He'd been relentless in his passion for her and lost count of how many times he'd brought her to bliss. He only hoped it was enough to banish the memory of every other man who had ever loved her.

He bent his head, taking one of her nipples into his mouth. A soft moan escaped her, and he did the same to the other nipple, nipping it gently and then licking it. He sat up and saw a kittenish smile appear on her face, and then she reached for him, pulling him down for a kiss.

Profound joy filled his heart with the thought of waking

every day like this. It would be a miracle if he could ever convince himself to leave their bed, but perhaps it would be easy because he would know that he would return to her at the end of every day.

"Good morning, *ma tendre*." He caressed her cheek with his knuckles.

She stretched like a cat and purred. "Come back to bed, Xavier. I feel a great need to remain in your bed the rest of the day." Her eyes sparkled devilishly, and his muscles tightened with expectation and frustration that he would be denied such pleasure.

"Unfortunately, we cannot, my darling."

Her eyes widened. She clearly had not expected his rejection. "And why not?" She lifted to her elbow, and he tenderly captured a lock of hair and tucked it behind her ear.

"Because there is a problem, and Madame Shipley needs us."

Jenee bolted up to a sitting position. "What is it? Has something happened to her or Violet? Please tell me they are all right."

He caressed her face. "Calm yourself, *mon amour*. They are unharmed, but there's been a robbery, and Constance, or perhaps it was Violet, has specifically requested my presence, which is probably their way of saying they request your return." He looked at her clothing scattered about the floor. "You should get dressed, as we need to be on our way. A fiacre is waiting downstairs." He handed her the cup of coffee he'd prepared for her.

"Do you know what was taken?" Jenee took a sip of the hot drink and sighed with pleasure.

"My deputy said a painting, but that's all I know."

Jenee's brow furrowed as she contemplated what he'd said. She took another sip and set the cup down. "I'll be ready in a few minutes."

Xavier rose and, taking her hands, pulled her up. She was naked, and he filled his vision with her delicious body and sinuous curves. He couldn't help but pull her against him. His cock had jumped to life at the sight of her.

"*Merde.*" He traced his tongue around the auricle of her ear. "You have no idea how much I don't want to leave this bed."

He was still figuring out the many ways to please her. Her shiver confirmed that her ears were particularly sensitive. Her eyes were closed, and she leaned into him. "We have to go, my darling. Constance and Violet need me."

"You are right. Friendship and duty call." He turned her around and patted her derriere. "Get dressed, *mon amour.*"

CHAPTER TWENTY-FOUR

May 17, 1900
Paris, France

THE FIACRE STOPPED just beyond the door of the house. Jenee kissed Xavier and jumped out of the carriage. "I'll meet you in the library." She picked up her skirt and ran to the French doors of the parlor, which were always kept unlocked for whoever wished to have tea or refreshments in the garden. She tiptoed through the hallway, up the servants' back staircase to the upper floor, and into her room. She sat before her vanity mirror, brushing her hair, and pinning it up as best she could until a gentle rap at the door distracted her. Her hair tumbled around her shoulders, and pins scattered across the floor. She was useless when it came to these early twentieth-century hairstyles. "Who is it?"

"It's me."

Jenee opened the door and let Iris in. "Are you all right?" She gave Iris a quick hug.

"Yes, I'm fine, as is Constance." Iris quickly assessed Jenee's hair dilemma. "Here, let me." She stooped to pick up the pins from the floor.

Jenee knelt to help. "I'm sorry I abandoned you and left you to deal with everything alone." She searched Iris' face for forgiveness.

"Don't be silly. You needed this time with Xavier, and no one could have known or predicted the robbery. Now sit, and we will see what we can do with your hair."

Jenee sat in the chair while Iris braided her hair and twisted it into a coronet.

"Constance was a complete wreck when the servants reported that the painting was gone," Iris said. "I thought it best to relieve her distress, so I made her a *refectu* and put her to bed. She has much fortitude when it comes to most problems, but a stranger's invasion of her home felt like a violation of her person and profoundly affected her."

"I can well understand why. It is a sickening proposition to think of yourself sleeping in your bed and being vulnerable in your home. Is she angry with me?"

"Of course not. I told her about you and Xavier, and she is happy for you. She adores you and wishes only for your happiness. I sent the request to Xavier so that I could get word to you as well. We need to take him into our confidence—I know we can trust him. Constance will also feel more comfortable with Xavier on the case. On the night of Madame Bernhardt's dinner party, she realized that the inspector possesses a certain, how should I say it, *je ne sais quoi?*"

Jenee grinned at the understatement. "He's a definite keeper, and he does exude confidence and strength, and you are right, we can trust him. I confessed everything to him, and he will help us. But I am worried about what lies ahead." Her smile faded as she thought about the danger they faced. "Am I correct in assuming you believe the vicomte is the thief?"

"No ifs about it—I know he is behind this. Thank goodness we convinced Constance to keep the original at the bank."

"Yes, but don't you think the vicomte will be furious at being fooled?" Jenee watched in the mirror as Iris curled a few strands around her face. Iris' handiwork never failed to amaze her.

"I'm sure he will be absolutely livid once he figures it out, and I worry for the poor soul he takes out his frustration and anger on." Iris stood back and examined Jenee's hair. "*Voila!* Let's get you changed, and then we will see how *Chef Inspecteur* Doumaz is fairing. Inspector Chauvet is not in any way as charming as your inspector, I'm afraid."

In the library, they found Xavier and another man standing before the empty picture frame that had held *Il Divano*.

"Inspectors, have you discovered anything of interest?" asked Iris.

The two men turned, and Jenee could see Xavier's eyes light when his eyes met hers. He quickly recovered his professional demeanor, and his eyes shuttered, conveying nothing personal or revealing. She appreciated his self-control, but her heart skipped a beat at his reaction.

"Mademoiselle Lazaar, how nice to see you again. May I introduce Inspector Chauvet," said Xavier. "I informed the inspector how we met at the unfortunate sidewalk collapse at the *Exposition Universelle*."

"Mademoiselle, the pleasure is mine. Such a tragedy that day. You are a lucky lady indeed." Inspector Chauvet reminded Jenee of Sir Arthur Conan Doyle, whom she'd Googled once out of curiosity. He had the same broad face, intense brown eyes, and mustache that curled upward and jiggled when he spoke. He held a pipe between his teeth, and puffed and spoke simultaneously to complete the picture. The spicy aromas of jasmine, roses, clove, cinnamon, and patchouli wafted around the library. Nothing could be done about it, but at least the French doors were open. She watched the smoke swirl to the open door and make its escape.

"*Le refect est pour moi*, Monsieur Inspector. Inspector Doumaz helped me through a most challenging time." Her gaze shifted from one man to the other. "I believe I shall become quite confused addressing two *inspecteurs*. I will refer to you as Inspector D and you, Inspector Chauvet, as Inspector C if you don't mind?"

Xavier's grin indicated he was amused by her jest. She was

sure he would never believe she could mistake Monsieur Chauvet for him. "I have no problem with that, Mademoiselle Lazaar. As to our discoveries, please allow us to take you and Mademoiselle Rousseau through the crime scene as we see it."

He strode to the French doors and pointed to one of the panes next to the missing doorknob. Outside, two policemen were brushing and dusting for fingerprints. One held a magnifying glass and studied the muddy shoe prints the thief had left on the stone terrace. Xavier had told Jenee about his admiration for Alexandre Lacassagne and Edmond Locard, with whom he often consulted on cases. They were France's leading figures in the new sciences of forensics and criminology and were based in Lyon.

Xavier adhered to the premise espoused by Locard that no matter how careful or precise a criminal was, there would always be something that he or she left behind that tied them to the crime. Whether the item was a button from a man's coat, a cigarette butt, or even a used condom, commonly known as a French letter, the smallest item could turn out to be vital evidence linking the criminal to the crime. Jenee was impressed by Xavier's collection of books and scientific articles on the ongoing developments in criminology and medicine, including discovering how to identify blood type. He believed that criminologists would one day use this science in identifying the perpetrators of crimes where blood evidence was found. Given Jenee's science and medical background, she would do everything possible to help Xavier. She looked forward to introducing him to the wonders of science, medicine, and technology.

"You will observe, *mesdames*, that the thief precisely cut a pane of glass from the door and, perhaps using a suction cup, removed the glass without breaking it, hence making no sound," Xavier explained. "Once the glass was removed, it was a simple matter of slipping his hand in and unlocking the door. Then he— I'm presuming it was a man by the size and markings of the shoe imprints—went to the painting and carefully cut it from its frame. In a matter of minutes, he made his escape without waking a soul. We must assume he knew exactly where the painting was situated in the house, as there is no evidence that he conducted a search of the outer premises. The footprints follow a direct path directly from the gate at the front of the property to this door. The thief is a professional, this is not his first theft, and I suspect he wore gloves, but we will collect all the prints here for elimination and future comparison."

Jenee and Iris exchanged glances.

"The question is," Inspector Chauvet interjected, "is there anyone other than the staff of *la maison* who saw the painting and could be considered a suspect?"

Iris' eyes blazed with assurance. "The Vicomte de Maurnier was here yesterday and saw the painting, and he was quite enthusiastic about it, and you should know that he is also an avid art collector."

Inspector C's brow furrowed as he puffed on his pipe. "Are you accusing the Vicomte de Maurnier, mademoiselle?"

Jenee could see Violet's growing vexation from the narrowing of her eyes. Why was law enforcement always hesitant to accuse powerful men of corruption or criminal behavior? She could imagine Iris' thoughts: *You ask for the truth, and because it doesn't suit your agenda, or it's troublesome, you wish to sweep it under the rug.* "You asked who knew of the painting, and I am stating the fact that the vicomte knew of it."

Xavier cleared his throat. "Is there anyone else we should be aware of? We do not want to jump to conclusions."

Jenee added what she hoped was clarification. "Several people were aware of the painting's arrival in Paris, including the playwright Edmond Rostand, the actress Sarah Bernhardt, the actor Constant Coquelin, the author Marcel Proust, and several others who were in attendance at a dinner party Tuesday evening. The soiree took place in Madame Bernhardt's suite following her performance at her theatre. Madame Shipley made mention of the painting at the party. However, none of the people at the gathering were privy to the location of the painting in the house, except the vicomte." She glanced at Xavier, whose face was an unreadable mask.

Chauvet stared at her with a penetrating gaze while emitting clouds of smoke from his pipe. It seemed that the more agitated or interested he became, the more frequent his puffs. "The vicomte was in attendance?"

"He was," said Jenee.

"You, Mademoiselle Lazaar, were not in residence last evening," stated Chauvet.

"No, I was visiting a friend and stayed the night." She could feel Xavier's stare, but no good could come from her confessing that it was him she had stayed with. Besides, it was personal and bore no pertinence to the case.

"I see." Chauvet looked from Jenee to Iris and finally to Xavier. "And it was Olivier, the butler, who discovered the burglary?"

"That is correct," said Iris. "First thing every morning, he unlocks the doors and opens the house. He is a trusted and valued member of the household staff," she added.

"Violet, did Madame Shipley convey to the detectives that the painting was a copy?" asked Jenee.

Again, Inspector C's brows hit his hairline, and puffs of smoke were emitted, reminding her of a locomotive barreling full speed ahead. "A copy, you say? Then we are investigating a stolen work of art with no intrinsic value?"

"True, but I might add that it is only because Madame Shipley had the wherewithal to hide the original at her bank, which was unknown to the vicomte," Iris said. "The thief, whoever he is, has no idea what he absconded with was a fake, and even though he failed to steal the real painting, it does not acquit him of criminal behavior. He will try again."

Jenee knew that Iris could not share the complete truth with Inspector C, that the vicomte must now know he had a fake. The painting he'd stolen was not a portal and was less than worthless to him.

"And you expect us to arrest the vicomte for a painting of no intrinsic value?"

Jenee felt her ire rise, and she wondered what trouble she would bring on herself if she stood toe to toe with the annoying Chauvet and gave him a piece of her mind. "Is it not the intent of the crime that matters here? We are certain that Madame Shipley expects you to catch the culprit, whether the painting is a copy or not. Besides which, I promise you he will try again."

"Before we can apprehend the thief, we must compile sufficient evidence, which is sorely lacking thus far." Xavier slid his gloved finger over the edge of the empty picture frame. "Do you find it odd that the thief removed the painting and was unafraid of doing it any damage?"

"It probably would be minimal. Madame Shipley has told us that in her experience in the art world, this is not an uncommon method when the thief is in a hurry," said Iris.

"Of course, you're right. What is Madame Shipley's plan for the painting? Surely she didn't bring it to Paris to keep it in a vault." Xavier knew the answer to that question, but by asking was forcing Iris and Jenee to take Inspector C into their confidence.

"She plans to preview it at a dinner party at Restaurant Brébant at the Eiffel Tower in a week," Iris replied. "Then it will be exhibited at the Grand Palais at the *Exposition Universelle.*"

Inspector Chauvet removed his pipe from between his teeth for the first time since he'd arrived. "If he is so inclined, it will be the perfect opportunity for the thief to strike again. We must have a plan in place and be prepared."

After the investigators concluded combing the crime scene and interviewing all the staff members, Inspector Chauvet bade them farewell and told Xavier he would get together with him tomorrow to discuss the case and the results of what evidence they had found. Iris offered to show Inspector Chauvet out, and then she wanted to check on Constance. She bade Xavier farewell and made a quick exit.

Jenee knew Iris had intentionally made an excuse to let her

and Xavier have a few minutes alone. With no one around, Xavier took her hands in his and pressed a kiss to her lips. She returned his affection, but she was a bundle of nerves.

"Inspector Chauvet will most likely insist on police presence at the preview dinner, which you know will only make it harder for Iris to take the painting. Why did you think this to be a good idea?"

"Jenee, the vicomte is dangerous, and I will need support."

"But the vicomte will not be receiving an invitation after abandoning us at Sarah's dinner party. Constance does not wish him to attend."

"Mark my words: he will make an appearance. Men like him don't quit their intentions; they simply reorganize and plot another way. I didn't tell you, but I've inquired with the Lyon police about Albert Archambeau."

"I vaguely remember that being the vicomte's name."

"Albert Archambeau is indeed the vicomte's name before he inherited his uncle's title and wealth. I should be receiving a detailed report tomorrow or the next day. I believe there is more to know about the man, and hopefully, something which will help us defeat him."

"I hope you are right, *mon amour.*"

CHAPTER TWENTY-FIVE

May 25, 1900
Paris, France

J ENEE AND CONSTANCE followed Hugo, the most beloved *refec d'Hotel* in Paris, as he squeezed through the rows of tightly packed tables where fashionably attired men and women were eating, drinking, laughing, and gossiping as they observed whoever had the good fortune to be seated in Paris' *belle monde* haunt of the beautiful and the blessed. The magnificent Art Nouveau interior glowed with hundreds of lamps adorned with rose-colored shades reflecting the splendor of white-linen-dressed tables set with sparkling crystal, polished silver, and bone-white china that bore the distinctive red logo of Maxim's. There was no better place to see or be seen in all of Paris.

Maxim's was the most famous restaurant in the world, and Jenee knew it was just what Constance's flagging spirit needed. The invasion of her home and the theft of *Il Divano*, even though it was a copy and not the original, was a traumatic experience for the Boston heiress. Jenee and Violet were at their wits' ends trying to cheer her up. Constance believed the ill deed to be a bad omen regardless of their assurances that the culprit would be caught. Sarah's invitation to lunch had come at the perfect moment, and Jenee, wanting to see her benefactress smile again, happily agreed.

Constance beamed with anticipation. "Maxim's has been closed for nearly a year and completely redecorated. I have heard that no expense has been spared readying it to open just in time for the *Exposition Universelle*."

"I've never been to Maxim's, and I am curious to see what all the hullabaloo is about," Jenee replied. Maxim's had always been beyond her parents' pocketbook, and she *was* curious to see the Art Nouveau masterpiece. But as she slipped into her seat, she felt a bit overwhelmed by the gaiety, the noise, the outrageous flirting, and the smoke from cigarettes and cigars that dominated the aroma of spices and herbs of the finely prepared food. She imagined it would be even more chaotic in the evening with the volume turned up from live music and dancing. Excitement rippled in the air, and everything and everyone contributed to the sensory overload that made her head spin.

Constance unfolded her napkin and laid it on her lap. "It certainly surpasses my wildest imaginings. The décor is *très chic*, don't you think?"

Jenee, studying the muraled walls painted with scantily dressed women in classical poses, nodded. "I'm not sure what I find more entertaining, the beautiful décor or the beautiful clientele."

"Hopefully, the beautiful cuisine. I am famished."

A formally attired waiter with a mustache and goatee arrived with a white linen napkin draped over his arm. *"Bonjour, mesdames*, can I offer you an aperitif?"

"Oui, monsieur." Constance turned to Jenee. "I believe we should order something special." She returned her attention to the waiter. "What do you suggest?"

"Bien sûr, a *Kir Royale* will be perfect to begin. Champagne and crème de cassis with a sprinkling of raspberries will prepare the palate for your gastronomical feast."

"Merci, we will heed your advice." The waiter nodded and was gone in the blink of an eye. Constance glanced around the room. "I wonder where Sarah is. I would never attribute tardiness

to her."

"Perhaps she was held up by something at the theater," Jenee said. "I imagine it is difficult for her to juggle the many hats she wears. I'm sure she'll be here soon."

"Yes, well, I'm starving, and the food smells and looks wonderful." Constance nodded to a nearby table, where the waiter removed the silver cloches, revealing entrees of *filet de sole aux moules* and *côte de boeuf aux pommes macaire*. "I think I fancy the steak and potatoes."

Jenee chuckled. "If you continue to go on about the food, we'll have to order everything on the menu." She surveyed the menu. "And these prices will set you back a good deal. Filet of sole and mussels will suit me fine, if you please."

"Oh, poppycock. It would take something far greater than a food menu to sink my ship." Constance chuckled.

Jenee noticed that everyone's attention had shifted to the entrance. "Ahh, there's Sarah now."

Sarah's eagle-eyed gaze swept the room and found them before Hugo could even greet her. He trotted behind her to the table, and every eye in the room followed. She wore a stunning light green worsted wool suit and a white ruffled blouse. Her bright golden-red hair that she'd cut short for her role in *L'Aiglon* bobbed as she walked, forming a halo of tousled curls around her face. Jenee didn't know how she managed it, but Sarah projected the appearance of a woman at least twenty years younger.

Jenee felt only admiration for the actress. Where most women in this era were dependent on men and forced to adhere to their rules, Sarah did as she pleased, charted her own course, and broke convention time and again. She was both admired and abhorred for her scandalous love affairs. Even in this era, all press, even bad press, was good.

Sarah bussed Jenee and Constance on each cheek before taking her seat and letting Hugo push her chair in. "Thank you, Hugo." She gave him a bewitching smile. "I am so sorry that I am late. Forgive me?"

"Don't be silly. Nothing to forgive," said Constance.

"I had to deal with the authorities because of an unexpected tragedy." Sarah dabbed at her eyes with her napkin. "I'm still in shock over the news."

Jenee knew the great actress could turn on a spigot of tears with little effort, but she could see that these were real tears, and Sarah was genuinely distraught. Constance and Jenee exchanged a worried glance.

"What is it? What has happened?" Something felt terribly wrong, and Jenee shuddered, feeling like someone had walked over her grave.

"You met her at my dinner party. She arrived with your friend Inspector Doumaz. My sweet young ingenue Lulu Lelouch…" Sarah's melodious voice cracked, and she was unable to continue.

"Lulu? What has happened to Lulu?" Constance looked completely confused at the mention of the girl who'd disappeared with the vicomte.

At that inopportune moment, Hugo reappeared and set down a glass of champagne for Sarah and cocktails for Jenee and Constance. "Is everything all right, Madame Bernhardt?" His perplexity at the crying diva was etched in furrowed lines across his forehead.

"Thank you, Hugo. I am fine, but I'm afraid a glass will not be enough today, and I require a bottle of champagne, *s'il vous plait.*" Sarah picked up the crystal flute and downed half of the fizzing liquid. She took a deep breath while Jenee held her breath impatiently, waiting for an explanation of why the police had visited Sarah and what Lulu had to do with it.

Finally sighing, Sarah continued. "Lulu's body was fished out of the Seine this morning, apparently a suicide." She picked up her drink and finished it. "I am terribly distraught."

Jenee's hand flew to her heart. "No, this cannot be true."

Sarah nodded, and a fat tear rolled down her cheek. "I'm afraid it is. The authorities arrived to notify me and question whether I'd noticed any signs that might indicate her mental state. Sadly, suicides of young women are routine, they told me, but Lulu showed no signs, and why would she? I'd taken her under my wing and was mentoring her. She showed such promise, and I believe she had a bright future. The young never consider the consequences of their actions. Of course, I am not one to talk, as I have made my share of unwise choices."

"The poor dear." Constance shook her head, taking Sarah's hand. Jenee knew Constance did not blame Lulu for the vicomte deserting her and was sincere in her empathy. Jenee wondered if Xavier knew, but of course he would. She imagined he would be devastated. She wished she could leave and go to him, but he was most likely in an official capacity dealing with Lulu's untimely death. After what she'd told him about the vicomte, did he suspect the vicomte to be the murderer?

What had promised to be an uplifting lunch turned into a solemn affair, blackened by the cloud of sadness that hung over them. Jenee and Constance did their best to raise Sarah's spirits, but Jenee only listened to the conversation with half an ear. Her thoughts were miles away, and all she could think about was Xavier. She made up her mind that she would take a taxi to the Île de la Cité after lunch and check on him.

Two hours later, Jenee entered the headquarters of the *Prefecture de Police* through an impressive porte-cochere. She felt heads turn at her entrance, and she garnered far more attention than she would have liked. She wished she was dressed a little less fashionably. She wondered how she would find Xavier among so many uniformed men, although, by their frank appreciation shown in smiles and the tipping of hats, she was sure any one of them would be more than delighted to help.

"*Excusez-moi*, I am looking for *Chef Inspecteur* Doumaz. Can you direct me to his office?" she asked the stout man sitting behind the main desk.

"I don't believe he's in his office," said the gray-haired official. The way he eyed her from head to toe made her feel like a strumpet soliciting a potential client.

"Do you know where I might find him?"

"If I'm not mistaken, he said he was going to the morgue." The man cast a steely-eyed gaze at her, daring her to ask him whether she might join Xavier there.

"It is of some urgency. I would appreciate someone taking me to him."

The sergeant, or whatever his title was, reminded her of a walrus with his bushy mustache and thick barrel build. He crossed his arms over his chest, only strengthening her picture of a walrus standing with his flippers crossed over a puffed-out chest. She fought not to giggle and gave him a placid smile. The walrus, however, was not beguiled.

"I'm afraid that's impossible." He offered no more explanation.

"May I send him a message so he might know that I am here?" She was losing her amusement and patience.

"Jean Claude," he called to a young officer busy behind him sorting piles of documents and placing them in wire baskets. "Can you take a message to *Chef Inspecteur* Doumaz at the morgue? I'm sure you won't mind leaving your current duties for a few minutes."

"*Oui,* monsieur." The young man's eagerness to do anything other than the mundane task he'd been assigned was evident. The walrus handed Jenee a piece of paper and a pen, and she wrote a quick note and handed it to the young man.

"Thank you, I'll wait here for a reply," she said. The file clerk ran off, taking a stairway down to a lower level. The walrus ignored her and returned to his work stamping and initialing forms.

Footsteps echoed on the marble floor as people came and went. Every emotion could be found among them. Some sobbed loudly while others cursed under their breath. She even witnessed a reunion between a man and his family, and watched them laugh and cry at his release.

The prefecture was a sizeable, stately building built as a barracks for the *Garde Républicaine* that later became the headquarters for the police. The immense complex was fashioned in a square, with a central courtyard containing gardens. Jenee imagined it would take time for the young officer to navigate the massive complex to where the morgue was. She wondered if there was a crime lab adjoining it.

The persistent glares of the walrus made her uncomfortable, and she decided not to be the focus of his scrutiny. She sat in a row of chairs along a wall and waited.

The interminable time waiting for Xavier to appear allowed her to marshal her thoughts. Her few encounters with Lulu played in her mind like reels of film on a screen. Could her dimpled smile, irrepressible flirting, and *joie de vivre* been an act? Was she, in truth, a tormented soul? She had attempted suicide before, or at the very least considered it. Jenee recalled that was how Xavier and Lulu met. He'd come upon her by chance and prevented her from jumping off a bridge into the Seine. Was it possible that it had all become too much? Did she suffer from depression? Jenee found it impossible to reconcile that tragic flaw with the state of Lulu's life at this time.

Lulu was not on a downward trajectory. Her dreams were within her grasp. She obviously had talent as an actress, enough to draw the friendship and support of an influential mentor. With Sarah as her friend, Lulu was poised on the cusp of success. Her beguiling looks and innocent demeanor would secure her plum roles. As to the security she sought, even though he was a venomous man, the vicomte's attention proved that if she wished to find a benefactor, there would be many a man who would be happily inclined, especially as she gained notoriety on the stage. Lulu throwing herself off a bridge did not make sense, but the taking of one's life never did.

Jenee couldn't help but ascribe Lulu's demise to the wicked vicomte. But if Lulu was murdered, why were the police so quick to attribute her death to suicide?

"Madame." The young officer came running back to her, out of breath.

"Yes, monsieur, I'm over here." She rose and waved.

"He left a while ago. *Chef Inspecteur* Doumaz told the coroner he was going home. He spent most of the night here in the morgue."

"Thank you, you've been most helpful." She leaned in and whispered, "The walrus behind the desk doesn't deserve you." She chuckled when she saw the confusion on the young officer's face, and then he got it and laughed with her. From the corner of her eye, she saw the walrus glaring at them.

She hurried out of the building, walked the short distance to Xavier's street, and climbed the six flights of stairs to his apartment.

She knocked for quite some time before he answered.

"Jenee, what are you doing here?" His voice, usually as comforting as a warm cup of chocolate, sounded gruff and distant.

She controlled her reaction, knowing he must be operating under considerable stress. "Will you not invite me in?"

It was apparent he was suffering. Dark circles surrounded his eyes, and his ordinarily robust complexion was drained of color. She also noticed he clenched his fists close to his sides. *He's blaming himself, or maybe he blames me.*

She could sense his reluctance, and it hurt her, but she swallowed that hurt like a bitter pill.

He opened the door wider for her to enter, and she walked in. Turning, she wrapped her arms around his waist and buried her face in his chest. "I'm so sorry, *mon amour*. I was at lunch with Sarah and Constance when I heard, and I raced to the prefecture to find you. They told me you'd gone home."

Xavier stiffened and then shuddered. His arms did not surround her as she expected, and she fought not to cry. Even though his aloofness swept through her like an arctic wind, she still held tight to him and, if anything, pressed closer.

When she looked up, his eyes were shuttered, revealing nothing, and she sensed a battle waging inside of him. She had a small opportunity to tear down the walls he was building between them, and she attacked them with no intention of failing. "Xavier, it is not your fault, and you must not blame yourself."

His voice, barely audible, resonated with ragged pain. "I should have been more understanding. I knew how she felt, yet I ignored it. Everyone I touch ends up destroyed." Looking into Xavier's eyes, it was as if she could see into his soul. "Don't you see, my loving you puts you in danger."

"The only danger for me is if you stop loving me." She cupped his face. "Look at me, Xavier. You are wrong to blame yourself. You are no more responsible for Lulu taking her own life than guilty of the deaths of your wife and child. That night at Sarah's, Lulu told me in no uncertain terms that I was a fool to let you go. She bore no ill will toward us. All Lulu cared about was your happiness. Only when I tried to warn her about the vicomte did she become annoyed and angry, and she told me I should stay out of her business. You recall saying she could take care of herself, do you not?"

"I was wrong, selfishly wrong. Somehow, I missed the clues. Yet even now, I can't recall any. I just don't understand why she would do this. She seemed so effervescent, so excited about the future."

"That was the impression she gave me too. It doesn't make any sense, and if something doesn't make sense, it may not be what you think. We need to consider that perhaps she didn't commit suicide."

"What do you mean?" he said in a husky whisper. "The coroner said there were no signs of trauma, struggle, or injury. She simply drowned."

"Xavier, there are other ways to kill a person or render them incapacitated. Lulu might have been drugged or poisoned and thrown into the Seine."

"But why, and who would do such a thing?" He turned away from her, raking his fingers through his hair, and began to pace.

Jenee considered this a positive sign that he was starting to think and weigh the possibilities.

"She left with the vicomte. We need to start there. Iris says the vicomte is a brutal serial killer of women, and he relishes committing violence." She swallowed to keep the bile from rising in her throat. "Have you heard the term psychopath?"

"Yes, I keep abreast of the advances in psychiatry. A Dr. Koch in Germany coined the word *psychopastiche*, which means a suffering soul."

Jenee nearly laughed at the insufficient meaning. "In referencing serial killers, the word has evolved to mean much more. These criminals are called psychopaths because they lack empathy. They display callous and manipulative traits. They are narcissistic and feel no remorse for their evil deeds. They take pleasure in the pain and violence they inflict. The vicomte is such a man, and Lulu may have been one of many victims. Iris told me he shot and killed her parents in cold blood."

"When did he do that?"

"In 1942, during World War II."

Xavier's eyes widened as he considered what she said. "But we have no evidence, no proof, no way to tie the vicomte to Lulu's murder. You heard Inspector Chauvet when Violet brought up the possibility that the vicomte should be considered a suspect. Bringing down a titled aristocrat who wields both wealth and power is no easy task."

"First, we must prove that Lulu was murdered."

"And how do you suggest we do that?"

"I must examine the body."

"But that's impossible."

"Nothing is impossible, *mon amour*," Jenee said. "Before I chose dermatology as my field of medicine, I thought about becoming a pathologist and did my preliminary studies in the field. All I need is to see Lulu's body and do an examination. Take some samples and perform some tests. A microscope would be helpful."

Xavier gaped at her in silence for a few moments. "I am speechless. Is there no end to your talents? I don't know how, but I will find a way to arrange it. Unfortunately, there is no way to go through legal channels. Not one of my superiors will approve a woman having access to perform an autopsy, even if she is a brilliant doctor." He took her hands. "But I am willing to risk it to know the truth and bring this monster to justice." He embraced her, and her heart soared. "Forgive me for my coldness when I greeted you. I was fighting my demons. You will have to be patient with me, *mon amour*. I am not a perfect man by any means, but I promise you I will strive to be the man you believe in." He gazed into her eyes with such love it brought a lump to her throat. She adored him.

"I know who you are, Xavier. Your anger and pain are natural, given what you've been through. We are all human. What kind of a partner would I be if you couldn't share all of yourself with me?"

Their lips met in a sublime kiss. It wasn't the "burning heat of passion" kind of kiss, but more the "heart's tender confession of love." It was the kiss she thought she would never find, and now it was the kiss she could never live without.

But when the kiss ended, she needed him to understand that there was a murder to solve and a devil to destroy. "How are you going to get me into the morgue?" she asked. "We are racing against time before the body decomposes and begins to hide its secrets."

"I have a plan."

CHAPTER TWENTY-SIX

May 26, 1900
Paris, France

THE BELLS OF Notre Dame rang out the midnight hour and moonlight cast long shadows as Xavier led Jenee through the empty streets of the Île de la Cité, the tiny island in the Seine River. A cool breeze blowing off the river chilled the beads of sweat on the back of his neck. He felt Jenee shiver beneath the cloak he'd given her to wear, and Xavier imagined she was as nervous as he was.

It had seemed prudent to disguise Jenee as best he could, so he'd dug out of his closet an old uniform. After the death of his wife and child, he'd lost so much weight that nothing fit him. Eventually, he'd regained the weight and forgotten about the uniform. It was still too big for Jenee, but they'd bound her breasts flat, then pinned, tucked, and tied a belt around her waist, so the uniform wasn't falling off her slender frame. Her hair she'd put in a ponytail and stuffed into one of his hats. Although she could never look like a man, she could pass for one from a distance. It was a precaution if they came across anyone at the prefecture. Xavier would distract them, and she would slip away and meet him back at his apartment.

The icing on the cake had come when Jenee broke off a piece of coal and drew a mustache. When she turned to him, he'd doubled over with laughter. She'd played it for all it was worth by sidling up against him and asking, "How about a quicky, monsieur?"

He'd shaken his head, not understanding. "What is a quicky?"

"I forgot that you know nothing of modern lingo. A quicky is, well, what it sounds like. It's a brief sexual encounter when time is of the essence." She winked seductively.

"You want me to make love to a little man with a mustache?"

Their mingled laughter relieved some of the tension. There was nothing to do but laugh at the insanity of what they were about to attempt. If caught, Xavier would undoubtedly be fired, and Jenee would be prosecuted.

Xavier left her in the shadows beside a little-used door at the back of the building that led to a service stairway. "I will come as quickly as I can, *mon amour*. Do not move." He kissed her and ran to the front of the building. Once inside, he nonchalantly walked through. He was dressed in his uniform, and the policeman who staffed the front desk merely waved. Jenee had told him about her encounter with the walrus. Xavier knew the man and had chuckled, telling her Monsieur Charles took his job very seriously and was very protective of his police force.

That evening, the man on duty behind the desk was, fortunately, not the walrus.

There was minimum staff working at this hour, and Xavier didn't have any interaction with anyone. He opened the door, Jenee slipped in, and he led her down the stairs to the basement where the lab and morgue were located. Because Lulu's identity was known, she would not have to be subjected to the humility of being displayed at the Paris Morgue in an ice room to be ogled by the public. The old morgue on the *Quai de l'Archevêché* was where the bodies fished from the Seine were displayed naked on slabs in hopes that someone might identify them. It had grown into a macabre tourist attraction that brought hundreds of visitors daily, including families with children. The author Emile Zola regularly visited the Paris Morgue and called it a "show that was affordable to all." Xavier found the practice appalling, as it stole the last vestige of human dignity from those poor, lost souls.

Xavier removed Lulu's body from the cold storage locker and rolled the gurney with her sheet-covered remains into the lab. Jenee shuffled her feet, waiting with her arms wrapped around herself.

"Here she is." He turned on the overhead lamp. "What do you want me to do?" He prepared himself as best he could for what was to come.

Jenee rolled the tray with medical implements over to the gurney. "I know this is difficult for you. Why don't you sit over there and give yourself a little distance while I examine her body?"

"No, we will do this together, and I will brace myself for the worst. Lulu is no longer here, her spirit has flown, and I know she would want us to bring the monster who did this to her to justice."

"Very well. I need to collect some samples, but first, I want to examine every inch of the body."

Xavier watched as Jenee pulled the sheet away and began her examination. He drew in his breath. He had seen Lulu when she was brought in wet and muddy from the river, but the coroner and his assistant were there, and he'd held his emotions in tight check. Now she was cleaned up, and her hair had dried, and even though Xavier couldn't see her dimples because her smile was gone, he could imagine them. His heart felt like a bloodless stone in his chest as he remembered her teasing and laughter. He had never loved her, but he had cared about her. His heart felt heavy, and his chest felt tight. Lulu was pale as moonstone, and her face gleamed bluish white in the light. He swallowed the thickness in his throat.

Jenee was intent on what she was doing. "Based on the lack of deterioration, Lulu wasn't in the water for very long. She isn't bloated, either, which means she didn't imbibe water. Lulu did not drown, and she was dead before her body was pitched into the water. Your coroner should have noticed that." She studied Lulu's hands and nails. "The capillary circulation collapses, making the body turn blue. There's dirt under her nails, which might include the murderer's skin, but the tests I would need to do involve DNA testing, and unfortunately, those tests won't exist until nearly a century from now."

Xavier knew that she was as much talking to herself as to him. He had heard mention of DNA but knew little about it, but from what she intimated, it was a science that one day would confirm a criminal's identity by traces of his skin and fluids.

Jenee lifted the eyelids and studied each eye. "The eyes are not dilated, and the pupils are constricted, indicating she may have been drugged." She looked up at Xavier. "That is a classic effect of opioids such as opium, heroin, and morphine." She continued her examination, checking between the toes, fingers, arms, and legs, presumably searching for any puncture holes that could have been made by a hypodermic needle. "Unfortunately, even if I cut her open and examined her organs, I wouldn't be able to accurately determine what kind of poison or drugs were used. Advances in science, technology, and lab screening are still years away in the future." She looked up at him. "Are you all right?"

"Don't worry about me. I promise you I'll stay standing."

"Actually, why don't you sit down over there." Jenee pointed to a chair against the wall. "I need to check something, and I'd prefer you not be standing over me."

"You can't cut into her, Jenee."

"I have no intention of doing anything other than a superficial examination. Besides, it wouldn't do me any good, as I have no lab to work in."

"I'm sorry. I wish I could do more."

"In London, our Vicomte de Maurnier was given the moniker of the Flower Girl Killer," she said. "Iris told me the serial killer was obsessed with flowers and left a rose with each mutilated victim. He went as far as to leave one of the victims in a field of flowers. Serial killers enjoy leaving calling cards. It's almost a signature of who they are. In London, it was a rose. I don't believe it is a coincidence that Iris' last name is Bellerose. In London, the last name she used was Desrosiers. She is his foil and stands in the way of what he craves most." She pulled the curtain, enclosing her and Lulu's body and blocking his view. "This won't take long, *mon amour*. Patience."

Xavier scrubbed his face with his hands. All he wanted was for this day to end, and he did not want to contemplate what Jenee might be doing behind the curtain.

She eventually pulled the curtain back, and he looked up. "Did you find anything?"

"I did." She held up one of the microscopic slides he'd given her.

"What is it?" She'd piqued his curiosity, and his investigative nature took precedence over the man who mourned his friend.

"Lulu's hair is red, the hair on her head and her vaginal hair. I found a silver-gray hair inside her, and it is not a pubic hair. The Vicomte's hair is silver-gray, and Lulu bears signs of abrasive sexual intercourse. It is exactly the kind of evidence that your Monsieur Locard points to in his theory that no two bodies can come in contact and not leave a trace. A fallen hair during an aggressive act of sex…" She shrugged. "It is easy to imagine, *n'est-ce pas*? We are lucky to have found it, as the river would have washed away any hairs that might have been on her clothing or skin. However, a hair that fell from his head and was inadvertently pushed into Lulu during sex or rape is a lucky break indeed."

"How do we prove it's his?"

"We need a sample from his head. Granted, even with a sample, I can't prove it's his without a reasonable doubt, but certainly, enough to narrow our search to him. We should also go to Lulu's building and interview the other tenants. We have not seen her since she left Sarah's with the vicomte eleven days ago, and perhaps someone saw something of her comings and goings."

"How do you propose we get one of his hairs?"

Jenee looked thoughtfully at the slide in her hand, then slipped it into her pocket. When she raised her eyes, he could see her determination. "His carriage. We follow him, watch him exit, and then lure his driver away while one of us searches. I'm sure we will find a strand of hair."

Xavier nodded. The woman he loved was clever indeed. One day, when this nightmare was over, there were so many questions about the future that he would love to ask her. The advancements in science and technology, to name two. He had no intention of disrupting the course of history, although he wished they could. What he wanted to know had more to do with how he could improve his investigations and bring more criminals to justice.

He still found the time-travel notion bewildering, but it had brought him Jenee, and for that miracle, he was grateful. Without realizing it, he'd come to believe, as she did, that they were meant to find each other. They were soul mates that had somehow been separated by time, and the error had been corrected by a supernatural twist of fate.

As he pondered his thoughts, Jenee observed him, and by the look on her face, he wondered if she could read his mind.

"I believe I have spent enough time in the morgue, Monsieur Chief Inspector. Take me home, *mon amour*."

"To Madame Shipley's *maison*?" He could not imagine being apart from her at this juncture, and he needed her as he needed his very breath.

Jenee giggled. "*Non, mon cher idiot.* Wherever you are is my home. I will not be parted from you now or ever again."

CHAPTER TWENTY-SEVEN

May 26, 1900
Paris, France

JENEE'S HEART THUNDERED in her chest. The vicomte's carriage was parked in the gravel entry to the house. Iris was correct: the vicomte would stop at nothing to take possession of the painting. That he would try to worm his way back into Constance's good graces after his shameful behavior at Sarah's party was the height of audaciousness.

She looked about and realized the driver was not with the carriage. The opportunity was more than she could resist.

She climbed into the carriage, stilled her shaking hands, and began to search. At first, she found nothing; the carriage was spotlessly clean. To give herself courage, she repeated Edmond Locard's principle: *"Wherever he steps, whatever he touches, whatever he leaves, even unconsciously, will serve as a silent witness against him."* She knew it had to be here, the one thing that would tie the evil monster to Lulu's murder.

She lifted the cushioned seat, and lo and behold, a silver strand of hair caught her eye. The tiny thread tempted her like the Holy Grail. *Let it be his undoing.* She carefully put it in a vial Xavier had given her and put it in her reticule. She pulled the strings tight just as a man cleared his throat. She nearly jumped out of her skin, her hand flying to her heart.

"Madame, can I help you?" The driver glared at her.

"Oh, monsieur, you frightened me."

"My apologies. May I ask what you are doing in the vicomte's carriage?"

A nervous laugh was the best she could manage. "I-I was in the carriage a week ago, and I-I lost an earring. Nothing precious, it was merely paste, but it was a gift from my dear late grandmother. When I saw the carriage, I thought I might look for it, which was silly. Of course, it wasn't there." Jenee climbed out of the carriage. "Please forgive my impertinence. It was rather foolish of me. I should have waited for your return and asked if you minded if I looked for it. I'll just be on my way."

"As you wish. Shall I mention the missing earring to the vicomte? I am sure he would be happy to replace it."

"Oh, dear, no, that isn't necessary. As I said, it was of no value, but *merci beaucoup*. Good day to you, sir."

Jenee didn't wait for a reply because the last thing she wanted was a confrontation with the vicomte. Without looking back, she hurried into the house.

"Ah, Mademoiselle Lazaar, there you are. Madame Shipley asked for you. She is in the library with the Vicomte de Maurnier." Olivier had the uncanny ability to appear out of thin air. On television, it was often said that an excellent butler had eyes and ears everywhere. If that was the case, then Olivier was an all-star.

Ever since Olivier had learned that Jenee had saved Constance's life, he had held her in high regard. He was fond of her and would do nothing to harm her standing in Constance's eyes. It was likely that her not returning last night was not known by anyone in the household other than the discreet butler.

"Thank you, Olivier. I assisted Chief Inspector Doumaz on a case, and we worked late into the night. I decided to stay in town." She didn't have to explain herself to the butler, but taking him into her confidence proved her trust in him.

"There is no need to explain, mademoiselle." He walked to the entryway table and retrieved an envelope. "This letter arrived for you this morning."

Jenee glanced at the thick cream envelope, her pulse pounding with excitement. The letter was from Eastbourne, England, and the return addressee was the Marchioness of Danbury. She wanted to tear it open but refrained and stuck it in her pocket. "Thank you, Olivier. Is Mademoiselle Rousseau in her room?"

"She is, mademoiselle."

"I will speak to her after I see Madame Shipley." Jenee could hear conversation coming from the library. She pressed her ear to the door.

"Really, Albert, I find it difficult to understand your behavior at Sarah's dinner party. Leaving with that actress after making that ridiculous excuse was very rude and hurtful of you." Jenee heard Constance sniffle.

"I apologize for the insult, but the girl was distressed and begged that I get her out of there. She said the inspector had used her unremorsefully and broken her heart. There was nothing for me to do but react as any gentleman would. I escorted the damsel home to Montmartre. By the time I saw her safely to her flat and listened to her tale of abuse and tears of humiliation, it was too late to return to Madame Bernhardt's soiree. You must forgive me."

Jenee rolled her eyes at the vicomte's blatant lies. He was very convincing, she'd give him that. He could rival Gérard Depardieu himself in the acting department.

How dare he slander Xavier and her with such blatant untruths? Jenee sucked in a breath to calm her sprinting pulse. It wouldn't do to play her hand yet and accuse the lying, murdering monster of his innumerable crimes. She couldn't imagine Constance believing any of this tripe, but the woman was good-natured and forgiving, and Jenee could sense her resolve melting into a pool of forgiveness.

"Why did you wait so long to tell me this?" Constance continued. "More than a week has passed, and I've had a dreadful time."

"I'm so sorry. What has caused you such distress?"

As if the bastard doesn't know. If only she had a gun. Jenee felt capable of putting a bullet through the parasite.

"My house was robbed, and my sanctuary breached. I don't know how I will ever feel safe here again."

"Was anything taken?"

Jenee nearly gagged. Listening to him was like drinking snake oil.

"My latest acquisition, *Il Divano*. The thief cut the painting from its frame and left without a trace."

"*Mon Dieu*, this is an outrage! Do the authorities have any idea who did this?"

"No, they are useless."

Jenee had heard enough. She opened the door and feigned surprise. "I'm sorry, Constance, I didn't realize you had a guest." She flashed a fake smile at the vicomte. "Your lordship, I would not think to see you here again."

"It's all right, Jenee," Constance said. "There was a misunderstanding, and the vicomte came to apologize and clear things up."

"Oh, I see, what a relief. We were deeply distressed to have lost your lordship's friendship. Will the vicomte attend the private dinner and preview of Allegretto's painting on Saturday?"

"But I thought the painting was stolen," he said, his eyebrows rising in surprise.

I bet you did, you slimy sonofabitch. "Didn't Constance tell you? She was clever to have stored the painting at her bank, and the simpleton of a thief could not possibly know that he stole a copy."

"How very clever of you, *ma chérie*." He took Constance's hand and kissed it.

"But it was—"

"No need to be modest, Constance," Jenee interrupted. "Well, I will leave you to your visit, vicomte. I'm sure I will see you on Saturday for the highly anticipated preview of Allegretto's masterpiece. I must speak to Violet." She nodded and, turning to leave, took two steps toward the door.

"Please give the dear lady my regards."

Jenee stopped in her tracks, turning. She was tempted to slap the sneer off the vicomte's face.

"I didn't know you and Mademoiselle Rousseau were acquainted."

"In fact, we are well acquainted. Please let her know that I look forward to seeing her again."

"I will convey your regards." Jenee strolled from the room as if she hadn't a care in the world. Once the door closed, she dashed up the stairs.

CHAPTER TWENTY-EIGHT

May 26, 1900
Paris, France

"V IOLET." JENEE RAPPED gently. "May I come in?"

The door opened, and Iris pulled Jenee inside her room. "Did the vicomte leave?"

"No, not yet. But he took great pleasure in telling me he knows you well, and he sends his regards to you and looks forward to seeing you soon. The bastard is baiting you."

"*Alors*, he's laid down the gauntlet, and we will do battle."

"Sooner than you think. As we expected, Constance has forgiven him, and he will be attending the dinner on Saturday. What are we going to do?"

"Nothing."

"What do you mean?" Jenee asked. "We have to do something. You must take the painting and return to Marco, and we must stop the vicomte once and for all."

"*Oui, oui*, that is our goal, but not at Restaurant Brébant."

"But I thought that was what we decided."

Iris began to pace the room. "Things change, *ma chérie*, and we must change with them. You were right in saying there will be too many people at the restaurant, and the painting will be the center of attention. We cannot risk the lives of everyone at the party. Remember, the vicomte cares not a fig for any life other than his own. We must confront him alone. I have already suggested to Constance that the painting return here after the preview at the restaurant. *Chef Inspecteur* Doumaz will stay the night and provide security. Then in the morning the painting can be transported under police escort to the Grand Palais.

"We will lure the vicomte in. Of course, he will take the bait and come for the prize. Between you, Xavier, and me, we will prevail. All I need is a few minutes to disappear through the portal, and the painting will disappear with me. The time traveler will be trapped here, and you can do with him as you choose."

Jenee sighed. "We must refine this plan of yours and go over it with Xavier. I'm sure he will have additional suggestions."

"Undoubtedly. And I'm sure we can adjust things to his satisfaction."

"Iris, I must tell you something else. A shocking and terrible tragedy has occurred," Jenee said, taking Iris' hand and leading her back to the sofa.

"What is it?" Iris' eyes showed alarm.

"Lulu, the actress who left with the vicomte the night of Sarah's party, has been murdered."

"*Mon Dieu!* That demon has struck again!" Iris' hands flew to her mouth.

"Yesterday, her body was pulled from the Seine, and I convinced Xavier to let me examine the body, and last night we snuck into the morgue." Jenee shuddered, remembering Lulu lying on the slab, her face so pale. She would never forget the sight.

"The time traveler takes his pleasure in murder. He is the devil's disciple. How did he kill her?"

"Her death was ruled a suicide by drowning by the coroner, but I found enough evidence that I am convinced it was murder. It is most likely she was drugged, poisoned, and sexually assaulted. I suspect an overdose of opioids could have been administered. Perhaps she imbibed it in wine. I can't say for sure because the body was submerged in water, making it more difficult to confidently ascribe the cause. But I did find a hair that wasn't hers inside her vagina." She opened her reticule and removed the vial containing the single hair. "And I found this silver-gray hair in the vicomte's coach. I'm going to compare the two under a microscope. If they're a match, and I believe they are, it should be enough to link him to her death. Xavier wants to see him tried, convicted, and guillotined. I want Xavier to find closure and the murderous time traveler to receive his long-overdue justice."

"I am confident your inspector will catch him."

"I hope so, because I feel much guilt involving Xavier in this. What we plan to do goes against everything he has dedicated his life to. I find solace in knowing that if we bring the vicomte down, Lulu and all the other women he murdered will have found their justice and can rest in peace."

"And we all will have a chance of happiness, *mon amie*," said Iris.

"That too." Jenee slipped her hand into her pocket, pulling out the envelope Olivier had given her. "I received a letter this morning from Eastbourne, England." She walked to Iris' desk, picked up her letter opener, and slit open the envelope. The stationery was thick, creamy, and embossed at the top with an R in a cameo. She skimmed the letter. "It's from Emily. She writes,"

Dear Jenee, I can't believe you are in Paris with Iris. I'm sure your ordeal has been as harrowing as mine to adjust to. I dare not write it out, but you know what I speak of. I will keep this brief. My husband Colin and I are coming to Paris. Can you believe I am married? At times I still find everything that happened impossible to believe, but I will share my travails with you when I see you, and I look forward to hearing yours.

Colin and I are planning to go to the Universelle Exposition. We thought about bringing the children, but they are still too young. Yes, we are blessed with twins, a boy and a girl. George is named after Colin's father, who died three years ago, and Cecilia is named after my mother. May God rest her soul.

As I was saying, we wanted to bring the children with us but felt they would be better off with their grandparents, a lovely couple who took me into their home when I first "arrived" in London and eventually adopted me as their daughter. It's a long story, but I shall tell you all when I see you.

Sometimes, I have to pinch myself, I am so happy. Thankfully, I am not pregnant, or Colin would have canceled our trip, and I am looking forward to seeing you! But if Colin has his way, I might be pregnant after a week holed up at the très romantique Ritz Hotel. Yes, I am still a little wicked, and yes, I'm as outspoken and determined as ever. I fear I drive Colin to distraction. Thank goodness he loves me beyond measure. I try, but I don't always succeed in not embarrassing him. For the most part, I behave honorably, as a privileged marchioness should.

Teehee ('ow do you like me title?). Who would ever believe that Emily, a descendant of smugglers, would end up an aristocrat? (Wait until you hear about my meeting with my great-great-great-grandmother.)

I think Colin is a wee bit nervous about meeting you, my BFF. Two self-sufficient, independent women might be more than he is equipped to handle, LOL. If only Gaby was here too! Dear Lord, poor Colin, if all three of us ever manage to be together again in one room. If we were flung back in time, I imagine Gaby was too.

In truth, don't worry, you're going to love Colin, my very own Lord Remington, and he will love you. I cannot wait to see you, and I am so excited to meet the extraordinary Inspector Xavier Doumaz. We have a million things to catch up on. Please tell Iris that I can't wait to see her too, and she can count on Colin and me for whatever she plans. We should be in Paris within two days of your receipt of this letter. Leave word for me at the Ritz Hotel.

Big kiss,
Emily

Time travel or no time travel, Emily certainly hadn't changed. Even though her bestie had jested of it, Jenee couldn't believe Emily was now an aristocrat, married to a marquess. Her only experience with anyone "royal" was the vicomte, and he was the most despicable man she'd ever met.

"What do you think?" she asked.

"I think we will make a most formidable team," Iris said. "Emily and Colin will be as determined as we are to bring that time-traveling bastard to justice. They are well acquainted with that monster. In London, the vicomte disguised himself as Seth Marlowe Wolfe. He usurped the wealth and title of the Duke of Shrewsbury. He murdered at least five women, one of whom was Colin's fiancée Daphne Carmichael, to whom he was engaged before meeting Emily, but better I should let Emily share that story."

"So, Colin is as anxious as Xavier to see justice served."

"Maybe even more so."

"Then as soon as Emily and Colin arrive, we must meet and devise our plan."

"I will send a message to the Ritz for Emily to contact us as soon as she gets in," Iris said. "And I will send an invitation for them to attend the preview of *Il Divano* at the Restaurant Brébant."

Jenee walked to the window and looked outside. "The vicomte has left, and I must change before Xavier arrives. We are going to Lulu's apartment house in Montmartre to see if anyone saw her and can tell us when she was last at her apartment." She turned back to Iris. "What about Constance?"

"I will make certain she is occupied. I will be going over numerous details with her about the dinner. We cannot allow her to fall under the vicomte's spell, and heaven forbid the vicomte gets his claws in her."

"We must do everything we can to keep her safe and to catch that beast, so he can never kill again."

CHAPTER TWENTY-NINE

May 26, 1900
Paris, France

JENEE LOOKED OUT the window of the fiacre at the rising dome of *Sacré-Cœur* as the horse clip-clopped across the Place du Tertre and came to a halt. They'd reached the butte. Xavier raised her wrist to his lips and pressed a kiss to her pulse point, sending a pool of warmth to her belly. He helped her alight from the carriage, then paid the driver to return in two hours. He took her hand in his, and they made their way up the steps to the narrow street where Lulu's apartment building stood.

"I can hardly believe it's been a month since I arrived in Paris. That first day, you brought me here, to Lulu's. So much has changed, and I have changed."

The most beautiful blue eyes she'd ever seen crinkled with his smile. "You are not the only one changed, *mon amour*. When the dust cleared from a collapsed walkway, I saw you and didn't dream that you could be the love of my life. Life can be strange and wondrous, *n'est ce-pas?*"

She leaned in and kissed his mouth. "We are fortunate, Xavier, to have found each other. I can't wait for you to meet Emily. I feel everything is coming full circle."

"Ahh, your marchioness friend. I am a plain man, a policeman. I hope she and her husband will not find me too bourgeois."

"That's ridiculous. There is nothing plain about you. You are heroic, romantic, and intellectual, and I love you beyond words. Emily will love you too. Don't you think I have my own fears about meeting her husband, the marquess?"

"Now it is you being ridiculous. Who could not fall in love with you, Jenee? We are all nothing compared to you. You have a far higher calling as a doctor."

"And just you remember that the next time you're vexed with me." She gave him a saucy wink.

Xavier chuckled. "We are here, and I will defer to your able judgment. There are not so many tenants that we can't knock on every door."

They entered the building and found an old woman with wiry gray hair mopping the floor. Jenee noticed she gave them a thorough once-over before dipping the mop in the bucket and pretending to ignore them.

She patted Xavier's arm. "Wait here." She approached the woman and smiled. *"Bon après-midi, grand-mère."* She pulled a five-franc coin out of her reticule and held it flat in her palm. The woman went to take it, but Jenee closed her hand before she could. "I can tell you know everything that goes on in this building. The coin is yours if you answer a few questions that for someone like you should be very easy."

The old woman gave her a smile that displayed several missing teeth. *"Oui,* madame, I am sure I can help you."

"Merci. There is a very pretty young woman who lives on the top floor, her name is—"

"Lulu Lelouch." The woman cackled and shook her hands as if they were on fire. "That one will get herself into trouble, but I have nothing bad to say about her. That dimpled smile of hers could win over a king."

"Of course you don't. You are not unkind, I can tell."

The woman nodded eagerly. "No, madame, never unkind."

"When did you see her last?"

The woman scrunched her brow. "I think it's nearly a week

since I've seen her, and I remember because it is very unlike her. For all her flirtations, she rarely entertains men here. Mind you, she could if she chose." She shrugged. "But perhaps the man she left with was someone special to her. Maybe she has moved into a grand *maison* and he has offered her a better life."

"Did you see the man?" Jenee's heart was beating so hard in her chest that she could feel it in her temples.

"I saw only the back of him. He was dressed all fancy and wore a top hat and cape, and his hair was as silver as that coin you hold."

"And you say they left together."

"Oh, yes, they must have been drinking because Lulu was giggling and leaning on him. I heard him call her his *fleur*. I have not seen her since. Maybe he has become her benefactor. I wish her well."

Jenee opened her hand, and the woman grabbed the coin. "*Merci*, madame, you have been most helpful."

Xavier waited, standing alert as ever. Jenee knew he would spring into action if they were accosted. She took his arm and nodded to the woman, and she and Xavier climbed the stairs in silence. He waited for her to reveal what she had learned when there was no possibility of them being overheard. When they reached the top floor and tried Lulu's door, it was locked.

"What are you going to do?" she asked.

"I will open the door with this." He pulled out a lockpick set and went to work. In seconds, he turned the knob, and the door opened. "*Voila, après vous.*"

Jenee half expected to see Lulu draped across her divan, and she couldn't help but recall the last time she was here, Lulu had greeted them adorned in her silk dressing gown, her adorable, dimpled smile, and a warm welcome. It was unbearably sad that the coquette's irrepressible spirit had been silenced forever.

Jenee took in the room with its lingering scent of Lulu's perfume. Xavier sat on the sofa, and after putting on gloves, he examined two glasses of wine left on the coffee table. He interrupted her thoughts. "What did the old woman have to say?"

"She saw Lulu leave with an elegantly attired man with silver hair. I'm certain it was the vicomte. She also mentioned that Lulu seemed inebriated."

"I don't doubt it." He lifted a wine glass with lip rouge on it and brought it to his nose.

"Be careful, Xavier. We don't know whether he poisoned her."

"Precisely." He picked up the other glass and sniffed it. "Lulu's glass has an astringent smell that I don't detect in the other glass. Here." He held out the glass with the ruby lip marks smeared around the rim. "What do you think?"

Jenee's brow furrowed as she inhaled. "I think I need to analyze the contents. Opium is known to have a vinegar-like smell. The woman downstairs said Lulu was very tipsy, but it doesn't look like she had much to drink." She looked around the room. "I wish we had something to take the glasses and wine back with us."

"Your wish is my command." Xavier pulled two vials with red rubber stoppers from his pocket. "I took these from the lab thinking they might come in useful."

"Clever man."

Xavier removed the stopper, and Jenee carefully poured the wine in. She handed back the vial, and he replaced the stopper.

"I don't suppose we need to take a sample of the other glass, since it was his, and there is nothing odd about the smell," he said. "We'd better take the glasses, though, so we can dust for fingerprints. But unfortunately, the thief wore gloves, and we found no fingerprints at Constance's *maison*, so we have nothing to compare them to."

"No, we'll also take a sample of his wine so we can compare them. It will be easier to narrow down the additive. Have you a chemist that you trust who could run an analysis?"

"I have just the man. Leave it to me. I want to do more looking around here before we leave. And then would you be in the mood for the man you love to prepare a bourride for you."

Jenee chuckled. "Am I to think that bourride will be your code word for lovemaking? It is rather clever of you. Whenever you are in the mood for love, you will ask me if I'm in the mood for fish soup?"

"I guess I am very transparent." He grinned. "You are the cure for all that ails me, and I find it hard to pretend otherwise."

"I promise you, it won't be happening here. I don't think Lulu's ghost would be amused if she's about, but, then again, she would be happy we are together."

"*Cher Dieu.*" He looked around, probably expecting to see Lulu's ghost watching from a corner. "For us to make love here would be sacrilege. Even as much as I desire you, I would never find my passion here."

"There was something else our friend downstairs told me."

"And what is that?"

"She overheard the man call Lulu his flower. The London serial killer's calling card was a flower, most often a rose. It must have amused him to call her his flower and know that he planned to kill her."

"I will not rest until that bastard gets what's coming to him."

"Then we must be very thorough in everything we do, and there will be no room for mistakes," Jenee said. "The time traveler is a formidable foe who has honed his skills for survival and has the mind of a master criminal."

"He thinks he may have the upper hand, but every criminal, mastermind or not, has a weakness, and his weakness is getting his hands on that painting."

CHAPTER THIRTY

May 29, 1900
Paris, France

CONSTANCE HAD ACCOMMODATED Jenee with the use of her carriage. Peering out the window, she sat on the edge of her seat, barely containing her excitement. The horses pranced in place, and the carriage rocked back and forth. Jenee's gaze was pinned to the doors of the eighteenth-century townhouse built in the grand style of Louis XIV. A white awning with blue cursive embroidery announced the impresario César Ritz's elegant signature hotel, the Ritz Paris. A couple exited, holding hands, and exchanged a kiss as they proceeded to walk up the Place Vendome toward the Rue St Honoré. The ambiance of Paris was always a boon to lovers.

"What an interesting couple," Jenee observed. "She appears so unpretentious, and he seems quite the dandy. Love can never be explained or given rules, and it knows no age or socioeconomic boundaries—and, judging by us, apparently no time difference."

"That is the composer Claude Debussy and the sculptress Camille Claudel," Xavier said. "My dear, that is not love, at least not the lasting kind. He is married, and Camille has been in an on-again, off-again relationship with the venerated sculptor Auguste Rodin for years."

Xavier helped Jenee out of the carriage and held her arm as they walked up the steps to the wrought-iron entrance. The tuxedoed doorman opened the door and welcomed them into an intimate reception area.

Xavier stopped at the desk and asked the man on duty to please let the Marquess and Marchioness of Danbury know that their friends had arrived.

"Ah, yes, I remember seeing a movie based on their lives." Jenee gazed up the white marble stairway with its magnificent black and gold wrought-iron balustrade that curved up to the second floor. A beautiful Empire desk displayed an exquisite oriental urn filled with an arrangement of white casa blanca lilies that perfumed the air.

"A movie about Rodin and Claudel? What is a movie?"

Jenee leaned in to smell the flowers and sighed. "Sometimes I forget where I am. Remember you mentioned that you saw the innovation of moving pictures showing opera and ballet that premiered at the exposition? In the next decades, that will evolve into a new industry and art form called the motion picture. It will have other monikers, feature films, movies, and cinema. Just as we attend a play or opera at the theatre, technology will enable stories to be captured on celluloid. Special buildings called movie theaters will be built to showcase these movies on a large, canvas-type screen. Then will come the radio. Not sure when that will be invented, but I'm sure it's soon. We'll be able to listen to stories and newspaper stories broadcast through a box in our homes and eventually in automobiles. That will lead to visual stories or little movies we can see in smaller boxes called television."

"*Mon Dieu!* As you know, I am a man who believes in the advancement of science and mechanical engineering, but it all seems incomprehensible that it should happen so quickly."

"And so much of it will happen in this lifetime."

Xavier grinned. "It is exciting, I must admit. I imagine the automobiles I'm beginning to see here in Paris will eventually replace carriages and horses."

"You have no idea how right you are." She smiled.

"I am an investigator, after all."

"Well, just you wait. This century is one of immense change."

"*Incroyable!* Your stories are almost as fascinating as you are." He leaned over and placed a light kiss on her lips. "I think it will take a lifetime for me to learn everything you know."

"Maybe we should have regular sessions? I could be your teacher, and you, my pupil," she said in a husky whisper.

Xavier arched a dark brow. "It has been many years since I was in a schoolroom, but the thought of you in a prim teacher's dress, with your hair in a tight bun, wearing spectacles and wielding a pointer, might give me a different sort of educational idea." He leaned in and nipped at her earlobe.

"You naughty man! One day I'll tell you about the pornography industry."

"*Mon Dieu*, I think we'd better talk about something else, or I'll be liable to reenact last night's adventures with you in the carriage when we return your friends to the hotel."

Jenee giggled. "All right, my love. So, enlighten me about Rodin and Claudel. I don't understand how you know about their relationship."

"I was called to Rodin's studio one evening to subdue Madame Claudel. She and the sculptor had a terrible row, and she was destroying both his and her sculptures. The end of love can be a terrible thing to witness. To see these two genius artists spew vitriol at each other is something I shall never forget."

"I can well imagine. I'm afraid that the story has a tragic end. I think that sometimes happens when people give their work and career all their passion and love. In Rodin and Claudel's lives, their art came first. Claudel's tragedy was she tried to find acceptance in a world where women are discounted."

"I promise you, Jenee, I will always put you before everything else in my life. I will never discount you."

What he said struck the very heart of her soul. She wanted to thank the gods of time travel that had whooshed her away to a time she didn't belong and placed her just where she needed to be.

"Thank you." She cupped his face and kissed him, and his arms flew around her, pulling her against his chest. "You are a man far ahead of your time. I love you, monsieur."

"I love you, mademoiselle."

"How did I get so lucky to find you, *mon amour*?" she whispered, holding his gaze.

"It is I who am the lucky one." He pressed a kiss on each palm. "The luckiest man in the world."

She blinked back tears. "Stop, or you'll make me cry, and then I'll look a fright when my friend arrives."

Xavier looked over her shoulder. "*Ma chérie*, I believe the moment has arrived."

Jenee turned toward the staircase, and a cry of joy escaped her. "It's Emily!" She ran to Emily, who was running down the steps to her. "I'm so excited to see you. I can't believe you're really here."

"I know. It's a miracle," Emily said.

They embraced, hugging, tears flowing. When they finally released each other, they held hands and looked each other over. Emily wore a cornflower-blue silk gown that was embroidered with rosebuds. Her hat was small by fashion standards and sported a small blue half veil that gave her an air of mystery. Her slender fashion model frame had become curvier, and her neckline revealed a full bosom and a line of cleavage.

"Motherhood must agree with you," Jenee said. "You look fantastic, your ladyship."

"Don't you start using that bloody title. I get that day in and day out. To you, I'm still Em and always will be." Emily gestured to her cleavage. "The babies did this, thank you very much. I finally have boobs."

"Well, you haven't changed. I can see you're still as unfiltered as ever." Jenee eyed the impeccably dressed man who stood off to the side with his arms crossed over his chest and a grin on his face.

Emily followed her gaze. "Oh, darling, I'm terribly sorry. Forgive my manners. Jenee, this is the love of my life, the Marquess of Danbury, Colin Remington, but because I know you will be fast friends, and I know he wishes it, you must call him Colin."

Jenee offered her hand, and Colin bent and kissed it. "My pleasure, Jenee. I have heard so much about you, and I feel I know you already."

Jenee laughed. "Oh, dear, I hope Em didn't share too much."

He winked. "I'm afraid she might have."

She felt her cheeks heat. "Em, I know you, and I'm sure all my secrets have been revealed."

"Oh, bollocks, I keep no secrets from Colin. Besides, you're the most remarkable woman I know. Of course I'm going to brag about you." Emily turned her attention to Xavier. "And you must be the man Jenee wrote me about who's stolen her heart." She held out her hand. "Chief Inspector Doumaz, am I correct? You, monsieur, have excellent taste in women."

"At your service, madame." Xavier bent and kissed her extended hand. "Please call me Xavier. And *bien sur*, I have not only good taste but good fortune." He beamed at Jenee.

Emily poked a finger in Xavier's chest. "And don't you forget it." His eyes widened at the invasion of his space.

"Don't mind my overly protective wife. That's how she is when it comes to those she loves. Jolly good to meet you." Colin held out his hand, and the two men exchanged greetings. "Please call me Colin. It seems the women we love are as close as sisters, and I imagine we will see a good deal of each other."

"A pleasure to meet you. How is it you speak perfect French?"

"My mother was French, so I needed to learn her native language. Emily and I speak to each other in French quite often, which has improved her skill."

Emily piped in. "Enough with the chitchat. What's the plan? We can't stand around here frittering away our day. Jenee and I will need a very long lunch to share everything that has happened to us since we last saw each other."

"Do you want to go to the exposition and then have lunch?" Jenee asked.

"The exposition can wait. Colin and I will go tomorrow, and you and Xavier are welcome to join us. How about a walk through the Tuileries Gardens? I'm dying for some exercise."

They left the hotel, and Xavier led them to the carriage. Opening the door, he said, *"Après vous, mesdames."*

Emily would have had them jogging if she could have, but as it was, she kept up a vigorous pace, and the humidity brought a soft sheen of perspiration to everyone's brow. Emily could never hide her management training. She was specific about where she wanted to eat for lunch and was adamant that she and Colin wished to treat Jenee and Xavier to something memorable— lunch at one of the oldest restaurants in Paris, Le Grand Véfour.

Like a beautiful woman's face, Le Grand Véfour had aged gracefully. The restaurant had survived the French Revolution, the Restoration, the July Monarchy, and France's return to Napoleonic dynasty rule. As both Jenee and Emily knew, it was a celebrated national treasure still going strong in the twenty-first century. With its Empire décor of red velvet and gold, Victor Hugo's favorite restaurant glittered like a newly opened jewel box. Jenee insisted they order the Marengo au poulet with its extravagant adornment of black truffles. As promised, it was divine.

"No one makes chicken like the French. The English haven't a clue," said Emily. She turned to Colin. "You're always spoiling me with tokens of your affection. If you really want to please me, you'll hire a French chef and bring him home with us. That would be simply swoon-worthy, and then you'd have perfectly prepared Dover sole the way you like it."

"I always knew you were a secret glutton, my love, when you picked food before love in Eastbourne."

Emily cocked her head and batted her eyelashes. "I knew I needed my strength for such an ardent lover."

Xavier chuckled. "Perhaps it is a common trait among women of the future. In Jenee's case, my bourride won her heart."

Jenee slapped Xavier's hand playfully. "Ah, yes, your code word for making love. 'My love, would you like some fish soup?'"

Xavier's eyebrows rose and his cheeks colored, and Jenee and Emily collapsed in laughter.

Jenee caught her breath. "Forgive me, my darling. I noticed you and Colin have joined forces rather quickly."

Xavier grinned, placing a quick kiss on Jenee's hand. "We men need to stick together in the face of such feminine power."

Jenee couldn't wait another minute to ask, "I am super curious. How did you and Colin meet?"

"Oh, you would have laughed your head off." Emily giggled. "I materialized in the middle of Piccadilly Road on a typical London pea soup evening and was nearly run over by the carriage Colin and his friends, the Carmichaels, were in. I fainted straight away, and when I awoke, I was in the arms of the most handsome man I'd ever laid eyes on"—she beamed at her husband—"who was none too happy with me."

"Darling, you can't blame a gent for not realizing that the moppet covered with horse manure, who'd just fainted in the middle of the road, would become his treasured bride. Ruined one of my best suits, but I wouldn't have it any other way." Colin bussed Emily's cheek.

Xavier laughed. "It seems time travel has a way of depositing its passengers in an inelegant way. Jenee arrived amid a collapsed bridge and was covered in concrete dust. However, I must confess her scent was not at all offensive."

"Jen, I hope I'm not jumping the gun here, but I am certain Iris has told you that you can return to our time," Emily said. "Have you decided to do that or remain here?"

Jenee nestled against Xavier and met his gaze. "If he'll have me, I believe I will remain."

"*Mon amour*, no one will ever love you more."

Emily clapped her hands. "We must celebrate. *Garcon*, champagne, *s'il vous plait*."

Xavier offered the toast. "First, let me toast my Jenee, who has pledged herself to me today. And to our mutual desire to see the Vicomte de Maurnier brought to justice. *À votre santé, mes amis*."

"So, what is the plan for that bastard?" Em asked. "If I know Iris, she is spinning a web to entrap him."

"It's taking shape, but I think the more minds, the better," Jenee said. "Why don't we forgo anything else today and go see Iris? And you can meet my guardian angel Constance. If Iris agrees, I've considered taking Constance into our confidence and explaining the whole sordid tale to her, and I believe she will wholeheartedly support our efforts."

"It will mean her loss of the painting," said Colin.

"Constance is a loyal friend, and money, which she has plenty of, would never come before her commitment to those she cares about. It wouldn't surprise me to learn that she knows more than she lets on about Iris and me."

"Then we will be off just as soon as I have my chocolate soufflé," Emily declared.

Colin's brows rose with amusement. "I'm afraid there will be no living with her if she doesn't get her dessert."

"Ah, but I could not agree with her more." Xavier winked. "It would be a tragedy not to indulge our senses with such a sensuous pleasure."

"Well, there you have it." Jenee giggled. "When you get down to it, everything begins and ends with sex and food, and we know it to be true when dessert becomes a sensuous pleasure."

"Hear, hear." Colin raised his glass. "I believe we have solved the ills of the world. We need more sex and more dessert, and all will be well."

Jenee and Emily locked eyes and fell apart with laughter, while Xavier and Colin looked on with amusement. Except for the looming confrontation with the monster time traveler, nothing had ever felt so right with Jenee's world.

CHAPTER THIRTY-ONE

June 2, 1900
Paris, France

ALLEGRETTO'S *IL DIVANO* took center stage at Restaurant Brébant. It hung from a heavy gold chain in front of the windows where, if it were daytime, the Champ de Mars Park would be seen. Instead, the starlit sky provided a sparkling background, illuminating the painting and making it stand out like a marquee above a Broadway theater.

The intimate gathering of guests sipped champagne and discussed the portrait that had been cordoned off with velvet ropes. On either side stood two plain-clothed policemen. Xavier had enlisted Inspector Henri Chauvet to provide security. The detective cast a withering gaze at anyone who dared to get too close to the masterpiece. On the other side of the painting, with his arms crossed over his barrel chest, stood a burly fellow with a surly grimace whom Chauvet referred to as *L'exécuteur*. Jenee suppressed her amusement when she heard Chauvet call him "the enforcer." Given the size and demeanor of the guard, there was no explanation for the sobriquet needed.

Dressed in a man's formal suit and holding a gold cigarette holder, the eccentric painter Louise Abbéma studied the painting. "I have never seen such realism and sensuality, and this could only be the work of a being caught in the throes of passion. *Il est extraordinaire.*"

"*Je suis d'accord.* If a man ever looked at me like that, I'd follow him to the ends of the Earth," Sarah breathlessly declared.

"Sarah, my love, you would never do such a thing. You are far too practical and far too independent."

But it was not only the painting that drew interest from the guests. Iris, whom few had met before, drew everyone's attention. None could be unaware of the startling resemblance to the woman draped across the divan. Daringly, Iris had returned her hair to its natural color, and it blazed as red as the woman in the painting. Everyone commented on the uncanny resemblance to Allegretto's subject and teased her that perhaps she was the artist's dream muse.

Her cheeks flushed pink. "It is uncanny, but I do see the resemblance," she admitted, and Jenee smiled, proud of her friend's courage for placing herself in full view of the vicomte.

"Perhaps you are the muse reincarnated," said Edmund Rostand.

"What a wonderful imagining," said Sarah. "The idea of recurring lives is soothing to the soul. I miss my beloved cheetah, Sylvie. It would be marvelous if I could be reborn as a cheetah."

"Oh, Sarah," said Marcel Proust. "We don't return as animals; we reincarnate into human form."

"How do you know, Marcel?"

"Siddhārtha Gautama, the Buddha, and his journey to enlightenment is an inspiration. His story is that he reincarnated many times and lived many lives until reaching his final incarnation as the Buddha. He tells of the journey to a godlier self and the ultimate gift of nirvana."

"So, like an aged wine, we improve with each rebirth?"

"Not if we don't let go of the need for material things and devote ourselves to spirituality and caring for others," Marcel replied. "My guess is that no one in this room would be considered an ascetic," he said with a chuckle, and everyone joined him. "We all carry our share of sins, I think. At least, I know I do."

Sarah, who looked ageless and stunning in a white satin gown with white feathers surrounding the neck and sleeve cuffs, kissed Marcel's cheek. "You may be a sinner, but I adore you, and I wouldn't trade you for any religious personage or flawless saint. Though I suppose you are right, my darling Marcel. I'm afraid we are doomed to an endless cycle of lives, since it is unlikely that you or I will ever give up our hedonistic pleasures. Perhaps I will come back as an actress again, which is something I do very well. I certainly have no intention of living like a monk and spending my life in prayer."

Constance clapped her hands and jested, "I am calling all sinners to the table. Let us eat and be merry while we are still here in this lifetime. Should we be taken tonight, which I pray not, at least we will go with a full stomach and a lightness of spirit."

Jenee was glad that Sarah had stolen the limelight away from Iris. The vicomte had glared across the table at the time-traveling artist's muse, but Iris ignored him as if he were the plague, which he was. She was clearly not afraid of him, and she shone with an inner light that captivated everyone in the room, much like her portrait.

JENEE HAD MARVELED at the whirlwind of planning and revelations since Emily and Colin's arrival. When they'd all gathered at Constance's *maison*, Iris revealed her secrets to Constance, and Jenee and Emily also shared their stories. It had been a great relief for Jenee to unburden herself to the woman who had been so kind and giving to her since she arrived.

Colin and Xavier sat in the library, sipping cognac and discussing their thoughts about the coming days, leaving the women to their confessions.

Constance had listened wide-eyed as Jenee, Emily, and Iris

told their time-travel tales. It was impossible for her to even consider that all three women had lost their marbles, as far-fetched as their tales may seem.

At last, Iris had come to the part of the story that was perhaps the hardest to believe. "The painting you own is not a painting but a magical portal, and it needs to be closed forever because it is being used by an evil killer, the vicomte."

"But how is that possible?" Constance asked.

"He is also a time traveler. The portals allow him to live like a shadow, appearing and disappearing at will. Without a way to stop him, he is free to kill. He slaughtered five young women in London, and now Lulu. He also killed my parents in front of my very eyes. He would have killed me if I had not been propelled through a portal. We must bring him to justice, or his killing spree will never end."

Iris spared nothing in the telling of her travails as a time traveler.

"A curse on the three paintings opened three portals, doorways that provide passage through time," she continued. "That monster is the minion of a powerful and evil woman in Florence. She forced a shaman to open the portals, and now she uses them to wield her evil. She will stop at nothing to destroy Marco and me, and she is desperate to get her hands on all three paintings and their portals."

"If we don't put an end to her and the vicomte, he will be free to continue raping, torturing, and murdering women," Emily added. "I have seen what he is capable of, and it would make your skin crawl."

"He was careful to leave no wounds, but he tortured Lulu as well, and I could see he made her suffer in my examination of her at the morgue," Jenee said.

Tears streamed down Constance's face. "That poor woman."

"Iris is in constant danger as well," Emily said.

"The vicomte has known all along that she is here, and this is why she has had to keep herself hidden as much as possible,"

Jenee added.

"If we do not stop this demon, he will continue to brutalize and murder," Iris said. "And I will spend the rest of my days trying to escape the vicomte's wrath. I need you, my dear friend, to help me." She clasped Constance's hand. "The only way to stop the vicious cycle is for me to enter and pass through the portal. When I do, the painting will disappear with me. The vicomte will be caught and brought to justice by Xavier and Colin, and I will return to Marco, at least for a while. Until it is time for me to seek the third painting. As I told you, there are three paintings and three portals. *La Sedia*, thanks to Colin and Emily, is returned to Marco, and its portal is closed, or it will be when he again possesses all three paintings. *Il Divano* is the second, and with your help, it too will be closed. I know this will be a great financial loss to—"

"Nonsense," Constance interrupted. "I have lived long enough to know that an object, regardless of its cost or beauty, is never more important than family, friendship, love, or loyalty. There is nothing that means more to me." She dabbed at the tears that filled her eyes. "The only loss that feels impossible to bear is the loss of you, my dear Violet. Oh, dear me, I mean Iris."

Iris threw her arms around Constance and wept tears of sorrow and joy. "Oh, Constance, the loss of your kind heart will be an even greater loss to me. After my parents' murder right before my eyes by the vicomte, I lost my faith and belief in the goodness of others. Marco returned my heart to me and taught me to love and trust again. You have taught me that friendship is greater than anything we might ever earn in this life. And you, Emily, and Jenee are the sisters I never had nor dreamed I might have. I can't help but believe that our goodbye will not be forever. Somehow, we will all meet again."

Jenee hoped Iris was right, and they would soon be reunited with Gaby. She reached under the table and clasped Xavier's hand. He gave her a reassuring smile, his pale blue eyes telling her everything in just one look.

Edmond Rostand drew everyone's attention when he mentioned Lulu's suicide. "Inspector, do you have any idea why she came to such a desperate end?"

"It was not suicide, *mon ami*. It was murder," Xavier declared, eliciting gasps from everyone around the table. His eyes narrowed and took on the hue of an ice-blue glacier as he stared piercingly at the vicomte. "And mark my words, I will bring the bastard who did this to justice."

"Murder! *Mon Dieu!*" Sarah exclaimed, her hand going to her heart. "The poor, dear girl. But it explains so much. It was beyond my understanding why someone with such a bright future would take their own life."

Marcel asked, "Inspector, do you believe it was a crime of passion? Perhaps a jealous lover or rival. Passions run deep in the theater, and it would not surprise me." The others nodded and looked to Xavier for an answer.

Before he could, Constant Coquelin's deep baritone ended the speculations about Lulu's death. "The loss of so young a life is a great tragedy and not something to be bandied about as dinner conversation. In any case, I'm certain the inspector will not likely answer your questions during an ongoing investigation. And we can all agree that, given the inspector's reputation, he will find the beast who did this."

"You would be correct, monsieur," Xavier said. "Until I have more definitive evidence, nothing should be revealed. As I learned from my mentor Edmond Locard, 'Every contact leaves a trace.'"

"Though I only met Lulu once or twice, Violet and I will be organizing her funeral," Constance said. "I invite you all to attend the mass."

"That is so generous of you, Constance," said Jenee. "I had no idea." She blotted the tears that stung her eyes with her napkin.

"I discussed it with Xavier. Lulu has no family, and I will not allow her to be buried in a pauper's grave. She deserves better than that."

The vicomte raised his glass. "I toast your kindness, Constance, and a special toast to Lulu. Such a tragic end to such a charming young woman. May she rest in peace."

Jenee and Emily simultaneously placed restraining hands on Xavier and Colin's sleeves. They could see daggers flying from both men's eyes, and feared that the men might leap across the table, wrestle the despicable murderer to the floor, and kill him with their bare hands.

Emily raised her glass. "Let us also toast that the monster who did this will be brought swiftly to justice. May he suffer his just rewards."

Jenee recalled Emily saying she found it amusing that the vicomte pretended not to recognize her and Colin. Emily said she would have loved to ask him how he'd healed from the bullet wound he received when she shot him.

"I second that," Albert said. "Here's to that bastard's demise."

Everyone raised their glasses for the toast. Jenee's gaze met the vicomte's as he sipped his champagne. He regarded her with a look of pure evil for a moment before returning to his usual placid smile.

CHAPTER THIRTY-TWO

June 3, 1900
Paris, France

JENEE, IRIS, AND Emily huddled together in Iris' bedroom, listening with their ears to the door. Jenee and Xavier had pleaded with Emily and Colin that they should return to the Ritz and leave the vicomte to them—they were parents of two small children, and the risk was too significant—but neither would be dissuaded. To leave Jenee and Xavier to face the evil time traveler alone was out of the question, and they would not hear of it. Exhausted from arguing, Xavier and Jenee acquiesced.

From the Prefecture of Police's arsenal, Xavier had procured for Colin and himself Modele d'Ordonnance Mle 1892 revolvers, and both men were resolved to use them.

It was a moonless night and pitch-black inside and outside the house. While Xavier hid in the library with the painting, Colin was hidden behind a rose-covered lattice panel in the garden near the French-doored entrance to the library.

Iris and Constance had had a tearful goodbye, and despite her protests, Constance was sent to bed. She'd promised to keep the windows and door to her suite locked. And now, Iris, Jenee, and Emily nervously awaited the arrival of the vicomte, whom they knew was sure to show up. After the dinner, he would know the noose was closing around his neck and that his time in Paris must end. He was most likely itching to disappear through the portal, taking *Il Divano* with him.

Jenee imagined his gloating in anticipation of stranding Iris in this era. He would rid himself forever of her interference in one stroke and deprive Marco and Iris of ever seeing each other again. The Contessa Farnese would reward him lavishly, and he would be free to satisfy his depraved pleasures of sexual torture and murder.

Constance had flawlessly executed Iris' clever ruse. In conversation with Sarah, Constance let slip that *Il Divano*, under police escort, was being transferred back to her *maison* tonight and would not leave for the Grand Palais until tomorrow. Iris was confident that the vicomte, standing nearby, would not ignore the bait, and Jenee held on to the notion that his twisted belief in his own invincibility and his overestimation of his cleverness would lead to his downfall.

"It would have been so much easier if you could have left already, Iris, and then he would have been stuck here," said Jenee.

Iris shook her head. "He is too powerful, and you don't have enough strong evidence to bring him to trial. He would have disappeared to another country and bided his time. No, *mon amie*, I must confront him and lure him into a confession. He survived a bullet last time and made his escape, which only stokes the flames of his treachery. His hatred of me and his inflated ego are our only hopes of unmasking and disarming him. His killing spree must end here. I will have my revenge for the murder of my parents."

"Dear Iris, please don't let his evil consume your quest," Emily said. "Don't let it destroy your goodness."

"Trust me, that will never happen, *ma chère amie*. To love and be loved is all I have ever wanted. With Marco, I will have achieved all that I yearn for. He is my rock." Iris, whose ear was pressed to the door, turned to Jenee and smiled. "I wish you could meet him, not as the mysterious supernatural hand reaching out of a painting, but as the man who sees beauty and cherishes it.

The man who embraces life with passion and brings that passion to life on canvas." She again pressed her ear to the door and placed two fingers over her lips. "Shh, I hear something."

XAVIER HEARD WHAT sounded like a knife slicing through paper. He tightened his fingers around the revolver's grip and curled his index finger around its trigger as he cocked the hammer with his thumb. A surge of adrenaline rushed through his veins, stimulating his senses into high alert. He couldn't see Colin, who was hidden just outside the French doors, but he imagined that he was experiencing the same heightened awareness and stood poised for action.

A soft pop and the tinkling sound of glass shattering announced the arrival of an intruder. Cool air poured into the room, and a slight chill hit Xavier's face. The barely perceptible creak of a hinge pricked up his ears. The broken glass crunched beneath a shoe, and he could just make out the outline of a darkly clothed figure that seemed more shadow than mortal man. Pointing the revolver in the direction of the shadowy figure, he slid his finger over the on/off switch on his flashlight and shined it into the intruder's eyes.

The shadowy figure raised his hand and chuckled. In less than an instant, he crouched and rolled, and Xavier did his best to follow his movements with the flashlight. The intruder knew the lay of the room and pulled the chain of a Tiffany lamp, and the room and everything in it became visible.

Both men blinked rapidly as their eyes adjusted to the light. Both held guns pointed at each other.

The vicomte, dressed in black like a cat burglar, sneered at Xavier. "How nice of you to wait up for me, inspector. You didn't really think your primitive flashlight would blind me, did you?"

"It is over for you, Monsieur Archambeau. Surrender yourself into my custody."

"I think not, monsieur. But just for my amusement, what am I surrendering for?"

"My investigation of you has borne fruit. As we speak, the body of your cousin the Vicomte de Maurnier is being exhumed and will be re-examined. After further analysis and a thorough autopsy, we found evidence of plant poison in Lulu Lelouch's body. We believe we will find that same chemical evidence in your cousin's body. The Lyon authorities are willing to reopen the case, and prosecutors in Paris are already building a case here against you."

The vicomte's laughter made Xavier's skin crawl. "Even if it were true, I will be long gone when your fruit ripens. You have no idea whom you're dealing with, and it will cost you your life."

"I'm afraid you're mistaken. If you do not surrender yourself at once, you will not be leaving this room alive."

"Inspector, I was rather enjoying our little *tête à tête*. However, I fear I'm beginning to grow weary. I will shoot you, and you will shoot me, but I will survive by simply disappearing into the painting. You, unfortunately, will not."

An English-accented voice interrupted. "And what will happen if we both shoot you?" Colin asked as he entered through the French doors.

The vicomte chuckled. "Why, this is rich. The pleasure of killing both of you is more than I could have wished for. Good evening, marquess. How nice of you to join us."

"You evaded your just reward in London, but your reign of terror is over."

"Again, I find your machinations amusing. You will notice that the gun I hold is not like any you have seen before. It is from the future and fires twenty rounds per second. By the time you wield those antiques you hold, I will have sprayed both of your bodies with bullets, and before the smoke clears, I will have the pleasure of watching you die."

"No!"

The high-pitched screams of Jenee, Iris, and Emily pierced the air as the three women burst through the library door and hurled themselves at the vicomte. But, as easy as swatting flies, he flung Emily across the room toward Colin, who dropped his gun when he caught her. Jenee tumbled head over heels toward Xavier, who tried to get off a shot but missed. The vicomte leaped with preternatural grace across the room toward Iris, wrapped an arm around her neck, and pulled her to his chest, shielding himself from any other fire. Iris struggled, kicking and flailing. Reaching back, she tried to dig her nails into his face, but it was useless.

He hissed in her ear, pressing the gun's muzzle to her temple. "Stop before I decorate the walls with your vile Jew blood. Have you forgotten how I dispatched your mother when the bitch dared to sink her talons into my face?"

"You bastard. Let go of me so I can kill you with my bare hands," Iris screamed.

"Ahh, and your father, spineless and worthless, made a show of bravery, but alas, he died like a pig without a squeal." The vicomte jerked Iris back toward the painting.

Xavier and Colin's guns were trained on the vicomte, but they had no way of getting off a clean shot, not so long as he had Iris in his clutches.

"Let her go," cried Emily. "Take the painting. It doesn't matter. Please don't harm her."

The vicomte's laughter was bloodcurdling. "I'm sorry, my dear, that I couldn't add you to my tally in London, and it is a shame I wasn't able to taste your sweetness."

"You are a venomous snake," Colin snarled.

"Thank you for the compliment." The vicomte tightened his grip around Iris' neck, and her lips opened and closed like she was a fish out of water struggling to breathe. "Do you know what both you, inspector, and the marquess share in common?"

"What in God's name are you talking about, you bastard?" Colin snarled.

"I'll tell you what you share. The knowledge that I raped and murdered Daphne, your first love, my dear marquess. And you, inspector, I had the pleasure of tasting that little coquette *amie* of yours. And what a delightful pleasure it was. Hearing their pleas for mercy while I satisfied my craving. In the end, I think they rather enjoyed it." The vicomte looked lustfully at Jenee and Emily. "I only wish I could have experienced the same pleasures with you, my dear ladies."

"I will see you in hell, I promise you," Xavier growled.

Iris' eyes bulged from the lack of oxygen. The vicomte had backed them up until they were in front of Allegretto's painting.

"What an exhilarating experience. Thank you, ladies and gentlemen, for tonight's entertainment. But now, I'm afraid I must be on my way, as I have another painting to recover. Oh, and I suggest you say farewell to your friend, as you will never see her alive again."

Xavier could not believe what he was seeing. A quick glance at Colin, and he knew his eyes were not deceiving him. Colin peered curiously at the vicomte. He saw the same thing.

The man in the painting had come to life. It was the artist himself, Marco Allegretto, who turned and looked out of the painting. His eyes were burning coals of hatred. It happened so fast that Xavier could barely register what was happening. The hands of the artist reached out of the painting and grabbed the vicomte, pulling back his head with one hand. In his other hand, a glint of steel caught the light, and with a swiftness and speed that was almost impossible to see, he slit the vicomte's throat with a dagger. Albert's eyes went wide with disbelief, and he pushed Iris away as his hands flew to his neck, desperately trying to stanch the gushing blood. Gurgling and groaning, he slid to the floor, smearing blood down the wall.

Iris stumbled, coughing and wheezing with relief from the release of pressure on her windpipe. Jenee and Emily ran to her side and helped her sit up.

"Are you all right?" Jenee said, examining Iris' neck to confirm there was no lasting damage.

"Yes, yes, I am fine," Iris rasped.

They helped her stand, and together they turned to view the now-dead vicomte, his face frozen in a mask of death.

Iris stepped forward and, with a bitter smile on her face, spat on him.

Above them, the painting radiated a luminescent glow. Iris looked up, and her eyes met Marco's. His dagger slipped from his fingers and hit the ground. The fiery embers that had burned in his eyes transformed to the dark blue of a deep-water sea, glowing with love as he held out his hand to Iris. "Come to me, *amore mio.*"

"*Un momento, tesoro mio.*" Iris opened her arms, and Jenee and Emily ran to her. The women embraced and rested their foreheads together for a moment. Then Jenee and Emily let Iris go and stepped back, nodding encouragingly. Iris smiled at Colin and Xavier. "Thank you. I pray we meet again."

She turned back to Marco and took his hands. "Take me home, Marco." Iris seemed to take wing, floating into the painting. Xavier blinked, and she was gone. The image, which had glowed vividly, slowly evanesced until all that remained was a blank canvas.

Xavier went to Jenee and enfolded her in his arms as Colin embraced Emily.

"*Mon amour*, are you all right?" Xavier whispered as he tenderly held the remarkable and courageous woman who had appeared out of nowhere a month ago and changed his life forever.

"I'm all right, my love. In fact, I am better than all right. I am home."

EPILOGUE

September 16, 1900
Eastbourne, England

JENEE'S KNEES SHOOK, and were it not for Colin and Emily's supporting her on either side, she wouldn't have made it down the white satin runner. The smiling faces around her were a blur.

She looked up and saw the most beautiful blue eyes she'd ever seen. Xavier, dressed in a navy-blue formal suit, his dark curls subdued as much as they could ever be, gazed at her as if she were the only thing in the world that mattered.

Ahead of her walked Emily and Colin's children, George and Cecilia. The future marquess carried a silk pillow with two rings, a determined look in his eyes. George was taking his duty as ring bearer with great seriousness. At the rehearsal, he'd complained that Cecilia was a baby and shouldn't be allowed to participate in the ceremony.

Of course, his protests were ignored, and now Cecilia skipped ahead, taking handfuls of rose petals from her basket and tossing them into the air. Most landed in her hair. Her impish giggles made the guests in attendance smile. Had she wings, she might be mistaken for an ethereal woodland sprite.

Her father and mother exchanged worried glances. Unlike her serious brother, she had already earned a reputation as a mischief-maker.

Jenee smiled at the two darlings as they stopped at the altar. She bent and kissed them both on their cheeks.

The demise of the evil time traveler and his aliases of Vicomte de Maurnier and the Duke of Shrewsbury was a cause for celebration for all. Still, the loss of Iris seemed an unfillable void to Jenee, Emily, and Constance. Before the ceremony, as Emily fussed over Jenee in her bedroom suite and Constance sniffled and repeatedly exclaimed how beautiful Jenee looked, the ladies had all raised crystal flutes and toasted Gabriella and Iris, with a hope for a future reunion. On this beautiful summer day in Eastbourne, overlooking the blue-green English Channel, there would be only tears of joy and a belief in a future bright with love and laughter.

Under the chuppah adorned with pink and white roses, the rabbi declared Xavier and Jenee man and wife to the resounding applause of the guests, but it was Xavier's kiss that fulfilled all of Jenee's hopes and dreams. If Jenee had learned one thing from Iris, it was that no matter what storms came their way, there was nothing she and Xavier could not overcome as long as they were together. Love was everything, and love would conquer all.

About the Author

Belle Ami writes breathtaking international thrillers, compelling historical fiction, and riveting romantic suspense with a touch of sensual heat. A self-confessed news junkie, Belle loves to create cutting-edge stories, weaving world issues, espionage, fast-paced action, and of course, redemptive love. Belle's series and stand-alone novels include the following:

TIP OF THE SPEAR SERIES: A continuing, contemporary, international espionage, suspense-thriller series with romantic elements. TIP OF THE SPEAR includes the acclaimed *Escape*, *Vengeance*, *Ransom*, and *Exposed*.

OUT OF TIME SERIES: A continuing, time-travel, art-thriller series with romantic elements. OUT OF TIME INCLUDES includes the #1 Amazon bestsellers *The Girl Who Knew da Vinci* and *The Girl Who Loved Caravaggio*, and the new release, *The Girl Who Adored Rembrandt*.

THE BLUE COAT SAGA: A three-part serial, time-travel, suspense thriller with romantic elements set in the present-day and in World War II. THE BLUE COAT SAGA includes *The Rendezvous in Paris*, *The Lost Legacy of Time*, and *The Secret Book of Names*.

The Last Daughter is a compelling and heart-wrenching World War II historical fiction novel based on the life of Belle Ami's mother, Dina Frydman, and her incredible true story of surviving the Holocaust. The story begins at the dawn of World War II and follows the Nazi invasion and occupation of Poland, focusing on the Nazi's six-year reign of terror on the Jews of Poland, and the horrors of the death camps at Bergen-Belsen and Auschwitz, where more than six-million Jews along with other vulnerable innocents were slaughtered.

Belle is also the author of the romantic suspense series THE ONLY ONE, which includes *The One, The One & More,* and *One More Time is Not Enough.*

Recently, Belle was honored to be included in the RWA-LARA *Christmas Anthology Holiday Ever After,* featuring her short story, *The Christmas Encounter.*

A former Kathryn McBride scholar of Bryn Mawr College in Pennsylvania, Belle, is also thrilled to be a recipient of the RONE, RAVEN, Readers' Favorite Award, and the Book Excellence Award.

Belle's passions include hiking, boxing, skiing, cooking, travel, and of course, writing. She lives in Southern California with her husband, two children, a horse named Cindy Crawford, and her brilliant Chihuahua, Giorgio Armani.

Belle loves to hear from readers—
belle@belleamiauthor.com
Twitter: @BelleAmi5
Facebook: belleamiauthor
Instagram: belleamiauthor